Ramón and Julieta

RAMÓN
and
JULIETA

Love & Tacos

ALANA QUINTANA ALBERTSON

JOVE
New York

A JOVE BOOK
Published by Berkley
An imprint of Penguin Random House LLC
penguinrandomhouse.com

Copyright © 2022 by Alana Albertson
Readers Guide copyright © 2022 by Alana Albertson
Penguin Random House supports copyright. Copyright fuels creativity,
encourages diverse voices, promotes free speech, and creates a vibrant culture.
Thank you for buying an authorized edition of this book and for complying
with copyright laws by not reproducing, scanning, or distributing any part of it
in any form without permission. You are supporting writers and allowing
Penguin Random House to continue to publish books for every reader.

A JOVE BOOK, BERKLEY, and the BERKLEY & B colophon are registered
trademarks of Penguin Random House LLC.

Library of Congress Cataloging-in-Publication Data

Names: Quintana Albertson, Alana, author.
Title: Ramón and Julieta / Alana Quintana Albertson.
Description: First edition. | New York : Jove, 2022. | Series: Love & tacos; 1
Identifiers: LCCN 2021036188 (print) | LCCN 2021036189 (ebook) |
ISBN 9780593336229 (trade paperback) | ISBN 9780593336236 (ebook)
Subjects: LCGFT: Romance fiction. | Novels.
Classification: LCC PS3617.U589655 R36 2022 (print) |
LCC PS3617.U589655 (ebook) | DDC 813/.6—dc23
LC record available at https://lccn.loc.gov/2021036188
LC ebook record available at https://lccn.loc.gov/2021036189

First Edition: February 2022

Printed in the United States of America
1st Printing

Book design by Kristin del Rosario
Title page art: Sugar skulls pattern © xenia_ok / Shutterstock

This is a work of fiction. Names, characters, places, and incidents either are
the product of the author's imagination or are used fictitiously, and any
resemblance to actual persons, living or dead, business establishments,
events, or locales is entirely coincidental.

This book is dedicated to my mother,
Diana Quintana Viramontes Chulick.
Thank you for always fostering my love of reading,
supporting my dreams, and loving me. I love you.

Ramón and Julieta

CHAPTER ONE

La Jolla, California

Ramón Montez relaxed in his leather chair and gazed out at the ocean from his home office. In contrast to his sleek, modern gray walls, the blue ripples undulated in the distance. Surfers dotted the coastline, catching the last breaks of the day, and Ramón wished he rode the waves with them, but he couldn't slip away from his desk. Not with a major acquisition for his company on the horizon.

He was confident that he would win the bid for the iconic block of property in Barrio Logan, an area that he loved. Barrio was home to Chicano Park—a Mexican-American historical site that had the largest collection of outdoor murals in the country. More importantly, it had been the center of the Chicano movement in the seventies when residents took over the land after the proposed park was slated to be turned into a California Highway Patrol station. Those protesters were heroes. The town was steeped in culture and community.

He needed to close this deal.

As CEO of the Montez Group, Ramón was responsible for identifying and taking over key properties throughout San Diego. With over two hundred Taco King restaurants in the country and tens of thousands of employees, the Montez Group had brought fast-casual Mexican dining to a whole new level.

To think, it had all started with Ramón's father, Arturo, and his surfing trip to San Felipe in the late seventies. One bite into an epic fish taco and Papá changed the course of his and his future family's life. He opened a small stand on the bay, and now the company was franchised throughout the United States.

"Ramón."

He recognized his brother Enrique's voice immediately. Ramón swiveled in his chair.

A deceased desperado donning a poncho and a perished pachuco decked out in a zoot suit popped their heads into Ramón's office.

Ramón took one look at his brothers and burst out laughing. It was a moment like this that made him glad he had agreed to buy this place together with them, despite the fact that they each could've easily afforded to purchase their own pads. But family was important to Ramón, and honestly, he couldn't shake the idea that he still needed to watch out for them, which was probably a lasting concern from protecting them his entire life from the disaster of their parents' marriage.

"Did I miss the memo on Chicano history day? Are we teaching at some school I didn't know about?"

Enrique gave a sly smile, but Ramón's attention was focused on his brother's ridiculous mustache, which curled at the ends. Dude definitely already won Movember, and it was only the first of the month. "Nah, just honoring our ancestors."

"Your usual Day of the Dead outfits weren't good enough this year?"

"No, hermano. These are custom-made." Jaime dramatically leaned back and placed his hand in the pockets of his oversized ballooning pants that tapered at the ankle. Ramón half expected Edward James Olmos to pop out of the closet and start singing. "They took two months to make."

Ramón gave a fake cluck of disappointment. "So, I can't get one at the last minute?"

Jaime pulled his phone out of his pocket and got his hand tangled in his double watch chain. "Let me put in a call to my seamstress. She might have something already made. I know a great—"

"Jaime, it's okay. It was a joke." Ramón shook his head. Jaime had been promoting the event on his social media, and Enrique would be giving a demonstration on how to grow your own altar flowers from a rare cempazúchitl seed he had cultivated himself from a cemetery in Jalisco. No doubt both were just ploys to pick up women, but at least they were somewhat representing the family business.

"I don't know why you two go to that party every year. It's just a bunch of tourists who don't know the difference between Day of the Dead and Halloween."

Enrique grimaced. "Well, I spent months growing the marigolds for the event. Besides, what would you know? You haven't been in years."

Enrique was a master horticulturist who had inherited their abuelo's love of landscaping. He had been lucky to turn his passion into a career and, surprisingly, had even convinced Papá to open a test kitchen garden. Enrique had big plans to streamline the way produce for the restaurants was being harvested at their main suppliers.

Ramón ran his hand through his hair. "Been to one Día, you've been to them all." Day of the Dead in San Diego had turned into another excuse to get wasted. It used to be a small procession to the graveyard, and now it was a three-day festival of hedonism. Half the people there didn't even understand the point of the holiday—to honor their deceased loved ones.

Ramón didn't need to party to honor his loved ones. He glanced at the altar he had built for his abuelo, a man who had practically raised him. Ramón had made the ofrenda himself and had purchased Abuelo's favorite bottle of tequila. A memory passed through his head of Abuelo teaching Ramón how to work on cars. Ramón had inherited his grandfather's prize possession—his 1967 Ford Mustang, which Ramón had restored and then converted into a slick and shiny lowrider. Ramón would toast to him tonight.

Jaime straightened the feather in his wide-brimmed hat. "No, dude. It's epic. You're missing out. Sexy dead brides and debauchery. What's not to love?"

Everything. Ramón envisioned a bunch of drunk influencers making TikToks in front of altars. He shuddered. No, thank you.

"Well, have fun."

Enrique nudged Jaime out the door. "We will. Later."

"Hasta."

Sometimes, Ramón envied his carefree younger brothers. They worked hard, but they played harder. Ramón struggled with that work-life balance. For Ramón, a self-proclaimed perfectionist, to give anything less than one hundred percent was unacceptable. It explained his bachelor's degree in Economics with a minor in English from Stanford University, and his MBA from Harvard.

He read over the numbers on his computer one more time. The only thing that mattered to Ramón was the bottom line. And the bottom line was that the Montez Group wanted a piece of Barrio Logan and a Taco King front and center on the main drag.

His cell buzzed.

Ramón answered on the first ring. "Apá. ¿Qué tal?"

"Good, Ramón. Good. I called to check on the Barrio deal. How's it going?"

Ramón smirked. It was like Papá could read his mind.

"Great. I've finalized the numbers for the offer. I'm ready to bid tomorrow."

"Ah, good." Papá hesitated. "You know, I could always check those figures, and—"

"Apá, isn't it time you retired? I'm the CEO now. You should be relaxing, kicking back with a beer on the beach tomorrow, not heading to a meeting."

Papá sighed as if he wasn't quite convinced. "I know, but I am chairman of the board."

Ramón sighed. There was no use arguing with Papá. "I'm confident we have this in the bag." And he was—extremely confident.

Papá exhaled. "I believe in you, mijo. I can't wait to close this deal. I've wanted a holding in Barrio for years, but it was never the right time . . ."

His wistful tone needed no explanation. There was a damn good reason why the Montez Group had never secured a property in Barrio Logan.

It was clear.

They weren't wanted.

Papá had been accused of being a sellout, which was just plain ridiculous. His father was a proud Chicano man who always gave back to his community. So what if he catered to the tastes of non-Hispanics? Sure, the restaurants served mild salsa, and the tortillas weren't made from scratch. Still, Papá had created jobs for Latinos and given to countless charities. And that was what mattered.

But Ramón understood the sting of not always being accepted by his community. He'd grown up rich and privileged and hadn't faced the struggles that many others had. He felt Mexican in his soul but wasn't always perceived as a real Latino. His cousins used to call his brothers and him coconuts—brown on the outside, white on the inside. Ramón's heart soared when mariachi music played but sank every time he spoke in Spanish to fellow Mexicans and was answered back in English. He had to constantly prove to his company and to his culture how Mexican he was. And he hated being called not just a gentrifier, but even worse: a gentefier.

But, as painful as it was to admit, he was one.

"Don't worry about it, Apá. I got this."

"I'm proud of you, Ramón. You remind me of myself at your age—young, passionate, full of ambition. But you have to remember to take a break sometimes. You know my work cost me my marriage to your mother."

Yup, Ramón was well aware of his parents' horrible marriage. His mother reminded him constantly. Though lately, she was too busy with her new love interest, a boy toy Ramón's age, to bother with her sons.

Ramón zoned out at his computer screen, which had a screensaver of Cabo San Lucas. The turquoise water rimmed around the natural rock arch. "After this deal closes, let's take a vacation."

"I'd like that." Papá paused. "I have one more favor to ask of you."

"Sure. What is it?"

"Would you stop by the party in Old Town? There will be reporters there and the mayor. I think since we are going to try to acquire in Barrio, we need to be present at cultural events to show we support our community."

"The Día de los Muertos party? ¿En serio?" The Day of the Dead party in Old Town was hands down the best fiesta for the holiday in San Diego, if not the state. Family fun, bro bashes, and cultural classes were all part of the event. There was something about the quaint, historic neighborhood that added genuine authenticity to the holiday. San Diego, which neighbored Mexico, was a true border beach town. With twenty percent of San Diego's 1.5 million population Hispanic, politicians were usually found circulating at these bicultural celebrations. Old Town was literally the oldest settled town in California—a place that could be the set for the next Zorro adaptation. Now it was a tourist mecca that consisted of sarsaparilla shops and tasty taquerías.

"Yes, I am. I'd go myself, but you are the face of the company, Mr. *People en Español*'s sexiest eligible bachelor."

Ramón groaned. That title had been nothing but trouble. All the gold diggers had placed a target on his back. Those women didn't like him for who he was, but instead for what he was worth. He'd never wanted to be the face of the company; he was proud of his work but craved anonymity. He'd gladly give that role to his youngest brother, Jaime, who was a model, influencer, and director of the company's social media platforms.

"Not sure that matters, because if I went, I would have to wear face paint."

Papá laughed. "Just go for a few hours, check in with some reporters and the mayor, take a few pictures, and leave. You never know—you could meet a nice young woman there. When I was your age, I always made time for the ladies."

Ramón exhaled. Papá's wild youth was no secret. As a little boy, Ramón loved listening to Papá's stories about hitchhiking through Mexico and surfing along the Baja coast. But Ramón's favorite story was about the spring break love affair his father had had with a señorita in San Felipe. It was there that Papá had first tried fish tacos.

Ramón had no trouble meeting women, usually through dating apps, if he ever managed to take a day off work, which was rare. He had no time to even think about starting a serious relationship with someone. And after his parents' nasty divorce, marriage no longer held any appeal for him.

Even so, sometimes, after he closed a big deal, he wished he could celebrate his success with someone. Toast champagne on his ocean-view rooftop deck or spend a romantic weekend in Paris. It would be nice to meet someone who was actually interested in him and not his money. But he doubted he could find such a woman, and he didn't even want to try. Women were a distraction—a fun one, but nothing more.

"Seriously, Apá. Can't Jaime do it? He will be posting his every waking minute anyway. And they look great in their outfits—they'll get so much press. He and Enrique just left."

"No. You know them. They will both be drunk and spend the night hitting on women. Definitely in no state to schmooze. There is nothing left to do on the Barrio deal. Take the night off. Please, do it for me."

Ramón had no choice but to agree. "Okay, I'll go. But only for a few hours."

"That's my boy. Do you have something to wear?"

Ramón exhaled. He did, but nothing like his brothers' new threads. "Yeah. I think my old charro suit still fits."

"Wonderful. Have fun. I love you. I'll see you in Barrio, mañana."

"See you tomorrow. Love you, too, Apá."

Ramón hung up, saved all his work, and shut off his computer. Papá was right; the best thing he could do for the Barrio deal was to go schmooze.

Ramón walked out of his office, through the long hallway covered with family photos and framed magazine articles, and strode over to his fully stocked rustic bar in the game room, where he took a shot of his stash of Clase Azul Reposado Tequila. *Hits the spot.* It was smooth, and it took the edge off the day perfectly. He filled a flask with some more and placed it by his keys and wallet.

Then he went to his bedroom closet. He searched in the back and

found his charro suit from when he'd played guitarrón with the Ma
riachi Cardenal de Stanford. The ingrained scents of dried tequila
and stale smoke from the fabric brought back memories of his college
years performing, which were the happiest times of his life.

The suit fit, surprisingly, even though Ramón had bulked up. His
daily workouts running on the beach and flipping tires in his custom
gym were his one outlet for stress.

Ramón went to Jaime's bathroom in their beachfront bachelor
pad, which, sure enough, had face paint strewn all over the white
marble countertop. Their maid, Lupe, would not be pleased. She
worked hard and fast, with a smile on her face, and Ramón always
made sure to clean up after any parties he and his brothers threw so
she wouldn't have to do any extra work.

Ramón had played at plenty Day of the Dead parties in college,
so he knew how to do the face paint. He shaved his face with a fresh
razor blade, used a white eye pencil to outline his eyes and nose, and
then spread white paint over his face. Black eye makeup and a spider-
web on his forehead came next. The perfect combination of beauty
and the macabre—life and death. To complete the look, he drew
black stitches over his lips to indicate that he was dead.

Papá was right—appearing at the event would be good for business. Ramón might even have a good time.

He quickly put the makeup away and wiped down the countertop.

Ramón secured his sombrero on his head. A final glance in the
mirror, and he was satisfied with what he saw—a man who would do
anything to close the deal.

He removed his guitarrón from the stand on the wall. One strum
of the brittle strings and the music beat through his heart and awakened his soul. When the notes sprang back to Ramón's head, he was

relieved that he hadn't forgotten how to play. He'd sung to crowds of women when he performed. Ramón loved being onstage, playing music, and singing love songs. He'd been a hopeless romantic, just like Papá.

But there was no time for women or music now.

He had a company to run.

CHAPTER TWO

Julieta Campos glanced around Las Pescas, bittersweet pride expanding her chest.

She had renovated the sea-to-table taquería as carefully as she kneaded her handmade tortillas. She'd selected every item inside the restaurant, from the custom-painted murals on the walls to the Talavera tiles underneath her worn clogs. Every Saturday morning, she went to the open-air fish market near Seaport Village to pick the freshest, most sustainable seafood available. From sea urchin to rock crab, Julieta never shied away from varieties that weren't typically served in Mexican cuisine. And she wasn't afraid to experiment in the kitchen.

Mexican seafood was her birthright. After all, her mother, Linda, had practically invented the fish taco in America—a fact that Mamá forced Julieta to keep to herself.

Mamá was a proud woman. She refused to talk publicly about how her recipe for San Diego's iconic fish tacos was stolen from her in the seventies by a smooth-talking Lothario who had strolled up to her tiny taco stand in San Felipe, captured her heart, and, after promising not only his undying love but also to return, ditched her to go back to California as soon as their spring fling was over. The jerk ended up founding a successful restaurant chain called Taco King, starring Mamá's signature tacos. That man was now a multimillionaire. Billionaire, in fact. Meanwhile, Mamá always struggled to make ends meet.

But Mamá was also a devout Catholic who hadn't sought revenge or even compensation for what had happened to her in her youth.

Instead, she'd just focused on her future. She'd met and married Julieta's papá, immigrated to California, started a family, and built her own legacy of authentic Mexican cuisine for the members of her community. Julieta was so in awe of Mamá and proud to continue in her footsteps. Though Julieta's parents had begged her to go to college, she'd always wanted to be a chef, ever since she'd worked in Mamá's restaurant cutting up carrots and radishes. Mamá knew the names of everyone who dined in her restaurant, and Julieta had vowed to be just like her.

After culinary school, Julieta trained at Michelin-starred restaurants and had even participated in a short stint on a reality television cooking show. But all she'd ever really wanted was her own place to serve her creations.

She had achieved her goal.

And *no one* would take it away from her.

An elderly couple dined on a whole fried fish baked in a tomatillo sauce in one corner. At the same time, a family with young kids munched on ceviche tostadas by the terra-cotta chimenea. In the heart of Barrio Logan, Las Pescas was more than a home for her; it was a community for her people.

Which was why, when she'd found out that her landlord, Señor Gomez, had decided to sell the property so he could retire and move near his kids, she sprang into action. He owned the entire block, and the buildings were for sale—she refused to allow a new owner to come in, triple the rent, and force all the stores out. Or even worse, not even give them a chance to pay the increased rent. They could kick out all the tenants, renovate the building, and lease it to corporate establishments. Lately, it was an all-too-familiar scene in Barrio—just last year the local bodega had been taken over by a big-box grocery store. Barrio Logan was now hip and ripe for gentrification. But the residents didn't want another chain store—they wanted to preserve their neighborhood.

Julieta had already applied for every small business loan she could find and had even made some calls to investors who were frequent customers of her restaurant. Señor Gomez had said the starting bid for his strip of buildings was eight million dollars! Julieta couldn't even fathom that type of money. Sure, there was a possibility that the new owner would allow her to stay open, but it was doubtful. Last year, an investor bought the land a street away, terminated all the leases, and built new condos. If Julieta could buy the entire block, they wouldn't have to close. Las Pescas had been around for twenty years. And since Julieta had taken over a few years ago, they were actually profitable. Now the restaurant had dedicated YouTubers and other influencers regularly posting pictures of their grub.

But none of that mattered if the building was sold and the new owners wanted to replace Las Pescas with a chain.

So far, nothing had panned out.

The sale hadn't been finalized yet. But she couldn't fret about that now, anyway—she had to cook tonight in Old Town for the Day of the Dead party. If she could garner enough good publicity, maybe that would attract an investor to save her restaurant. After all, she had beaten out one hundred other taco vendors for this prime location at the event by being voted San Diego's Best Tacos. Though the kiosk would be small, the hut reminded her of her mamá's original stand in San Felipe. It was kismet.

And she had been so wrapped up with this crisis that she hadn't even been able to properly celebrate the holiday.

Today was her first Day of the Dead without Papá. Día de los Muertos had always been her favorite holiday. As a girl, she loved helping Mamá set up the offerings for their deceased relatives—the liquor to quench their thirst after a long journey back to the living world, the toys for the younger children who had passed, the bread of the dead that was topped with skull-shaped mounds, which were sometimes in a round pattern that represented the circle of life. Day of the Dead was not Mexican Halloween—this celebration was full of joy and remembrance, honoring the loved ones who were no longer here on earth.

Tears welled in her eyes as she tended to the altar that she'd built for her beloved papá in the corner of the restaurant. She had spent hours preparing the ofrenda—from picking the finest marigolds to baking the pan de muerto to hand-dipping candles in his honor. She'd even placed a pack of cigarettes and a shot of tequila on his altar, despite Mamá's objections. Smoking and drinking may have killed Papá, but she'd be damned if she didn't offer him some comfort in the afterlife.

Mamá yelled at her from the back door. "Julieta! ¡Vámonos!"

Julieta gulped. Mamá's silver-streaked black hair, normally pulled back in a tight bun, was long, loose, and wild under her lace veil for the holiday. For a moment, Julieta's childhood fears of being kidnapped by La Llorona sprang to her mind.

Julieta grabbed her chiles and loaded them into the back of her catering van with the rest of the ingredients as Mamá climbed into the driver's seat. Julieta joined her in the van, and they set off toward Old Town. Mamá shot her a disapproving glance. "Where is your costume?"

Julieta sighed. "In the back. I don't see why I have to wear it. I'm working here, not picking up men."

It was Mamá's turn to sigh. "Julieta, it's Día de los Muertos. Show some respect to the dead. Like your papá."

Julieta looked out the window toward the water. "Fine. I'll change when I get there."

"Gracias. I'll do your makeup. It will be nice to see you wearing something besides an apron and flour."

Julieta read the subtext loud and clear. *Perhaps then a nice man might notice you.*

"Amá," Julieta sighed again. "Men my age are only interested in hookups. No one writes poems or sends flowers. They don't serenade women, like Keanu Reeves did in *A Walk in the Clouds*."

"Your papá did."

Julieta's heart ached. How had it already been almost six months since he'd died?

"Yes, he did. I wish I could find a man half as good as him. I miss him." She closed her eyes and pictured his smile. She could almost hear his laughter bellowing through the movie theater on their weekly film dates. Though the memories of Papá were bittersweet, they still brought Julieta joy. She opened her eyes and saw tears in her mamá's. A lump grew in Julieta's throat.

What would it be like to have a love like the one her parents shared? Papá had bought Mamá flowers every week until the end. And Mamá always made sure to make his favorite flan once a week. How had they possibly kept the spark alive for so many years?

Julieta doubted that she would ever know.

The only songs men sang these days were on TikTok. And even those were lip-synched.

Romance was dead.

They pulled into a crowded parking lot in Old Town. Luckily, they had a reserved parking spot, because the place was packed. Even so, that didn't stop a bum from trying to scam them to pay a parking fee. Mamá tossed him a twenty to ensure he wouldn't key their vehicle. Julieta reluctantly squeezed into the back of the van and changed into the Day of the Dead costume that Mamá had handsewn for her years ago. Despite her reluctance to wear it, she did love the ornate, formfitting white bridal gown, with accents of black and red lace. Unfortunately, the neckline was cut low, revealing Julieta's ample cleavage, which she usually kept safely hidden under salsa-stained aprons.

Julieta hopped out of the van and did an obligatory swirl for Mamá, who clapped.

"You look so beautiful."

"Well, this is probably the closest you will ever get to seeing me in a real bridal gown, so you might as well enjoy it." And Julieta wasn't lying. She would be thirty next year. She had long given up any hope of ever finding her soul mate.

Mamá shook her head. "Well, with an attitude like that, you're probably right." Though she was in her early sixties, she didn't look a day over forty. She was petite and curvy, and her beautiful brown skin was smooth. She had minimal lines around her eyes, which she swore was due to her daily use of eye cream. Despite Mamá's outside appearance, Julieta constantly worried about her health. Mamá had lupus, and even though they had health insurance, if the building was sold, Mamá's medical bills would be a huge financial burden they may not be able to afford.

Julieta pointed to Mamá's makeup palette, which Mamá clutched in her hand as if it was their secret taco recipe. "Let's just hurry. We have to set up."

Mamá didn't waste any time. She ran a brush across Julieta's cheek. Julieta closed her eyes, the gentle swipes soothing her. Rhinestones were stuck around her eyes, then more makeup was applied. For the finishing touch, Mamá affixed a floral headpiece with an attached veil to Julieta's long black hair.

"Mija, you're gorgeous." Mamá shoved a mirror into Julieta's hand.

"Thank you." Julieta saw her reflection and gasped. She really *should* be thankful. Mamá had made her skin shimmery, and the embellishments Mamá had put on had enhanced her dark eyes. Even her intricate tattoos matched the look. Julieta had a Catrina sleeve watercolor tattoo on her arm, much to Mamá's disapproval. What did Mamá expect? Julieta was an award-winning chef, not a nun.

"De nada." Mamá called the event coordinator, and staff was sent to help them gather the food containers. The scents of spicy cumin and sweet cinnamon filled the air as Julieta made her way through a maze of revelers dressed for the event. Ballet Folklórico dancers with elaborate, colorful costumes performed in the square. Young children were getting their faces painted.

Julieta paused at an altar filled with intricately woven marigolds and ornately decorated sugar skulls. There was a picture of a man who resembled Papá above it. A chill filled her soul; she yearned to hold his hand just one more time. Julieta said a quick prayer, did the sign of the cross on her chest, and then forged on to the venue.

They finally reached their stand, which had been decorated with blooms overhead and papel picado, and the staff helped them set up. Julieta reached into the cooler she carried and pulled out the fish. On the menu tonight was a high-end fish taco—an ode to Mamá. With a seared sea bass in an al ajillo sauce, this fish taco would be nothing like anything anyone had ever tasted—definitely not like the cheap farmed tilapia taco the Taco King chain restaurant used for their tasteless version.

Julieta began placing the other ingredients on the table.

¡Mierda! The most important one isn't here.

She tapped Mamá on the shoulder. "I'm going to go back to the van—I forgot my chiles."

Mamá nodded, and Julieta turned around and headed toward the parking lot.

Julieta reached the van and grabbed the chiles. But before she went back to Mamá, she took a brief detour. She needed a moment to herself before beginning the exhausting shift.

She opened a gate and strolled through a public garden adjacent to the main street. Normally, this area was busy, but tonight, everyone was in the plaza for the party. The bright bougainvillea draped the walls like magnificent curtains, and there was a colorful Talavera birdbath in the center. She dreamed of owning a home with room for a garden. She would grow all her own herbs and vegetables, and even some flowers. And maybe she would be blessed with kids who she could teach to care for the plants.

Ha! Kids? Who was she kidding? She couldn't even find a boyfriend. She supposed she could have them on her own, but she really wanted to find a partner. And Mamá never ceased to remind Julieta that her only hope to have grandbabies rested with her. Maybe she could take some time off from work and focus on her personal life.

One day.

She just hoped it wouldn't be because her restaurant was closed.

Why wouldn't any of the banks give her a loan so she could buy the buildings instead? She was a successful chef. She was an upstanding citizen, for goodness' sake—was she truly seen as a flight risk? Julieta's hands clenched into fists.

Just breathe.

She couldn't get worked up like this now—not when she had a cooking pop-up to focus on.

She bent down to smell a red rose when a deep male voice interrupted her, causing her heart to leap into her throat.

"'A rose by any other name would smell as sweet.'"

Ay, Dios mío. Her pulse ratcheted back down. Did he really just quote *Romeo and Juliet*? What a player. She looked up.

Whoa—sexy dead mariachi alert! Was she dreaming? Her heart stuttered.

A tall man with a strong jawline and twinkling dark eyes framed by impossibly long eyelashes stood before her. He was definitely handsome, even though his face was obscured by makeup. His charro suit seemed painted on his muscular body.

He winked at her, which caused her to grin unabashedly.

The shiny silver buttons on the sides of his tight black pants outlined his legs. She couldn't help staring at his strong thighs . . . and that huge bulge in his pants.

Breathe, Julieta, breathe.

He held a guitarrón by his side. Julieta loved that big instrument with its deep, rich sounds. Papá used to play it and sing lullabies to her when she was a little girl.

Julieta stood and examined the big Mexican guitar closely. It had six thick strings and a beautifully ornate rosette around the sound hole. It had to be expensive. Maybe this guy was some famous mariachi musician.

She pulled herself together. "That's a gorgeous guitarrón. Can you actually play that thing? Or did you just buy it as a prop to get some likes on Instagram?" Julieta prided herself on her sarcasm, a trait cultivated from years in the restaurant industry reacting to the idiots who didn't believe that she could be successful.

Her words seemed to amuse him, judging by his sexy laughter. He didn't say a word, instead lifted the instrument into position and began to strum.

Bold music filled the air, and Julieta's hips swayed to the music despite herself.

¡Ay, Dios mío! Was he playing "Abrázame" by Julio Iglesias? It was one of her favorite songs ever. Mamá had played that song over and over when she was a child.

The beautiful notes rang out from his seductive strings, and chills ran through Julieta's spine as he opened his mouth and serenaded her.

Just like in that movie she'd loved as a child.

Her lips parted in response; a warm flush came over her body.

And there, under the San Diego moonlight, Julieta's heart skipped a beat.

Maybe romance *was* alive on the Day of the Dead.

CHAPTER THREE

The words Ramón hadn't sung in ages echoed through the night air. Sure, serenading a señorita on Day of the Dead while dressed as a mariachi was a bit cheesy, but the truth was that he loved playing the guitarrón. Especially for a beautiful woman.

Guau. The girl in the garden was breathtakingly gorgeous. She had a petite frame, dark iridescent skin, and magnetic energy. Her haunting espresso-colored eyes hypnotized him. Ramón had to force himself to stop staring at her fabulous cleavage. But her curves didn't stop there. That ass was the kind that songs were written about. He could write one about her right now.

He studied her tattoos—a welcome change from the straitlaced women he normally dated. Maybe she had even more tattoos hidden underneath her clothes. Ramón would find out later tonight.

His body flooded with warmth. He didn't give a damn that he was making a fool out of himself—it would all be worth it if this girl went home with him.

Make that *when* she went home with him.

The chica danced fluidly in time with the music and kept smiling at Ramón. Their eyes met—Ramón held her gaze and raised his brow. She blushed and turned away.

Yup, he had this in the bag.

Should he have picked a shorter song? Probably, but he had gone with a classic—one his father used to sing to his mother, back when they hadn't despised each other. Papá had taught Ramón to play it years ago.

Ramón stared directly at the girl. She sang along with him, her voice sweet and soft.

Like an angel.

She knew the words? Impressive. Most girls he met didn't know any of the old-school songs. His college sweetheart had hated mariachi music and had never come to his shows. She had always wanted him to sing pop songs to her in English, but Ramón believed that the lyrics sounded better in Spanish.

The final notes left his mouth, and Ramón placed his guitarrón down. He knelt, plucked a single red rose from the garden, and presented it to her. "Eres bella."

Her hand brushed against her cheek.

O that I were a glove upon that hand, That I might touch that cheek!

"Gracias. Wow. You're really talented. I love that song. I didn't think anyone our age played the guitarrón. Where did you learn?"

"Well, my father taught me guitar, but I picked up the guitarrón at Stanford. I was in the student mariachi group there."

Her pupils widened. "Stanford? You must be smart."

Women like confident men—never downplay your abilities. He leaned into her and grinned. "I am. And you have great taste in music—that song is a favorite of mine. What's your name, beautiful?"

The woman paused.

Uh-oh. Why was she hesitating? Probably because she didn't want to tell some stranger in a dark garden her name.

She twirled a lock of her hair. "What's yours?"

He paused also. The name Ramón Montez was well known in the Mexican-American community in San Diego. Once women knew who he was, they just saw dollar signs.

"Romeo." He teased.

The girl laughed.

"Right. Then I'll be Juliet."

Cool. She liked to play, too. Maybe she wanted a no-strings-attached affair, also. Otherwise, she surely would've pressed him on his real name. "Hola, Juliet. Mucho gusto. Are you here with a date?"

He had already done a ring check, so he didn't think she was married, but the last thing Ramón needed was some angry boyfriend to come around and ruin his night, or worse, start a fight with him. Ramón could defend himself—hell, he had a black belt in Tae Kwon Do—but he didn't want any bad press. Best to get that discussion out of the way now.

The rhinestones on her face shone in the moonlight. "No, my mom came with me. I'm actually working tonight. And I have to go. But you have a beautiful voice. Thanks for the song." She took a step away.

Nope. Ramón wouldn't give up on her that easily. "Working?" He threw his hands up. "Where?"

She pointed to the plaza. "Obviously here."

Right. "Got it, Juliet. When do you get off? I'm working tonight, too." And he was, kind of. He still needed to find his brothers and make some appearances.

She covered her mouth with her hand. "Nine."

"Well, tell you what. Meet me back here at nine thirty."

She shook her head. "I don't think so. Besides, didn't you read

Romeo and Juliet? '*For never was a story of more woe than this of Juliet and her Romeo.*'"

Her lips widened into a coquettish smile. "It's hopeless. We can never work out. We're star-crossed lovers."

He laughed and grinned. He liked her sass. He walked to her side and cautiously brushed a lock of hair off her delicate shoulders. "Let's do a rewrite."

"Nah, why mess with a classic? And I don't know anything about you. You could be a serial killer."

He shrugged. "Fair, my lovely maiden." He didn't blame any woman for being worried about her safety. But he was a gentleman, not that she could possibly know that. He took a step closer to her—her sweet cajeta scent filled the air. "But I'm not—far from it. It's a glorious night. Get to know me. I'd like to spend some more time with you."

She pursed her lips and tilted her head like she was considering him. "What's in it for me?"

He smirked. He liked a challenge. These days, he could get laid with a simple swipe on his phone, which was, frankly, boring. Ramón missed the thrill of the chase and, ultimately, the sweet taste of victory. "If you come back, I'll sing you another song."

Her eyes met his, but she quickly looked away. "I'd like that, but I don't think that's a good idea. Have fun tonight, Romeo."

He took her hand and kissed it. "I will," he laughed. "With you."

"Good night! '*Parting is such sweet sorrow.*'" She giggled and ran off. She disappeared outside of the garden.

Should he follow her to see where she was going?

No. Definitely not. That would be creepy.

Where did she work? He could tell by her sexy outfit that she wasn't a waitress at his restaurant in the square, thank God. That would be awkward. And inappropriate. Ramón never mixed work with pleasure. Sleeping with an employee was a lawsuit waiting to happen.

Maybe she was a salesgirl in the candy store or a chandler at the candle shop. But it didn't matter what she did for a living—all that mattered was that she came back tonight.

Ramón grabbed his guitarrón and walked out of the garden. As he made his way into the crush, he searched for her face. Would he ever see her again? He hoped so.

He took a moment to marvel at the beauty of the celebration. He had been to many Day of the Dead celebrations throughout the United States and in Mexico, but the gathering in Old Town San Diego was by far his favorite. Despite what he'd said to his brothers about the event, it was intimate. It wasn't Old Town's fault that tourists who knew nothing about the holiday invaded the celebration. The organizers did their best to keep it authentic. Respectful. Real. Gigantic, elaborately costumed Catrina skeletons lined the street in their own intricately made altars. Some had bright flowers in their hair, some wore pearls, all were magnificent.

The ground vibrated beneath Ramón's feet from the many dancers tapping their toes. Ramón hadn't felt this at home with his people since he had been in college. With his makeup and his clothes, his identity could remain a secret until he had to face the press. And now, he had the prospect of a romantic liaison on the horizon.

He was glad Papá had forced him to come—not just to celebrate but also because Ramón had met "Juliet."

A song rang out in the plaza. His heart skipped when he saw a group of mariachis playing in the main square. Ramón would love to still play music regularly, but he just couldn't justify taking the time away from work. But tonight, dressed in his suit and holding his guitarrón while serenading a beautiful señorita, made him wistful for his music-making days. What would his life have been like if he had chosen another path? Could he ever have made it as a musician?

It was doubtful. And unpractical. Besides, these days, mariachis were mostly relegated to quinceañeras, weddings, and Mexican restaurants. Very few people respected mariachi music. Hell, even his own brothers made fun of him for playing it.

Speak of the bastards . . . Jaime and Enrique emerged from the historic Wells Fargo building with their cousin Benicio, friend Mateo, and a handful of scantily clad women. Should he pretend he hadn't seen them?

Ramón wanted to schmooze with the mayor, talk to a few reporters, grab a bite to eat, and check on his restaurant before returning to the garden in the hope of Juliet's return.

Before he could even make a decision, Mateo ran over to him. "Ramón! I recognized your suit. Man, I haven't seen your guitarrón since college. I didn't think you were coming tonight."

Mateo had been Ramón's roommate at Stanford. He was now a successful architect, but Ramón had been so busy with work lately that Mateo spent more time with Ramón's brothers than he did with Ramón. "Well, I wasn't, but I'm here. My dad wanted me to butter up some politicians and meet the press because we're closing the Barrio deal tomorrow."

Benicio glared at Ramón as he joined the conversation. "Hold up—you are putting a Taco King in Barrio Logan?"

Ramón's throat scratched. He might as well tell him now. "Yeah, we are."

"Are you serious?" Benicio kicked the dirt on the ground. "Are you stupid?"

Ramón clenched his jaw. Benicio grew up in the heart of Barrio Logan, accepted by his people and his culture. Ramón had always been an outsider, no matter how hard he had tried to fit in, especially as a child. Benicio's father was Papá's younger brother. Once Papá had become successful, he had asked his brother to work with him, but Tío Miguel had refused. He had raised his kids very differently from the way Papá had raised Ramón and his brothers. Tío Miguel's wife, Tía Rita, was a stay-at-home mom. Ramón, on the other hand, had spent little time with his mom and was raised by his nanny. When Ramón had been a little boy, he had loved going to his uncle's home and staying there during the summer when his parents went on their annual vacation to Europe. Tío Miguel's home didn't have a pool or maids, but it had something that Ramón's house had never had.

Love.

"I'm not stupid. I know there will be protests. But we got it under control." And they did. Nothing could go wrong. Ramón had been preparing for the deal—and its guaranteed backlash—for months.

Benicio held his hand up like a stop sign in front of Ramón's face. "Whatever you say, primo. You know how they feel about the Taco King. How *we* feel about you. We don't want you there."

His words stung. Benicio was part of Ramón's own family. But that part of his family had always considered Arturo a sellout.

Enrique inserted himself in between them. He placed his hand on Benicio's shoulder. "Relax, man. Those buildings on that block were going under anyway. If we didn't buy it, someone else would have. We're not the bad guys."

Benicio just shook his head. "Whatever you need to tell yourself." His eyes darted away from them. "I'll see you guys later."

Benicio walked away from the group and toward the crowd. Ramón's chest constricted. This night had started out on such a high.

Jaime playfully strummed Ramón's guitarrón. "Don't worry about him. He's always like this."

Ramón nodded. "Yeah, but he's right. They don't want us there."

Enrique knocked back some tequila from his flask. "This isn't news. You got this. Anyway, I'm glad you showed up. You work too hard. Take the night off."

"I plan to—after I meet with the mayor."

Mateo pointed back at the women Ramón had seen them talking to. "Come join us. We are meeting their other friends down the street. They said they want to party."

It could be fun. But Ramón had to work. That was why he was here, after all.

And there's a certain brunette I'd love to see again a little later . . . "I can't. I have to meet with the mayor and some reporters."

Jaime tugged on Ramón's sleeve. "Come on! They're hot. I call dibs on the pachuca chola."

Ramón glanced toward the women. How Jaime had found a woman who was also dressed in the 1940s zoot suit style was beyond Ramón. Her obviously dyed flame-red hair was styled into a bouffant that probably concealed the requisite razor blade. Definitely Jaime's type. The two of them would make a viral video swing dancing before the night was over.

"I would, but I already met someone. I'm seeing her later." Ramón was confident Juliet would come back to the garden.

Enrique's eyes bulged. "Damn. You didn't waste any time. Bring her along with us."

Ramón smirked. He shared enough with his brothers—his home, his cars, his privacy. "Nope. I want her all to myself. Good night, gentlemen."

Ramón walked back into the center of the square and in the direction of the main stage. On his way, he looked at his phone.

Seven thirty p.m.

In two more hours, Juliet would be his.

CHAPTER FOUR

Julieta inhaled the rose that the sexy man had given her. The floral scent made her woozy.

Or maybe her giddy state was because she was high on his testosterone.

She took a deep breath and grounded herself back in reality.

That song in the garden had probably been planned. She was just the lucky—or unlucky, depending on how you looked at it—girl who had walked into his trap.

He'd said his name was Romeo. What a joke. Clearly, he was a player. She'd been completely enamored when he sang and strummed the guitarrón for her, but once he gave her a fake name, her walls went up.

Or maybe he was just being playful. But playful was not what Julieta wanted. She wanted honest. Hardworking. Humble. A man who didn't play games.

And she hadn't lied exactly—Juliet *was* her name. Well, a version of it, but the J sounded like an H.

That romantic prelude had been a fun distraction, but it was time to get back to work. She raced to the stand and found Mamá frying tortillas with a scowl on her face.

"Where did you go? You left fifteen minutes ago!"

"Lo siento. I just needed a moment to myself." She wasn't actually sorry, but the apology rolled off her tongue anyway.

Should she tell Mamá about the handsome stranger?

No. She would have Julieta married off by the end of the holiday. Especially if she told her that Romeo had sung "Abrázame." The power of a classic Spanish ballad wasn't lost on Mamá. And who could really blame her?

"Ay, Julieta." Mamá threw her arms around Julieta, pulling her into a hug. "I know you are worried about our restaurant, but don't give up on me now. Let's focus on the food."

Food. Yes. Tacos. Fish tacos. To showcase why they made the best tacos in San Diego. That was why they were here. Not to fall for gorgeous masquerading mariachis.

Julieta prepared her sauce. She ground the spices together and diced the chiles, but her mind wandered back to Romeo.

He'd said he attended Stanford, but he also mentioned that he was working at this event. What did he do? Maybe he owned the new bar up the street. Maybe he was an actual mariachi at one of the restaurants. Wherever he worked, he probably had no intention of meeting with her later and would instead serenade the next pretty young thing he met, and there were plenty of candidates milling around tonight. Men these days had no attention spans. Why get to know someone when you could just swipe to meet the next woman on the never-ending assembly line of love?

The crowd began to gather at the stand, and Julieta cooked as fast as she could. Onions were chopped, limes were squeezed, tortillas were fried. At least this event was always a blast—the attendees were mostly dressed up in elaborate costumes, and some of the makeup applications deserved Emmys. Kids painted sugar skulls on rocks; Latin musicians played onstage as lovers danced. It was magical. Julieta was blessed to be part of the celebration.

But it would be nice to come here at least once in her life and not have to cook at the event.

Maybe next year.

For as long as she could remember, her parents had brought her along to help, which she'd loved. But now that she could lose everything that she'd worked so hard for, something had to change. Maybe she needed to strengthen the other areas of her life. Laugh more. Play more. Love more.

Take more risks.

She could start tonight with that handsome stranger . . . but was he the type of challenge she was after? Normally, the only gambles she took were with her cooking.

That way she would never get hurt. Or even worse, lose her focus on her business by being distracted by a man.

Ah, but he was so hot. Wasn't he worth the distraction?

An hour into the pop-up, Julieta glanced up from her frying pan. She looked toward the main street. Her gut wrenched.

Hundreds of people carried candles to the graveyard to honor their dearly departed loved ones. Julieta should've been in that procession, honoring Papá, instead of cooking for tourists.

Mamá dabbed her face with a paper towel as the crowd walked by.

"Mamá?"

"It's the onions."

Ah, the onions. Always there to blame for your sorrow. Another benefit of being a chef.

Julieta squeezed Mamá's hand and went back to cooking.

"Julieta!"

Despite his makeup, she recognized her cousin Tiburón immediately from the colorful shark tattoo on his neck, an ode to his name, and his generous smile.

Growing up without siblings, Julieta would have yearned for a big brother, had Tiburón not gladly fulfilled that role. If Julieta had a problem with anyone, Tiburón would take care of it.

Julieta left the stand and crossed the crowd to greet him. "Hey, Tib! Dig the zoot suit. Red's your color." She hugged him. "Who are you here with?"

He looked over his shoulder and pointed to some guys. "Just my bros."

A gang of dead pachucos were gathered in the square. Julieta loved the clothes from that time period.

"Are you hungry?"

"Yeah, I can eat. I'll never turn down your cooking—especially now that I've lost my job."

"Again?" Julieta sighed. Why couldn't he seem to find regular employment? Julieta would hire him at the restaurant, but with the building sale looming on the horizon, she didn't want to waste his time when they could be out of business.

"It is what it is. I cannot be tamed."

Julieta shook her head and walked back over to the stand.

"Hey, Tía Linda!" Tiburón stepped behind the window on the stand and kissed his aunt on the cheek as she clucked her tongue.

Julieta quickly prepared a dozen tacos for Tiburón and his friends.

Tiburón nudged her. "Do you want to hang out after the event? Pablo has the hots for you."

Julieta looked toward Pablo, who stared right at her. Julieta gave a friendly wave and Pablo grinned.

Pablo was handsome, no doubt, and a great guy. They had grown up together and were friends. Good friends, even. And he was super close with his family, and hers, and his mother loved Julieta.

But Julieta felt nothing when she hung out with Pablo. No sparks. No nerves. Just a big fat . . . nothing. Maybe that was okay. Julieta's expectation of being hit by a romantic jolt was unrealistic. Maybe Julieta was just numb when it came to relationships.

Except she wasn't numb. Fire had pulsed through her veins when she had listened to Romeo sing. But that was just lust. Nothing more. There was no such thing as love at first sight.

But why then would she prefer seeing the likely Casanova again instead of a man who was rock steady?

She shrugged. "Pablo is so sweet. But I'm not sure about tonight. I'll probably be tired after the event. Anyway, I'm stressed about to-morrow."

Tiburón hugged her. "Don't worry about it. I won't let anything happen to Las Pescas."

Julieta winced. "Thanks, I appreciate it. But let's see what happens."

Tiburón sometimes ran with a rough crowd. She wanted to keep her restaurant in Barrio Logan more than anything, but she didn't want anyone, especially people in her community, to get hurt. If the people in Barrio Logan protested, make that *when* they protested, then the police would come. And Julieta didn't trust the cops. No one in her neighborhood did.

She handed him the bag full of tacos. "Here you go. I gave you plenty of hot sauce."

Tiburón grinned. "You're the best, prima. Come party later."

But what about Romeo? "I'll think about it. I'll text you when I get off."

"Okay. Have a good night." He hugged her, then walked away.

Thousands of tacos later, the event finally wound down. It had gone wonderfully, and everyone had loved her food. She'd even had a well-known critic from *San Diego Magazine* stop by and sample her cooking. He'd raved about it, so Julieta hoped she would get a good review. Or at the very least a shout-out on Instagram.

The stars overhead illuminated the night. This was it. The final decision. Should she go home and be responsible? Or meet the handsome stranger in the garden?

Julieta was always dependable and, well, boring. What would it be like to be reckless for once? Follow her heart instead of her head? Lose herself in the moment instead of stressing about the future?

Julieta closed her eyes and focused on her breathing, a technique she had learned when she had been stressed working at her previous high-end restaurant.

When she opened her eyes, she wanted to see Romeo again.

Now she just had to ditch Mamá, which was easier said than done. Ever since Papá had died, Julieta had spent all her extra time at home with Mamá—they even lived together. Julieta had begun to accept how codependent they were. Especially with the prospect of her restaurant closing, she needed to expand her horizons and her circle of friends. Her life was work and her family. With Papá gone and her restaurant endangered, how would she fill her days? Watching telenovelas with Mamá?

Julieta wrapped up some extra food. Why let it go bad? She prepared two more fish tacos and covered them in foil. Mamá flashed her a suspicious look but remained silent. Romeo had given her a rose and sang her a song—the least she could do was feed him. As Mamá always said, "Barriga llena, corazón contento." Julieta agreed, the way to a man's heart was through his stomach.

As Julieta packed up their mobile kitchen into the van, she turned to Mamá. "Do you mind going home alone? I want to stay here for a bit."

Mamá's brow furrowed. "By yourself? Who are those tacos for?"

"For me—I didn't get a chance to eat. And I won't be alone. I'll catch up with Tiburón," Julieta lied, and instinctively touched her nose. Thankfully, it didn't grow any bigger.

"Ay. With his friends? Those borrachos."

"They're not drunks, Amá. That's not fair. They're young. They drink. I doubt they'll end up like—"

Julieta literally bit her tongue. She would not disparage Papá on the day she was supposed to honor him.

Mamá leveled Julieta with her eyes.

Dammit. Why had Julieta said that? It was true, but still. Guilt consumed her.

She should call it a night and go home. She had to prepare herself for whatever would happen tomorrow.

But right now, she just wanted to forget about her problems.

Mamá shook her head. "I don't think it's a good idea."

This was harder than Julieta had thought it would be. She was a twenty-nine-year-old woman, not a child. She didn't have to ask permission, of course, but she still did so, out of respect. "People are hanging around. I'll be fine. Tiburón will drive me home."

Mamá threw up her hands. "Fine. But be safe. Stay in well-lit areas." She dug into her purse, grabbed something, and handed it to Julieta. "Take this."

Julieta looked down. "Mace! Amá, I don't need Mace."

A homeless man walked by them and spat in their direction.

Well, on second thought, maybe she did.

"Fine." She tucked it into her purse and kissed Mamá on the cheek. "Buenas noches."

Mamá waved goodbye and drove out of the parking lot.

Once she was out of sight, Julieta leisurely walked back to the garden . . . already second-guessing her decision.

What was she doing? She was so foolish. Romeo was probably not there. And even if he was, did she want to share secret kisses with a man who was clearly a professional Don Juan?

Ugh, yes. Yes, she did.

Even so, she should've gone home with Mamá. Or met with Tiburón. And Pablo. Yes, Pablo. He was a good, safe choice. And at least she knew him. Knew his family. Hell, knew his real name.

But by this time tomorrow, she would probably lose everything. Didn't she deserve one moment of happiness? One wild, passionate night before her world came crumbling down?

But as she turned the corner, her breath hitched.

Romeo.

His black hair shone in the moonlight and framed his ruggedly handsome face. His lips were plump, and she wanted to feel his mouth on hers.

Her pulse pounded so deeply she was sure Romeo could hear it.

Romeo's gaze started at her face and then slowly moved down every inch of her body and back up to meet her eyes. He gave her a devilishly handsome grin. "I didn't think you'd return, Juliet."

"That makes two of us. Did you have a good night?"

"It was okay." He walked closer to her, and she could smell the lust burning between them. He was like an intoxicating drug, and she wanted to get high. "But now that you're here, I'll make sure it's a night we'll never forget."

CHAPTER FIVE

S he came back.
I knew she would.

He couldn't explain it, but there was something special about his Juliet. Most of the women he dated were like his mom's fine china—gorgeous to look at but very fragile and too focused on appearing perfect and acting like prim and proper ladies. They always wanted to talk about the two Fs—the future, in which they saw a big ol' wedding, and his finances, which Ramón wasn't keen to discuss.

Tonight, Ramón wanted a different kind of F.

F . . . un. And to not think about his job.

A gust of cold November wind caused Juliet to shiver. She hunched her shoulders and covered her chest with her hands.

Always the gentleman, Ramón took off his jacket and shook it out grandly. "Here, put this on."

She pulled it over her dress. "Thank you. That's really kind of you."

"Don't mention it."

She beamed at him. "Oh, I brought you something." She handed him a plastic bag.

Ramón was taken aback. He was used to giving gifts, not receiving them. He reached into the bag and pulled out two packages of foil. He unwrapped the first one to reveal a fish taco with a slice of lime.

He stared at the taco for a moment—did she know who he was? Or was this just a coincidence?

"I didn't know if you'd had a chance to eat."

Probably a coincidence. They were in Old Town on Day of the Dead—tacos were currency here. "I hadn't. Thanks. That was very thoughtful of you." Ramón sat on the lip of the tiled fountain, doused the taco in the side of hot sauce that was in the bag, squeezed some limón over the fish, and took a bite. She sat down a few inches away from him.

Whoa. These tacos were incredible! They were nothing like the ones they served at his restaurants. The full irony was that the entire idea of Taco King came from Papá eating the most incredible fish tacos made with fresh ingredients in Mexico. And when the business had first opened, they'd stayed authentic to that recipe. But over the years, cost cutting and catering to gringo palates had turned their taco into a shadow of its former self. The fish was now frozen, the tomatoes came from a can, and the tortillas were mass-produced in a factory. Ramón imagined that the taco he was eating now was close to the original one his company was based on.

This fish was so fresh and was coated in some type of spicy batter. The tortilla was crispy and light. And that sauce! What kind of chiles were used in it?

"Where did you get these? They are amazing."

She smirked and tossed her hair. "Oh, just some stand I passed on the way here. Glad you liked them."

Liked them? Ramón loved them. But more importantly, he was touched by her sweet gesture.

Normally, people he met only did nice things for him if they wanted something in return—usually his wallet. This woman didn't know a thing about him. She didn't know how rich he was or what kind of car he drove.

Maybe she would like him for who he was. Was that even possible? Who was he without his wealth or name?

He finished both tacos in a flash. Damn, he wanted another.

He reached out to take her hand, and he was pleasantly surprised when she didn't pull it away. "That was really kind of you. Let me repay the favor. Can I buy you a drink? There's this new bar up the street," he offered.

She placed her hand on his chest, which caused Ramón's heartbeat to accelerate. "Not so fast, Romeo." A playful grin spread across her face. "I'm still waiting for my next ballad."

Ramón laughed. He needed to take it slow, woo her. The entire time he had spoken with the mayor, his mind had been elsewhere—right here, with her. Juliet's hand lingered on his chest, which Ramón puffed out like a proud peacock. Her fingers were so delicate, so soft, so sensual.

"Romeo? The song?"

Right. The song.

"I'll play whatever you like."

She bit her lower lip. "Hmm. Well, you probably don't know the one I want to hear."

"Try me."

"Fine." Her mouth curled into a mischievous smile. "'Me Estoy Enamorando' by Alejandro Fernández."

Wow. This girl loved the same old-school music he did. But before he could start playing, her hand touched his. "No, seriously, I'm just giving you a hard time. Just play what you'd like."

Ramón was about to rock her world. He held the guitarrón and plucked the notes. She squealed when he began to sing.

Her response invigorated him.

Ramón had wanted to be a rock star, not a businessman. He'd grown his hair long and spent all his time rocking out to Metallica. He'd even joined a band that had played in local bars. But Papá had always reminded him that music was just a hobby, not a career. As the eldest son, he had a duty to carry on the family business.

Once, in a fit of teenage rebellion, Ramón had started a big fight with Papá. He'd told him that he hated the restaurants and was never going to work in the company. Papá hadn't joined Abuelo's gardening business—why shouldn't Ramón forge his own path? Become his own man?

Eventually, he cooled down—Papá was right. Ramón was grateful to have the privilege and the opportunity to be the CEO of a restaurant group at such a young age. He owned an oceanfront home in La Jolla and drove a lime-green McLaren sports car. Financially, he had everything he could possibly want. He had made the right choice, pushing away his dreams of rock-stardom to support the family business.

Even so, seeing the gorgeous woman in front of him singing along to the song he belted out and looking at him like he was a rock star performing in front of a sold-out crowd gave him more satisfaction than closing a multimillion-dollar deal ever had.

After he sang the last word, he put down the guitarrón.

She dramatically fanned herself. "Romeo, oh Romeo. You're so amazing! I'm super impressed. Do your parents listen to that type of music, too?"

Yup. Before they'd divorced. "They used to."

"Well, my mom still does."

"How about your dad?"

A pained expression appeared on her face. "He did. He passed away recently."

Ouch. "Lo siento." He couldn't make it better—but perhaps he could be there for her now. He could listen—if that was what she needed.

"It's okay. I mean, it's not. I'm kind of a wreck about it. It's my first Día de los Muertos without him."

Ramón squeezed her hand. "It must be tough."

She gave a small smile. "It's not easy. And I was working during the parade. I feel like I didn't do enough to honor him."

Well, Ramón could help her do just that.

He gently placed his arm around her shoulders and was pleased when she didn't pull away. "Come with me."

"Where?"

"Just trust me."

Juliet gave him a considering glance and then clutched her purse closer to her chest.

Dammit. She didn't know him. Of course she didn't trust him. New approach.

"Sorry. I should've been clearer. It's just somewhere I visited earlier tonight. There will be lots of other people there. We won't go anywhere you're not comfortable."

She exhaled. "Okay."

Ramón led her out of the garden, and they slowly strolled down the main marigold-lined street, which still buzzed with energy. Though most of the children had gone home, the adults were ready to party. Ramón was pretty sure that Enrique and Jaime were already wasted somewhere, making jerks out of themselves.

He glanced at the woman by his side. *Thank God I am here with her instead.*

Ramón stopped in front of his restaurant, which was still open. "I'll be right back. Wait here."

Juliet looked at the Taco King awning and crinkled her nose.

"I'll just sit on this bench until you come back."

She walked a few steps away, sat down, and grabbed her phone.

Great. She hated Taco King. Which meant she would probably hate him.

His throat constricted. Many Mexicans disliked the restaurants, especially the Old Town location because it was set up to attract tourists. The waitresses all wore traditional Mexican gowns and kept their hair braided with brightly colored ribbons. There were roaming mariachis in classic garb. Margaritas were served in glassware the size of birdbaths. Ramón had to admit the restaurant was a bit gaudy. The place had been accused of cultural appropriation, which was bullshit. Mexicans always ripped off other Mexicans in the food industry—once a trend hit, every taquería in San Diego started changing their menus. And Mexican regional specialties had origi- nated in other cultures anyway—pan dulces were influenced by the French, and al pastor was based on lamb shawarma from the Leba- nese. Cooking was about experimentation and innovation.

Not that Taco King did much in the way of innovation. They stuck to the tried-and-true classics and gave Americans what they wanted—basic Mexican food at affordable prices.

Maybe it was for the best Juliet didn't know his true identity. She may not be so interested in spending time with him if she blamed him for tarnishing the name of good Mexican food.

Ramón opened the door and went inside. Would Juliet even still be waiting when he emerged?

Despite being in costume, the waitress immediately recognized him. Though he was rarely at this location, a picture with Papá, Ramón, and his brothers adorned the wall.

The woman batted her eyelashes. "Hola, Ramón. How can I help you?"

He glanced at her name tag. "Hey, Ana Maria. I need two candles, a box of matches, two pieces of paper, a pen, and four shot glasses, por favor."

"Got it. One second."

She went to the back and quickly returned holding a bag.

"Here you go. Need anything else?"

"Nope, that's it. Thanks."

"Anytime, Ramón."

He left the restaurant and was pleased to find Juliet still sitting on the bench. He stopped to stare at her for a moment before he approached. Her long black hair cascaded down her back, ending right above her curvy hips. He was a lucky man that someone else hadn't come by and seduced her away from him.

He walked over to her and handed her a candle.

She eyed him. "What are you doing? The procession was at eight. They walked right by me."

Ramón nodded. He had watched earlier as hundreds of people carried candles and walked en masse to the graveyard. The community coming alive to respect the dead.

"Well, we will do our own. For your father."

"Really?" Her mouth opened and closed. "Thank you."

"De nada."

Ramón struck a match. The flickering flame cast shadows across her face as he gently held it to the wick of her candle. She cupped her hands around it, a giant smile on her face as if the two of them shared a secret.

Ramón lit his own candle for Abuelo, then gestured toward El Campo Santo Cemetery. "Shall we?"

"Yes. Thank you." She nodded, and slowly, respectfully, they walked out of the plaza, down San Diego Avenue for a few blocks, toward the most sacred of grounds.

Something about this moment—it was so right. Normally, this wouldn't be his idea of a first date, but he wanted to do something special for this enchanting señorita in the moonlight.

Juliet covered the flame with her hand as they walked, finally arriving at the cemetery. The tragic beauty of the graveyard gutted him, reminding him again how lucky he was that Papá was still here. The crosses were decorated with marigolds, and the colorful papel picado lined the white fence cheerfully, despite the aura of sadness that made his heart feel heavy in his chest.

Juliet placed her candle in an empty glass holder by one of the altars. Ramón put the guitarrón down.

"Did your dad drink?"

Juliet cast a downward glance. "Too much."

Got it. "Shall we give him some liquor?"

Her eyes widened. "Yes. He'd love that."

Ramón took out his flask of tequila and poured a shot into the glass for her father and another one for Abuelo. "Want to toast him?"

Juliet nodded as he handed her the glass and she placed it at the altar.

"Who is the other shot for?"

"My abuelo. He was a great man."

Juliet nodded. It was nice to share this moment honoring their relatives with someone else who respected and understood this holiday.

Ramón then poured two more shots and handed her one, a tiny fission of excitement thrilling through him as their fingers touched.

Juliet raised the glass to her lips. "¡Salud!"

"¡Salud!"

They downed the drinks.

"I also have paper and a pen if you want to leave your father a note."

Juliet exhaled. "Yes, please. Thank you."

He handed them to her and collected her glass. She placed the paper on top of one of the altars, scribbled some words, and then folded it over. She wrote "Alejandro" on the top and tucked it under a sugar skull. She handed Ramón the pen, and he quickly wrote his own note to Abuelo and placed it near a candle.

She knelt at the altar and made the sign of the cross on her chest before standing up to face Ramón.

She bit her lip. "Can I ask one more favor?"

"Sure. Anything."

"Would you sing a song for him? He loved music. He used to sing to me as a little girl . . ." Her voice choked up.

Damn. He hadn't planned to sing another song tonight but wanted to make her happy. "What did he sing, beautiful?"

"¿Y cómo es él?"

Ramón gulped, grateful that he knew that song but reluctant to sing it due to its meaning. Though many people thought this was a song about a betrayed man, it was actually written by a father who finds out his daughter is to be married and wants to get to know her future husband. Definitely an awkward choice for Ramón to sing. But how could he say no to her? "Of course." He picked up his guitarrón and strummed and sang. The lyrics hung heavy on his soul. *What is he like? Where did he fall in love with you? Where is he from?* The words had even more meaning in Spanish. It was almost as if Juliet's father was trying to get to know Ramón from beyond the grave.

Juliet wiped the tears from her eyes and touched Ramón's face. "That was one of the nicest things anyone has ever done for me."

"Don't mention it. We can stay as long as you like."

"I'd like that."

Ramón picked up his guitarrón and held her hand as they walked through the graveyard, looking at the other altars. Juliet marveled at a massive, colorful three-tier ofrenda filled with sugar skulls, pan dulces, and flowers. Ramón preferred the simpler ones, monochromatic with black-and-white pictures, candles, and items that represented what the deceased loved in their life.

Juliet turned to him. "I'm ready to go now."

Okay. He studied her heart-shaped face and got lost in her chocolate-colored eyes. He couldn't read her. Did she want to go home with him after such an emotional night? Probably not, and he couldn't blame her. Ramón wouldn't push his luck. At this point, he wanted to get her number and ask her on a proper date.

"Would you like to go to a bar and have a drink? We can get to know each other better."

She shook her head no.

Dammit. Where had he gone wrong? Maybe she just didn't want to get drunk, which was fine by Ramón. He wanted to remember this night.

Think, Ramón. The night slipped through his hands.

"Or we could go get dessert. There's this bakery that's open late. We could sit there and talk and get to know each other."

"I don't want to talk." She leaned into him, and Ramón quickly shifted the strap of his guitarrón from his side to his back. He pressed into her, feeling her tight body next to his. He smelled cumin and chiles on her—did she work in a restaurant? That was doubtful, since he'd met her only a few hours ago. No way would she have a shift that short.

He didn't know; he didn't care. He couldn't wait another moment to kiss his Juliet.

She tilted her head, and Ramón cupped it with his hands.

"Romeo?" she said, breathily.

"Yes?" His lips were a whisper from hers.

"Bésame." She leaned up and glanced her lips over his, soft and sweet.

His heart pounded. He took her softly at first, appreciating the subtle beauty and joy in that first kiss, a moment that could never be repeated with her again. Desire stirred inside him, and Ramón took no prisoners. He kissed her hungrily, and she responded with a fiery passion. She tasted like tequila and lime and lust. He wanted to get drunk on her lips. This kiss in the graveyard was hauntingly beautiful, just like her.

She pulled away first and looked deep into his eyes. "Do you live nearby?"

Yes.

"Close enough."

"Let's just go back to your place."

Ramón grinned. "I thought you'd never ask."

CHAPTER SIX

Her lips still were on fire from that kiss. *Oh, that kiss.*

That kiss was like one of the songs he'd sung to her earlier in the night—passionate, romantic, emotional, sexy. Julieta had never been kissed like that. Most of her dating experiences had been awkward, drunken hookups with men she didn't really know or care about. Which wasn't really her fault at all. She was a chef. She worked seven days a week, from an hour or more before her restaurant opened until an hour after it closed. Sex to her was stress relief, with little to no time to establish any semblance of an emotional connection.

Not that she knew Romeo. Hell, she still didn't know his real name.

He took her hand and led her to the parking lot. She was dizzy with lust and anticipation, though her nerves were on high alert just in case her instincts were wrong and he was some kind of psychopath. She clutched the Mace through her purse, thankful she had taken it from Mamá.

Why had she suggested going home with him? She never did that. She'd probably ruined her chance of having any sort of decent relationship with this man by not only agreeing to go home with him but asking to.

Dammit. He had offered to buy her drinks and dessert, not to take her to bed. He must think she was easy, or worse, desperate.

But tonight, she didn't want to think about being responsible. Or even having a future with this soulful man who sang to her heart. She just wanted to forget about the fact that she could be losing everything she had worked so hard for. She wanted to numb the pain of missing Papá.

She wanted to get lost in lust and pretend that her life wasn't imploding.

He pressed a button on his keys, and a shiny tomatillo-green sports car beeped.

What the hell? What kind of car was that? She studied the silver emblem on the back. A McLaren? Julieta had only ever seen one in her life, and it had been inside a showroom in La Jolla. What kind of man drove a car like this?

Maybe he was some trust fund baby. Maybe it was his father's car . . . though maybe not. He did say he went to Stanford. Maybe he had a high-paying finance job. Who else would spend a quarter of a million dollars on a car? Only a multimillionaire who had cash to burn or an idiot who lived above his means and tried to impress people.

He opened the door for her, and his hand brushed against her back as he helped her into her seat. Well, at least he was a gentleman. Or a player. Or both.

The cold, hard truth was that Julieta didn't know a damn thing about this man she was about to go home with. Mamá would be so ashamed.

But this wasn't about Mamá. This was about Julieta, for once in her life, taking a risk on something other than her cooking.

A risk on romance.

He popped the back of the car open and carefully placed his guitarrón in its case.

Once he got into the driver's seat, Julieta touched his thigh. It was hard and muscular. "Nice car." The tan leather was buttery soft.

Ay, Dios mío, please don't let my makeup stain the interior.

"You like it?"

"Uh, yeah. Who wouldn't? I've never been in a McLaren."

"Most people haven't. I know it's showy." He flashed a playful grin. "But I work hard. I deserve it."

Well, at least he was confident. "You must." What was his real name? Julieta wouldn't ask again. It would surely come up as the night progressed.

They left Old Town and headed in the opposite direction of her home in Barrio Logan. Where did he live? La Jolla? Del Mar? Rancho Santa Fe?

They exited toward Pacific Beach. Yup. La Jolla. Definitely La Jolla.

As they drove down the main drag, Julieta looked at all the carefree college girls, sauced-up sailors, and mischievous Marines partying at the bars in Pacific Beach with a smattering of vagabonds on the side of the street. Julieta ached for the homeless. Housing in San Diego was expensive. So many people were one paycheck away from living on the streets. Julieta would probably find another job if her restaurant closed, but what about her employees? If they lost their jobs, many of them wouldn't be able to pay rent. And what about Tiburón? He needed a job. Someone to take a chance on him.

Julieta focused her attention back on the sorority sisters and immodest Instagram influencers mingling with the muscular military men and blasé beach bros spilling out of bars and onto the busy sidewalk.

She had never gone to college, so she had no idea about that lifestyle. "It's packed here. Is it normally this busy?"

"Yeah. Every weekend. Do you not go out much?"

"No, I don't. I work nights."

"So do I. Nights. Afternoons. Mornings. All the time."

She smiled. She liked his work ethic. A rush of feelings came over her in a wave—maybe they were compatible. Julieta may not be wealthy, but she was top of her game in her career. She was a badass, and she knew it. "Well, I guess we have something in common then. What do you do, Romeo?"

"I run a business group. We have several properties throughout San Diego."

"That's cool." That sounded both impressive and boring. Julieta didn't understand the appeal of crunching numbers all day and schmoozing at golf courses. She preferred to be creative. She loved experimenting with classic cooking techniques and swapping in nontraditional ingredients. She had just perfected a recipe of lavender flan that she planned to put on the menu next week. Well, if there was a next week.

But clearly, he was successful. He drove a McLaren, and she had an old Honda with two hundred thousand miles on it. Not to mention she was about to lose her job, her restaurant, her life.

Stop. Stop thinking about it. Just for tonight.

He interlaced his fingers with hers. Her breath hitched. "Tell me more about yourself. What do you do for a living? And tell me your name, sweetheart?"

She didn't think he'd believe that her name was Julieta, after the whole *Romeo and Juliet* thing. And she didn't want to tell him about her restaurant. She was afraid she would just start crying. No more tears tonight.

"I create things. And I already told you my name. It's Juliet."

He winked. "Sure it is, babe."

The car hugged the road, and then he turned off the main street and snaked around the corner, driving along the beach.

She tugged on her hair. "I assume you like the beach since you live out here?"

He smiled, revealing his dimples, and she melted. "Yeah. I surf every chance I get. How about you?"

"Nope. I've never surfed. And I never go to the beach." She considered diving into a long diatribe about how her community in Barrio Logan used to have access to the beach until the Navy expanded their bases and moved the community inland. But it wasn't time for a San Diego history lesson.

"That's too bad. I'd love to teach you."

Julieta smirked. His words didn't seem like a line, but Julieta's guard was up. Even so, the thought of this handsome stranger in board shorts teaching her how to ride the waves drove chills up her spine. But tonight, all she wanted to ride was him.

He finally pulled up to a stunning modern mansion. It was sleek and massive, with an oceanfront balcony, and a rooftop deck with a hot tub.

Who was this guy?

The garage opened. It had more cars in it than an auto lot, including a Tesla SUV, a Porsche, a Lamborghini, a classic lowrider Mustang, and a pimped-out Ford Raptor. She stared at the Mustang. She was certain she hadn't seen it at La Vuelta, the car cruise in Barrio Logan. He parked, exited the car, and opened her door. His thoughtfulness was refreshing.

It didn't matter. This was a one-night stand—it was obvious to

Julieta that this Romeo, whoever he was, was completely out of her league.

And that was fine. This was one night. One night of shiny McLarens and beachfront mansions in her beater-cars-and-dilapidated-casas world.

He helped her out of the car, closed the door, and then pressed her up against the vehicle. Julieta loved the way he took control, and she melted in his arms.

His mouth covered hers, and she tasted the desire on his lips. He bit her bottom lip, and Julieta bit his back. A hungry look spread across his face.

She could feel every hard inch of him pressed up against her thigh. His tight charro pants left little to the imagination, and Julieta was excited that if the night went as she planned, she wouldn't have to wait much longer.

He pulled away with a devilish grin on his face. Then he retrieved his guitarrón case from the sports car.

He motioned for her to follow him to the door leading into the house and pressed his index finger to the screen on the side of the door, which caused it to magically open. Julieta had only seen locks like that in the movies.

But the keyless entry was not remotely impressive compared to this house.

The living room was literally overlooking the ocean.

Julieta sometimes scrolled real estate websites for fun. This house had to be worth at least six million dollars, probably more.

Was Julieta on some type of hidden-camera show? This night was completely insane. It was one of those fantasy dates from *The Bachelor.*

He placed his arm around her shoulders as she marveled at his casa. She clasped her hands in front of her face and scanned the room, every piece of art, every piece of artisan furniture causing her jaw to drop further and further. "Nice bachelor pad."

"Thanks. My brothers and I bought it together."

Ah, that was so sweet. Many people would find it odd for a man to live with his brothers, but not Julieta. Many Latinos lived with their families until they were married. She loved that he was close to his siblings. "Oh, are they here now?" This place was so big, they could probably be in another wing and Julieta wouldn't know.

"No. They are still partying in Old Town. We could've each bought places by ourselves, but we'd rather live together. After our parents' divorce, we were all each other had."

"Wow. That's cool you are so close." Julieta swooned. As tragic as his statement was, she was thrilled he was opening up to her. Maybe this had potential of being more than a one-night stand.

"How about you? Do you have any siblings?"

"Nope, I'm an only child." Julieta wished she had a brother or a sister. All she had were her cousins. Granted, she had nine of them on Mamá's side alone, but she was closest to Tiburón and Rosa.

"That must have been lonely. My brothers and I fight, but I still can't imagine life without them."

He stared at her like he saw right through to her soul, to the long nights she'd spent by herself.

But Julieta just imagined that—he didn't know anything about her.

"It wasn't too bad." She shrugged coquettishly and stepped closer to the gray suede sofa, as seduced by the soft material as she was by the view. "There are benefits to spending time by yourself."

"And indeed, to spending time with others." He stepped toward her, and the air sparked between them.

Kiss me.

Surely, he would kiss her again now. His lips, so full, so soft, so

close. His muscles bulged underneath his outfit. She couldn't wait to
see him naked.

"Let me make you a drink." He stepped back, breaking this tense
dance between them. "What would you like?"

He gestured to a marble bar in one corner of the room. Behind it,
a myriad of colorful liquor bottles shone in the golden glow of the
overhead lights. Hell, most of the restaurants she'd worked at didn't
have a bar like this one. "I'll take a paloma."

He smirked. "Good choice. Paloma coming right up. Make yourself at home."

Ha. I wish.

If Julieta got comfortable, she would never leave. "This place is
immaculate. I would never believe that three men live here."

"Well, I can't take credit for that. We do have a maid."

But of course he did. A pit settled in her stomach. She couldn't
imagine hiring someone to clean up after herself. She shook it off.
She wouldn't allow her prejudices about his wealth to ruin this night.

"Hey, can I use your restroom? This makeup is driving me crazy."
She wanted to wash it off before it ended up ruining his sheets, which
probably had a thread count higher than her bank balance.

"Sure." He pointed to the right. "Second door on the left."

"Thanks. I'll be right back."

She walked along the hallway and studied the art. There were
many cool pieces from up-and-coming Latino artists, including one
painting Julieta recognized as having won some huge award. It had
even been displayed in the White House—she was sure of it. She had
seen a television show during Hispanic Heritage Month about the
artist.

Then another photo caught her eye. A framed magazine cover of
an older man with three younger men beside him, one of which had
to be Romeo. All three men shared the same strong jawline and

dreamy dark eyes framed by even longer eyelashes. They all looked similar—probably his brothers and perhaps his father. She stepped closer to the picture and read the headline.

"Arturo Montez and Sons. The Taco King's Family Tells All."

What?!

Julieta's head spun, and heat pulsed through her.

The Arturo Montez? Owner of Taco King?

The man who had stolen the recipe from her own mother?!

It couldn't be. What were the chances of that? She stood closer to the picture and read the subtitle.

"Founder of the Taco King franchise with his sons, Ramón, Enrique, and Jaime."

Of course he was a Montez. He had even stopped by Taco King. Ay, how could she be so stupid? She should've ditched him then.

Panic tore through her as she became impossibly hot.

What had happened? Was this a setup? Did Romeo, who was probably Ramón, though she couldn't be certain due to the makeup and the fact that all three men looked alike, know who she was? Did he plan to seduce her and steal another one of her recipes for his crappy chain?

No. No. That was ridiculous. He had no clue who she was. They had met in masquerade. And she'd stupidly brought him tacos—though she didn't tell him that she was the one who had cooked them.

Either way, she had to get out of there.

She dashed back down the hallway.

Romeo clutched a drink in his hand. "You okay?"

"No, I'm not. This is a mistake. I need to go."

His face twisted with confusion. "What happened? I . . . We were having a good time."

"We were. I . . . I just have to go home. Now."

"Are you sure? We can just talk."

"No. I want to leave."

Romeo exhaled loudly and ran his hand through his hair. "Fine. I'll drive you."

"Nope. I'm good." If Romeo drove her home, she'd lose all control of her mind, give in to her hormones, which did not care if he was a Montez, and end up doing him in the back seat. Well, his McLaren didn't have a back seat, but that was beside the point. "I'm calling an Uber."

He shook his head as she reached into her purse and ordered a ride.

Breathe, Julieta, breathe. He had been a gentleman. The least she could do was be civil. "It was nice to meet you, Romeo. You have a beautiful voice." She paused and threw in a small jab. "You're really talented. Maybe you should've pursued music instead of business."

And with that, she opened the front door of his home and left. She checked her phone and confirmed her ride was on the way.

The salty ocean air blew through her hair. She would've liked to have spent a night out here in paradise, but it wasn't meant to be.

Julieta's fists clenched. At least she hadn't slept with the enemy.

As she waited, she savored the taste of the beach on her lips. A soft, lilting melody rang through the air—her favorite song, which he'd played earlier.

She looked up at the balcony. He sat on a chaise, holding the drink he had prepared, staring right at her.

Man, he was hot. And better yet, he had been kind.

Her ride pulled up and she hopped in.

She didn't belong in his beachfront mansion. And just like a rejected bachelorette, she headed home. Back to the barrio, where she belonged.

CHAPTER SEVEN

Ramón sat on the balcony of his condo and watched Juliet get into a car.

What had just happened? The night had been going great. She'd been totally into him until she'd gone to the bathroom. He'd thought for sure she would spend the night with him. What could have set her off?

He downed the drink he made for her in one shot and went back inside his house.

Women, man. He would never figure them out.

Ever.

Confusion coiled inside of him. Had he come on too strong? No, dammit. She had been the one to ask to go back to his place. Ramón hadn't even tried to take her home with him at that point. He had intended to buy her a drink, then hopefully win her over.

He threw his hands up in the air. It was probably for the best that she went home. The last thing he needed was an all-night-long sex fest to distract him from his mission—owning the property in Barrio Logan.

Even if that distraction was in the shape of a very charming chica.

It wasn't meant to be. He would celebrate tomorrow instead. But it would unfortunately be without Juliet.

Ramón undid the silk tie on his charro suit and exhaled. As he headed down the hall to the bathroom, he scanned the walls, seeing what she had seen. There was just some art and some pictures with his brothers—how could those have bothered her? Most women liked to see a guy who had taste and who was close to his family. Right?

He paused at the framed magazine picture of Papá, Enrique, Jaime, and himself on the wall. Could *that* have bothered her? Maybe she didn't like that his father had founded Taco King. Lots of Mexicans thought that Papá was a sellout, and she'd certainly turned her nose up at the joint earlier.

Well, Ramón guessed he would never find out why she'd left. He doubted he would ever see her again.

He couldn't find her if he wanted to—he didn't even know her real name.

Not that he had given her his.

Her words to him earlier in the night rang in his head—a prophetic warning.

It's hopeless. We can never work out. We're star-crossed lovers.

Just like the real Romeo and Juliet, Ramón and his star-crossed señorita were doomed.

Ramón entered his bathroom, stripped off his tight outfit, and hopped in the shower. He scrubbed the paint off his face. The hot water cascaded down his body, and his thoughts again turned to the captivating and mysterious girl who'd fled his house. He hadn't even seen her face without makeup, though he wished he had. Her lips were full, her breasts were beautiful, and her ass was round. And the way she kissed with her delicious mouth had driven Ramón wild.

His hand reached down to stroke his throbbing cock. Oh, how he wished it was her delicate fingers wrapped around his length, or better yet, her mouth.

Yeah, that was it. He wanted to fuck her mouth.

The soft tongue of hers licking his tip, teasing him until he couldn't resist her any longer. Juliet on her knees in front of him, deep throating him. Her eyes locked on his as she took him deeper and deeper.

Juliet!

Ramón gasped, the aftershocks of ecstasy still thumping deep inside of him. He finished his shower, brushed his teeth, and climbed into bed.

Tonight was a bust—but at least tomorrow he would be successful in closing the deal.

R amón woke the next morning bright and early. He looked out the window of his bedroom toward the ocean. The waves rippled, a perfect break. After he bought the building, he would reward himself and go surfing. He needed it, especially after striking out with Juliet last night.

He took a quick shower and then dressed in his custom-tailored suit. The bright blue color was a bit over-the-top, but having the best clothes, watch, and acumen helped intimidate the other competitors.

Ramón entered the garage and wasn't shocked to see that his brothers hadn't come home last night. He was sure they'd both partied their asses off. He slid into his McLaren and headed to Barrio Logan. As he left the shores of La Jolla behind, he reflected on the day ahead. Was this deal a good idea? That neighborhood hated change, but if he didn't bid, someone else would. If he succeeded, he would own an entire block of buildings on the main shopping street. There were several businesses that currently leased space there. A sea-to-table restaurant, a café, a panadería, a pharmacy, and a small bookstore. Ramón wasn't a dick—he would try to work with the businesses to see if they could stay there. But he knew most of them wouldn't be able to afford the new rent increase.

The current tenants had all been paying under-market rent for years. If they had to relocate, then that was sad but just business. He would revitalize the street and bring in new ventures. A flagship Taco King, one that was a bit more authentic, would anchor the street, no matter what. And maybe he could convince Starbucks or a small-format Target to lease the other open spaces. The possibilities were endless.

Ramón exited off the freeway. The vibrant Aztec warriors on the murals greeted him. Cultural pride beamed in his chest. The artwork in Chicano Park was legendary. His own father had once protested to preserve the park when the city of San Diego wanted to turn it into a parking lot for a future California Highway Patrol station. Papá had joined other Chicanos and made a human chain around the bulldozers. The irony hung heavy on Ramón—Papá had once fought hard to preserve the culture of this community, and now he would battle to strip the town of its vibe. Ramón's stomach grumbled—he couldn't tell if he was hungry or consumed with guilt.

Ramón shook off his conscience and focused back on the street. Wow, this area had changed so much already. Ramón came here as a little boy when there was nothing but local taquerías, panaderías, and bodegas. Now, the place was filled with construction. There was a group of work-and-live lofts to the right of the street and a brand-new brewhouse to the left.

Perfect. The new and improved Taco King would fit right in.

Ramón parked his McLaren in front of one of the buildings he hoped to acquire. A big sign greeted him—Las Pescas. He'd never eaten here, but supposedly, the hotshot chef made the best fish tacos this side of the border. Though he couldn't stop thinking about the tacos Juliet brought him last night. Too bad he'd not found out where she had purchased them. Those had been incredible.

The meeting for the auction was next door with the owner of the buildings, but since Ramón was early, he decided to check out the menu plastered to the black brick wall. So many authentic, hearty, classic Mexican dishes. Maybe after he and Papá completed their task, they could eat here.

As soon as he got out of his car, Papá pulled up behind him—in a brand-new Bentley convertible.

Ramón embraced Papá. Though in his mid-sixties, Papá looked younger than his years. His hair was black without a strand of silver, and his body was in shape thanks to his daily boot camp workouts. "Nice ride, Apá. When did you get that?"

Papá grinned at Ramón and pointed to the car. "I picked it up the other day. I would love to take it up the coast to Santa Barbara. It would be great if you, Enrique, and Jaime would join me."

Ramón winced. The song lyrics from "Cat's in the Cradle" rang through his head. Papá had always been slammed with work when Ramón was a kid. And now, Ramón and his brothers were the ones who were too busy. They didn't spend enough time with Papá, who was lonely. "I'll go with you, when things cool down at work. Maybe you should take some of your own advice and make time for the ladies."

"That would be nice. I hope to one day meet a beautiful woman."

It was only a matter of time before Papá would start dating again. Hopefully, he would find a good woman who was interested in him, not his money. The last thing Ramón wanted was for his father to become a sugar daddy. But he did want him to be happy. After his divorce, Papá deserved to find love again.

"Gotcha. Are you in the market for a trophy wife?" he said with a smirk on his face.

"Now Ramón. There is nothing wrong with taking time out for romance."

"I'm teasing. I want you to be happy, Apá. Now let's go buy this block."

Ramón and his father walked into the building for the auction. Normally, these things were done online, but the owner had insisted on meeting the buyers and looking them in the eye. That requirement rattled Ramón. He wanted his offer to stand out because it was the best business decision. Would the owner choose a lower offer to preserve the current landscape of the community? Ramón hoped not.

Ramón scanned the room and checked out the other suits. He recognized most of them from similar commercial real estate ventures that he had done.

To them, this was just another deal. To Ramón and his father, owning a piece of Barrio Logan was essential to the future of their company. This location was up-and-coming and had historical significance.

The owner entered the room, which fell silent. He was around the same age as Papá, but he had laugh lines around his face and distinguished silver hair. Ramón couldn't shake the thought that this man looked happier than Papá did.

After the owner shook everyone's hands, he gave a speech about what the block meant to him and his family. How he hoped that whoever bought it would preserve the culture and the authenticity of the block. The man's gaze lingered hopefully on Ramón and his father. They were the only Hispanic investors in the room. Surely the owner thought he could trust them.

But could he?

Each bid was submitted in an envelope, and the owner took them into his back office. Ramón exchanged a knowing glance with Papá.

Twenty minutes later, the man walked out of the room. He extended his hand toward Ramón.

"Congratulations, mi hijo."

Yes! Pride radiated through his body. He had done it! All those early mornings he'd spent crunching numbers, all those sunset surf breaks he'd missed, all those nights of hard work . . . it had all been worth it.

Ramón hugged the man. "Gracias, Señor Gomez."

"De nada, Ramón. I chose you because I believe you will do right by our people and invest in our community. It's great to see a successful Mexican-American businessman. You remind me of myself when I was your age. I trust that you will maintain the integrity of our street."

Dammit. Ramón's throat itched. "I will make you and the residents proud," Ramón lied. He hadn't planned to mislead Señor Gomez but was caught up in the moment.

Señor Gomez placed a firm hand on Ramón's shoulder. "Treat my tenants well."

Ramón forced a smile. "I intend to." He had to get out of here before Señor Gomez asked him detailed questions about his plans. Señor Gomez had to assume that they were putting a Taco King on the block—why else would they have bought it? Did he really think that Ramón had just spent eight million dollars as some sort of charity project? Señor Gomez was a businessman—he couldn't possibly be that naive.

The other people in the room extended their congratulations to Ramón and his father.

Ramón and the now former owner exchanged some information about their lawyers, and then said their goodbyes.

Once they had exited the building, Papá hugged Ramón.

"We did it! I'm so proud of you."

"Thanks. Let's go celebrate."

Ramón opened the door to Las Pescas. The restaurant was packed with people.

"Table for two?" a hostess whose name tag read Rosa asked. "Right this way."

Rosa seated them at a small table near the fireplace and handed them the menus. Ramón held her gaze for a second. Something about her reminded him of Juliet, but she looked younger. She had the same shade of brown eyes and a similar shape of mouth. But she had no tattoos on her arms. Ramón pushed Juliet out of his head.

This place was nice. Ramón loved all the Talavera tiles and pictures. They would be perfect for the Taco King's flagship restaurant. He would buy them from the owner after he shut the restaurant down.

The waitress came out and took their orders—Carnitas Eggs Benedict with Chipotle Hollandaise for Ramón and Huevos Divorciados for Papá. The name of Papá's order made Ramón laugh.

Arturo scanned the decor. "This place will make a great Taco King."

Ramón agreed but shushed Papá. They were here to eat, not announce their takeover loudly and alarm the current tenants.

After twenty minutes, a pretty woman came out holding two plates of food. Same color eyes as the hostess, and similar shaped mouth.

And nose.

And long dark hair.

It couldn't be. His eyes were betraying him again because he so badly wanted to see Juliet once more.

Ramón focused on the beautifully intricate Catrina tattoo on her arm.

Just like the one . . .

Whoa. Was that her? Surely not . . .

His eyes locked with hers, and there was no doubt.

Ramón had found his dead runaway bride.

"Juliet? It's me. Romeo."

Her mouth slowly opened as a flicker of recognition spread across her face. She dropped one of the hot plates, ceramics and salsa splattering everywhere.

The other customers turned to stare.

Her brow furrowed and her jaw dropped. "What are you doing here?" The look on her face turned from confusion to rage. She clenched her hand in a fist. "Did you come to steal one of my recipes for your crappy restaurants?"

What? Why would she say such a thing?

Arturo's face contorted, and he leaned across the table. "What is she talking about, mijo?"

"I don't know. I'll handle it, Apá." Ramón stood up to face Juliet, who was now even more breathtaking to him without last night's makeup. Man, she drew him in like a flame. He almost forgot what he was going to say when he was face-to-face with her magnetic beauty. Oh right, she had just accused him of trying to steal a recipe. What in the— "I don't understand why you would think that. Do you *work* here?"

She let out an audible huff and then raised her chin proudly. "I'm the *chef* here, 'Romeo.'"

Holy shit. Ramón's jaw dropped and his gut clenched. "It's Ramón, actually. I didn't know this was your restaurant."

The patrons turned to witness this train wreck.

An older woman ran out from the kitchen. "Ay, Julieta, what is going on here?"

Juliet-a? The Spanish version of fair Juliet. Of course, that's her name.

"Nothing, Amá." Her voiced cracked. "These guests were just leaving."

Papá gazed at Julieta's mom. His eyes widened, and he tilted his head. He stood up and stepped toward her.

"Linda? Is it you? It's me! Arturo!"

Wait, his dad knew her mom? "Apá? You know her?"

Linda clasped her hands together in a prayer position, and her eyes widened in surprise before they narrowed in rage. She took a deep breath and straightened her apron. "My daughter was right. Get out! You are not welcome in here."

Ramón's thoughts raced. What had just happened? Why were they both so mad? How did Papá know her mom? Ramón didn't have a clue, but he would figure it out. Clearly, there had been a big misunderstanding. Everyone just needed to take a deep breath and calm down.

Ramón sat and wiped some salsa off his suit leg. "I'm sorry, but I don't understand what is going on here. Why are you both so upset?"

Linda pointed to Arturo. "It does not matter. You have caused me enough pain and suffering. Just leave."

Ramón had had enough—who was this woman to talk to his father that way? He stood up. "We will do no such thing. We own this building now. We're your new landlords."

A look of horror flashed across Julieta's face. She threw the other plate on the ground and stormed back to the kitchen.

Rosa ran after Julieta.

Linda's lip quivered. "How could you do this to me, Arturo? Again! Have you no shame?"

She followed Julieta into the kitchen and left Ramón and Papá standing there amidst the shattered plates.

Chapter Eight

A shard from the plate was wedged in Julieta's ankle, but that pain was nothing compared to the stab in her heart after Ramón's announcement.

Rosa pointed one of her ornately manicured nails at Julieta. "Julieta! What was that about?"

Julieta just shook her head. She couldn't tell her prima about the masked man from the night before. Rosa couldn't keep a secret, and her entire family would be in Julieta's business, not like they weren't all the time anyway. Especially now that Romeo—er, *Ramón*—was the son of Arturo Montez. And even worse, the owner of their block.

Julieta watched from the kitchen window as he and his father left the restaurant.

Ay, Dios mío. She couldn't even form the words to express her emotions. Her rage. Her confusion. Her helplessness.

Julieta hobbled into the bathroom and pulled the ceramic piece from her skin and rinsed the wound in water. Blood swirled down the sink along with her hope.

Mamá stormed in and hovered over her. "Julieta! How did you know that man?"

"I don't know him, Amá. I met him last night at the Day of the Dead party." She left out the part about how he'd serenaded her in the garden, how he'd helped her honor Papá, how he'd kissed her under the moonlight, and how she had gone home with him. None of those details were relevant at all.

All that was important now was that Romeo, aka Ramón Montez, was now her landlord.

"Is he the reason you stayed behind last night? Did you know that he planned to buy our block? Did you know who he is? Who his *father* is?"

Julieta shook her head. "Ay, no. Of course not, Amá. I didn't know anything. It was Día de los Muertos last night. We were in makeup, remember?"

"So, the son of the man who stole my recipe forty years ago randomly met you last night and just happened to buy our block?"

Julieta grabbed the first aid kit and doused her wound in hydrogen peroxide. She winced at the sting. "Pretty much." She let out a deep breath and covered her cut with a bandage. "But none of that is relevant. He owns the building now. He will raise the rent and replace us with a Taco King. We will have to shut down."

Mamá nodded. "Yes, it seems like that will be the end result."

"Maybe I can change his mind." Julieta didn't believe for one second that Arturo, a man who had ruthlessly stolen Mamá's recipe decades ago and never given her any credit, would somehow grow a conscience. But Ramón seemed different. He was kind last night, and thoughtful. But he was probably just trying to get laid.

Julieta screwed the lid back on the peroxide and then turned and leaned her back against the sink. She stared into Mamá's brown eyes, now framed with fine lines. "What exactly happened between you and Arturo? You never told me the story. How did he steal the recipe?"

"It's irrelevant. What is done, is done." Mamá rushed out of the bathroom, shaking her head.

Why was Mamá so tight-lipped about her affair with Arturo? Julieta used to think it was because Mamá didn't want to disrespect Papá. But he was dead now. Why wouldn't Mamá tell her what had happened with Ramón's father?

Julieta put a Band-Aid on her foot and went after Mamá. There was no sign of her in the kitchen. Julieta found her cleaning up the mess in the dining room.

Julieta grabbed a broom and a dustpan from the utility closet and joined Mamá.

"Amá," she said under her breath, not wanting to draw further attention to their drama in front of their customers. "This is important now. Tell me."

"Fine." She pursed her thin lips. "Let me clean this mess up, then we shall go for a walk."

Uh, okay. Mamá never liked to leave the restaurant during the day, but Julieta had been dying to hear this story since she was a little girl, even more so now that she had met Arturo and Ramón, so she didn't question her.

Julieta poked her head in the kitchen and told the cook that she'd be right back.

Then she took Rosa aside. "Rosa, Mamá and I are taking a walk. If those men come back, tell them we are unable to serve them. And then text me."

Rosa nodded, and then her eyes widened. "Okay, but dímelo. Did you hook up with that guy? He's so fucking hot."

"Rosa! Who cares if he's hot? He's a Montez."

"So, you did sleep with him?"

Julieta grasped Rosa's shoulders. "No, I didn't." But Julieta had wanted to.

Rosa tossed her curled black hair. "Well, you should've. I would've. What a waste."

Julieta leveled Rosa with her eyes and turned to Mamá. "Okay, let's go."

Mamá pushed open the glass door and strode onto the busy main street.

Julieta was right behind her. And the first thing she saw was Ramón's guacamole-colored McLaren, but luckily, no sign of him. Where was he? Terrorizing another one of the shops he was going to destroy? Ay, Dios mío. Had he no shame flaunting his sports car here, knowing that he was going to buy their building and send panic through the community? A small crowd had gathered around the vehicle, and one chica, who was dressed up like a fifties-style pinup complete with salsa-red hair, was even posing for pictures in front of Ramón's beloved McLaren. The residents of Barrio Logan were car connoisseurs. One of Julieta's favorite events was the biweekly La Vuelta Lowrider Cruise. Classic cars would line the streets, music blasted from the radios, and drivers would bounce their automobiles, defying gravity.

Julieta loved her town.

She greeted everyone she passed on the block. Children from the local day care slid down the slippery slide at Chicano Park. Toddlers' laughter rang through the air, and Julieta smiled. She would often make the local kids bean and cheese burritos for lunch. Many of their parents couldn't afford food and their siblings' only meal of the day was at the local elementary school. But the people in the community always took care of one another. No matter what.

What would happen when they were all displaced?

Julieta and Mamá stopped at a fruit vendor, and Julieta indulged in some fresh mangoes with chamoy and Tajín. Mamá ordered some sandía with chile and limón. They grabbed their cups of frutas and sat in the park under her favorite mural that had the words LA TIERRA MIA painted above a Mexican worker wielding a pickax.

Chicano Park was the heart of her community. Nestled under the Coronado Bridge was the most magnificent artwork. It was full of historic Chicano murals featuring Mexican-American leaders. The scent from the dream sage in the herb garden mingled with the sweet smell of her mango. A little girl's ball bounced and became stuck between the bronze legs of Mexican revolutionary Emiliano Zapata. Joy flushed through her. She remembered coming here every week with her parents. This place was the brightness in their concrete jungle. She had been pushed in a swing here, learned how to ride a bike here, and had even had her first kiss in this very park. This place was glorious. And since it was a historical landmark, it was the one area that the gentefiers could never take from them.

"Okay, Mamá. Spill."

Mamá exhaled. "I had just convinced my papá to let me open a small taco stand of my own. He had a bigger restaurant down the street, but I wanted a simple menu. Fish tacos and beer. It was slow at first, because most of the gringos didn't want to try fish tacos, but business had picked up. One sunset, this young man stopped by and ordered two tacos and a beer. He was so handsome. His son looks just like him, but Arturo's skin was darker, and his hair was longer. He was a surfer"—Mamá gave a wistful sigh—"and he didn't wear a shirt."

And Ramón had told her he was always a surfer—just like his dad. What would Ramón look like shirtless? His body had been so firm against hers . . . Would his abs be chiseled into a six-pack? His chest warm and kissed golden-brown from our ancestors? She bet he had a sexy happy trail that led down to his—

No, Julieta. She had to stop thinking about him that way.

Mamá continued. "He loved the food and asked me out. Of course, I said no. Your abuelo was very strict and didn't want me to get used by an American man. He was worried that if Arturo loved me and left me, no man would ever want me again."

That was pretty misogynistic of him, but Abuelo lived in a different country and a different time. She had fond memories of him. He always wore a hat and would give her candy when her parents forbade it.

"So you snuck out?" Julieta asked.

Mamá shook her head and took a bite of the watermelon. "No, I didn't. I agreed, and Arturo came and met my father. We had a chaperone, my Tía Viola, accompany us on our date. And wow, was Arturo a charmer. He taught me how to surf and would read poetry to me. He sang to me on the beach. I loved him."

Poetry and music sounded heavenly. Ramón quoted Shakespeare and had even offered to teach Julieta how to surf. Like father, like son. "So dreamy. What happened? He seems perfect."

"He was. We spent two weeks together, and he had to go back to San Diego to graduate. He promised to return when school was out. I waited for him, and he never came. I finally had to accept that he would never come back. So, I forced myself to move on." She paused, her face turning warmer. "Your father had always loved me. He had been my best friend, and my family adored him. I finally realized that I loved him too—that our friendship was stronger than any fleeting, irresponsible passion. The basis of a lifelong partnership. He asked my papá for my hand in marriage. My father was thrilled, and we wed."

Julieta pursed her lips. Mamá's relationship with Papá was like Julieta's relationship with Pablo. Strong, steady, based on similar values and upbringings, not lust and liquor. And her parents had been so happy together.

"Well, you definitely chose the right man. I'm selfishly glad Arturo didn't come back, or I wouldn't be here."

Mamá held Julieta's hand. "Me too, mija, me too."

Julieta still had unanswered questions. "But why do you think he stole the recipe?"

"I don't think he did, mijita, I know! I had it in a recipe book. And then it was gone. Poof. Vanished."

Julieta wasn't convinced. "Are you sure? How did he know it was in there?"

"I had invited him to dinner and showed him the recipe book. He knew where it was. He had asked about it many times, and I joked that it was a family recipe. That he would have to marry me to get it. He had always dreamed of opening a restaurant. But he wasn't a chef. I was."

Julieta sucked the chamoy off the mango. She loved the tart, salty taste mixed with the sweet. "And you never talked to him again?"

"No, it was the late seventies. We didn't have emails and cell phones. We had letters. He never wrote. I never saw Arturo again— until today. I never wanted to, not even when he stole the recipe. It was easier to just forget—less painful. You understand."

Julieta hugged her. "I'm sorry, Mamá. That must've been hard. But why didn't you go after him later? When you came to the States? You could've sued, Amá. You would have some claim to his profits. They are millionaires." Julieta considered mentioning Ramón's McLaren and his house in La Jolla but decided against it.

"I didn't want to come off as a scorned woman. Who would have believed me? And I was so happy with your papá. And you. You were my dream. The money didn't matter."

"But it does matter. If we had their money, we could've bought the block."

"I know this new situation seems impossible, my love. But we will come out smiling, no matter what."

She wiped her brow furiously. "So, what you are trying to tell me is that it's okay to lose the restaurant."

"I'm just saying that whatever happens, happens. There is more to life than work. And holding on to your anger isn't healthy. Papá wouldn't like it."

Mamá's words hung in the air, annoying Julieta. She refused to just resign herself to losing the restaurant. She needed to fight for what was rightfully hers.

Running Las Pescas was her calling.

She'd worked so hard to build her own place—and she wanted Mamá to be able to retire soon, not have to start over again.

Besides, the problem was bigger than just her. The whole community would suffer if she didn't do something. And the Montezes had stolen from her family before and profited off their hard work; she wouldn't let it happen again.

They finished their fruit and walked toward the restaurant. Julieta was ready for war—she would give all she had to save Las Pescas. It was her right. It was her legacy.

And she was still in complete shock that Ramón was the one who'd bought her building.

Ramón was a gentefier—no doubt about it. Who the hell did he think he was—buying up land in Barrio Logan? He was Mexican, dammit! He should know better.

Maybe Ramón would do right by the neighborhood and by her.

He'd seemed kind enough last night. He hadn't done a single thing to offend her or pressure her. He could be a good guy. He couldn't force *all* the tenants out of their businesses—could he? What if he infused money into the community instead? He could keep the rent affordable and invest in improving the buildings.

But deep in her gut, she didn't believe that. Julieta had been to Ramón's lavish house, a detail she hadn't shared with Mamá.

A man who drove a McLaren and lived in an oceanfront mansion in Bird Rock didn't strike Julieta as the type to be focused on helping his community.

She hoped she was wrong.

What would happen next? Would Ramón feel like he could show up at her business anytime he wanted since he was her landlord? She did not want to see or deal with him.

Even though he had looked so ridiculously hot in that suit, even hotter than he had last night. Now she could see his chiseled face, his strong chin, his dark eyes, there was no more question—he was dangerously and devastatingly handsome.

But nothing could ever happen with them. She laughed thinking about how they met. They truly were Romeo and Juliet. Two strangers who shared an intense connection and who were from families who had a bitter feud with each other.

The Montezes and the Camposes.

Two households, both alike in dignity,

In fair Barrio Logan, where we lay our scene . . .

Once they arrived back at Las Pescas, Mamá went into the kitchen to braise the carnitas. Julieta greeted the guests and then snuck to the back to check her email on her phone.

There was a message from Ramón Montez to the restaurant's contact email.

Her heart raced as she clicked on it.

Julieta,

I am sorry for shocking you this morning. I truly had
no idea you were the chef at Las Pescas. I would like
to talk to you about the future of your restaurant.
Could we meet for dinner?

Sincerely,
Ramón

He wanted to have dinner? As in, a date? Was he mad?

Chapter Nine

Ramón stared at his phone after he'd sent the email. He couldn't believe that the enchanting woman he had met at the Day of the Dead party was the chef at Las Pescas.

He waited for a reply, but there was nothing.

After getting kicked out of Las Pescas, Ramón and Papá had settled on coffee and pan dulce at the neighboring coffeehouse. He chose a table in the far back of the café, hoping no one would recognize him from the scene at Julieta's restaurant. Ramón sipped his café de olla, which was sweet and spicy and quite strong, and took a bite of his crunchy concha, which was equally delicious. This place was another hidden authentic gem, and the ladies here were not throwing dishes at him, so that was a plus.

Ramón studied Papá. His left hand shook, and his eyes were wide and wild. Papá downed his coffee like it was a shot. "Apá, how do you know Julieta's mom?"

A faraway look graced Papá's face. "It was another lifetime ago, mijo. I met Linda in San Felipe before I started Taco King."

Ramón's eye's widened. "*She's* your Baja beauty?"

Papá nodded and his smile widened into a cocky grin. "The one and only. I can't believe it's her. She's still as beautiful as she was the evening I serenaded her on the beach."

Guau. Like father like son. Love songs for the win.

"Did you love her?"

Arturo patted his chest. "With all my heart."

Ramón couldn't believe Papá's words. In previous retellings of this story, Papá had always made it sound like it had just been a fling. "Then why didn't you go back for her?"

"I did. But I found her with another man."

Ouch. That had to hurt.

"Did you beat him up?"

Arturo shook his head. "No, of course not. I wanted to, Ramón. I wanted to rip his throat out."

Wait—Linda said he had hurt her.

"Why did she say you made her suffer?"

Arturo threw up his hands. "I don't know. Probably because she thinks I never came back for her, but I did. After I saw her with that guy"—Arturo closed his eyes tightly as if he was fighting his memory before opening them again—"I wanted nothing to do with her."

Ramón swallowed. Wow. Seeing Papá react so strongly to Linda rattled him. What had he been like when he was younger? Romantic and passionate like Ramón was? Had Linda's betrayal of Papá cast a shadow over Ramón's parents' relationship?

"I'm sorry."

"It's in the past. I'm over it."

But Ramón didn't think that Papá was over it. By the hurt expression on his face and the anger in his voice, Ramón was certain that Papá was still holding on to some bitter resentment.

What a small world. Now Ramón had the hots for Linda's daughter.

How could it possibly be that the beautiful woman he'd kissed in the moonlight and had bonded with about being workaholics was the chef of this restaurant? He was thrilled that he had found her, but now they had no chance together. She hated his guts; their families were enemies. What a cruel twist of fate.

But maybe he could fix this.

He was a problem solver. He listened and was compassionate, probably from the years he'd spent consoling his younger brothers when they missed their parents, who were always traveling when they weren't fighting. As for Julieta, he would start by taking her to dinner tonight—that was, if she agreed.

But first, he had to figure out what his plan was for Las Pescas.

He had intended to turn it into another Taco King—it was in the best location for a restaurant on the block. But now, he had his doubts.

He also now assumed that the tacos she'd brought him in the garden were ones she had made herself. Ramón typed on his phone. A few seconds later, his suspicions were confirmed—Las Pescas had a taco pop-up in Old Town last night.

He wished she hadn't dropped his plate of eggs—he could pretty much guarantee that they would have tasted incredible.

Just like her.

He studied Papá, who was surveying the place, no doubt planning the fate of this café. Papá's mind was as sharp as ever.

"So, what are we doing with Las Pescas?"

Papá sighed. "What do you mean, what are we doing with Las Pescas? We talked about this, Ramón. We are turning it into a Taco King. Our flagship store. We will hire a chef to create a specialized menu. Add some new food items. Have the girls wear traditional out-fits. It will be stellar."

A bitter metallic taste filled Ramón's mouth, and it wasn't from the sweet pastry he ate. "Like the Old Town location? It feels almost offensive here. Old Town is more of a tourist location—Barrio Logan is a community. I don't think dressing the waitresses in Mexican clothing is appropriate."

Arturo folded his arms across his chest. "Ramón, Old Town is our most lucrative restaurant. People come from all over the country to experience some of our culture. We can do the same for Barrio Logan."

But Barrio Logan didn't want to be some tourist trap. Papá should understand that. Ramón had to think of a solution that would ap-pease everyone.

Ramón's head now ached. If they went ahead with Papá's vision, he would never have a chance with Julieta.

But more importantly, Taco King would be replacing a beloved local independent restaurant run by a local chef who lived in the community with a reviled chain. Ramón had known this all along, but the issue hadn't been abundantly clear to him until today, when he had seen Julieta and been inside her restaurant.

"Right, Papá. But this community is already resistant to us. I saw Benicio last night. He told me they don't want us here. And he's right. So we need to ease our way in and build trust. I'm not sure we should just go around changing everything. At least not immediately."

Arturo's brow cocked. "I want a Taco King in Barrio Logan. That is the whole reason we did the deal, why we purchased the entire street. We need a location here. A marketable one. It's nonnego-tiable."

Ramón gritted his teeth. There was no way that Papá would

budge, and until he retired, Papá had the final say on everything. And Ramón couldn't really blame him.

How had he not thought this all through while making the bid? Ramón had spent hundreds of hours researching the numbers in Barrio Logan. He had even driven by here a few times. But he had missed the mark. He hadn't truly spent time here since he was a kid. He hadn't realized what made it tick. Basically, he had completely fucked up.

But at least he was willing to admit his mistake and fix it.

"I got it. Don't worry, I'll handle it." Ramón looked around at the café. One wall featured a mural of a sexy chola clasping a rosary and a painting of some shiny purple lowriders. The place smelled like cinnamon and spice. A Juanes song played over the sound system. Ramón couldn't help but tap his foot. This café had so much character. It had so much heart.

Ramón smiled at an older woman making coffee behind the bar. Was this her café? Was he about to crush her dreams and kill her livelihood? "What about this place? Are we going to close it?"

"Raise the rent. If they can afford it, they can stay. If not, we can approach Starbucks."

How could he shut this café down? For a soulless Starbucks? He glanced at the merchandise—they sold hand-painted cups and local artisan crafts. What would the new place sell—a Starbucks Barrio Logan mug with a drawing of Chicano Park?

Ramón's stomach clenched, but he blamed himself for getting into this mess. This had always been the plan for the block; nothing had changed except that he found out that Julieta was the chef at Las Pescas. Why hadn't Ramón listened to Benicio, or more importantly, consulted with him about the project? Spent some more time here before he pursued the deal? Eaten more conchas at this café, dined at Julieta's restaurant, understood the implications of this transaction?

"Do we have to destroy every business here? Maybe we can work something out with them. Apá, we want the community to like us."

Papá glared at him. "Look, mijo, don't go getting all soft on me because you want to sleep with Linda's daughter. How do you know her again anyway? Did you meet her when you were doing research on this deal?"

"Nope." Ramón smirked. "I met her last night." Ramón didn't go into details, but he was certain whatever Papá imagined was more scandalous than what actually happened.

"That's my boy! She is beautiful, just like her mother."

"Yes, that she is. But now, it's awkward."

Though Ramón normally thrived on his father's praise, this time Papá's words had the opposite effect. Ramón had closed the deal. He should've been ecstatic. But, instead, he was racked with guilt.

But why? Was it just because he had the hots for Julieta? A woman he didn't even know? He just lusted after her—that was all.

Or maybe it wasn't all. Ramón flashed back to how she'd looked at him in the garden when he sang, how she was thoughtful enough to bring him food, how she seemed to like his company even before seeing his McLaren and knowing how rich he must be. He didn't just want to sleep with her; he wanted to get to know her better.

Papá pointed at Ramón. "Unfortunately, things will not work out between you two due to my history with her mother and our owner-ship of their building. There are many other beautiful women, espe-cially here in San Diego. No matter what, never mix business with pleasure."

Ramón heeded Papá's words, but that didn't mean that he had closed the door on Julieta.

He still wanted her.

He checked his phone. A message from Julieta awaited.

Mr. Montez,

As your tenant, I will agree to meet you to discuss the future of Las Pescas. But I need to be clear—this is not a date. I have no desire to have dinner with you. You can meet me at the restaurant tonight at six p.m.

Sincerely,
Julieta Campos

P.S. I apologize for dropping your food.

Yes! She agreed to meet him, though Ramón realized that she really didn't have much of a choice.

Ramón's first instinct had been to buy her roses and take her to dinner at the most romantic restaurant across the bridge in Coronado, but he could see that plan was completely inappropriate. He did not want to make this already uncomfortable situation even more awkward. Or make Julieta feel that he was sexually harassing her.

So he would keep it professional.

For now.

Dear Miss Campos,

Thank you for agreeing to meet with me. I will be there tonight at six. No apology necessary for earlier. I understand how shocked you were—as was I. Though, to be honest, I'm glad I found you.

Sincerely,
Ramón Montez

He downed the rest of his drink and turned to Papá. "I'll be meeting Miss Campos tonight at six to discuss the future of Las Pescas. Who knows? Maybe they will be able to pay the new rent."

Ramón enjoyed testing Papá.

Papá took a sip of his second Mexican mocha, then licked the whipped cream off his upper lip. "If they can pay that amount, then raise it until they can no longer pay, Ramón. I want to take over that restaurant. I *will* take over that restaurant. That space will be a Taco King. This is nonnegotiable."

Ramón grabbed his phone and his keys. "Got it." Frustration laced his words. "Well, I have to get back to work and prepare for my meeting with her tonight. I'll see you soon."

Papá stood to hug him, but Ramón turned toward the door. After they said their goodbyes, Ramón exited the café. On the way out, he left a one-hundred-dollar bill in the tip jar. The lady smiled at him, and guilt consumed Ramón. She had no idea that he was about to destroy her business.

He licked the final remnants of that pastry off his lips. He should've bought more, because once he shut this place down, he would be eating stale blueberry muffins and prepackaged frozen and dethawed egg sandwiches at the future chain coffeehouse instead.

Before getting into his car, Ramón strolled down the street. Though the coffee and pastry were both great, Ramón was still hungry. He stopped in a cool hot dog shop named Barrio Dogg that had a gallery of artwork and a sick lowrider car out front.

This place was so cool—the perfect blend between American and Mexican culture. He ordered a beer and a bacon-wrapped hot dog topped with chili con carne, manchego cheese, jalapeño peppers, salsa verde, a slew of other spicy peppers, and a menacing-sounding house-made chili oil called Dragon Tears.

He sat facing the street so he could experience the vibe of the block.

The sun shone and reflected the bright colors of the artwork on the buildings. He took a picture of a mural of Selena painted by a local artist. People greeted each other with hugs. The owner knew his customers by name.

Pretty much the opposite of La Jolla.

The owner served him his beer. Ramón sipped it and thought back to his Stanford classes about Chicano history. How the government destroyed this community by allowing the military to take its beaches and by rezoning it for industrial uses. He gazed at the bottom of the Coronado Bridge, which was like a concrete roof that covered most of Barrio Logan.

Back then, Ramón had been dedicated to embracing his culture and fighting for its survival and growth. He had marched for farmworkers' rights, worked on immigration reform, campaigned for bilingual education.

Now he was responsible for tearing his community apart.

His food arrived. The colors from the chiles and the condiments made this dish look like a work of art. He took the first bite of the hot dog and the heat from the peppers burned his lips, but in a good way. The flavors partied in his mouth, and Ramón was in complete heaven.

Thank God they hadn't bought this building.

Ramón finished his meal and headed back to his car.

He strolled past a paleta vendor, the sweet smell of his frozen treats lingering in the air.

"Watch out!" the vendor cried out.

Ramón darted to the side just as a gaggle of kids raced past him, chasing a soccer ball down the pavement. He shook his head and kept walking until he came to a jewelry artist set up in a small stand.

He took a closer look at one of the pairs of earrings. They had red roses with some beads hanging below. He couldn't help but think that Julieta would like them, but he was in no position to be giving her gifts. Ramón slapped down a twenty and bought a pair anyway.

He stopped and stared around the block—*his* block. He had done months of research on Barrio Logan, and had even visited a few times, but he had never truly gotten a sense for it as he did today. Behind the numbers and data, he had missed an important element.

The people.

People like Julieta. People like her mom. People like the elderly man pushing a paleta cart. People like the barista in the café. This neighborhood was ripe for gentrification. But Ramón stopped for a second and said a prayer for the culture—his culture—that he was about to betray.

Chapter Ten

Julieta read Ramón's reply on her phone.

He would come over tonight.

She made the sign of the cross on her chest and said a quick prayer.

But her momentary calmness quickly dissipated. How could she pull off her plan? Her throat constricted.

She had asked him to meet at her restaurant—now she needed to give him a meal he would never forget.

She barged back into the kitchen, where Mamá obsessively scrubbed food off a plate.

"Amá, Ramón is coming back here. Tonight."

Mamá cocked her head to the side. "What are you talking about? El Banco is not welcome here. He and that pendejo father of his."

Julieta threw her hands up and had to stop herself from laughing at Mamá's new nickname for Ramón. "Amá, stop. Don't you see? This is our only hope of saving the restaurant. He bought the block;

he owns the land. That is final. There is nothing we can do about it. He can shut us down. Unless . . ."

"¿Qué?"

"Unless we can somehow convince him to let us stay."

Mamá turned the water off, wiped her weathered hands on her apron, and faced her daughter. "Ay, Julieta. De tal palo tal astilla. He is just like his father—he does not care to be honorable. He only wants money. He's greedy. He doesn't care about his people, his culture. They are not like us."

Maybe Mamá was right, but Julieta didn't want to admit it. She only had a glimmer of hope to keep her dream alive.

"But Amá, he will love my cooking. *Love* it. Their food sucks. If he puts a Taco King in here everyone will revolt. And he's a smart man. He knows this. I read his biography online—he went to Stanford and Harvard."

"He may be a good student, but he has no street smarts. And he must not care about bad publicity."

"Oh, I think he cares about his image. If he didn't, he wouldn't be driving that car. Did you see it?"

"I saw it. Why do I care about his car?"

"It's a McLaren. Do you know how expensive that car is?"

"No, and I don't want to. And you are wrong. He drives that car because he wants to draw attention to himself. Flaunt his money. But he doesn't care if we revolt. He will get richer while we lose everything." Mamá shook her hands dramatically as if painting a scene before them. "People will still come to eat at his crappy restaurant. He will probably hire a tour bus to bring them here from the airport. Put a donkey out front for pictures. He will attract tourists that don't know the difference between tacos and tostadas."

How could someone not know the difference between tacos and

tostadas? One was folded; one was flat. It was simple, really. "I don't know. Maybe you are right."

But maybe she wasn't.

Julieta didn't know what would happen. But she did know one thing.

She hadn't spent much time with him last night. Hardly any at all, in fact. But he had come alive when he'd played the guitarrón. How he'd worn that instrument proudly strapped to his chest; how he'd sang in beautiful Spanish; how he'd beamed with pride when she'd cheered him on.

She had seen his soul.

And he was kind. He'd led her to the graveyard to honor her father. Hell, he even sang to her dad. That couldn't have been an act, could it?

If he could connect to those lyrics through music, maybe he could connect to their culture through food. And she wasn't dumb— he wanted her. Maybe he would at least consider giving her restaurant a chance to survive for his ulterior motives. A man like him always got what he wanted—and he wanted her.

Julieta had to try to save Las Pescas. She refused to give up that easily. "I'm going to try."

"Don't waste your time. It's not going to work." Mamá scrubbed a pan.

"Stop with the dishes, Amá. I need some help."

Mamá turned the water back on, reached over to the radio, and blasted some Maná.

"Real mature, Amá."

Ay, Julieta would have to go at this alone.

Which was fine.

Mamá was many things—a great cook, a loving wife, a protective mother, and a loyal friend, but she wasn't a fighter. If she had been a fighter, Julieta wouldn't be in this position in the first place. Mamá should've confronted Arturo years ago, when she came to the States. She should've asked him if he stole the recipe. Sued him. Taken the money and then created a great life for her family.

But Mamá didn't like conflict. She valued peace and love and family.

Julieta valued those things, too, but she wouldn't go down without a fight. As her father's daughter, she always stood up for what she believed in, no matter what it cost her.

And with that, Julieta pulled out all the stops. Lure Ramón in with her food and beg him to keep Las Pescas open.

She quickly surveyed her ingredients. Pumpkin, fresh fish, and almost every spice and chile imaginable. What to do, what to do?

Julieta could go high end with a bougie tasting menu composed of expensive ingredients with minuscule portions, so he could pretend he was in one of those pretentious restaurants where it took months to get reservations. Maybe then he would feel at home.

Or, Julieta could flip the script. Go truly authentic and regional. Huge servings of traditional fare that could rarely be found this side of the border.

Neither of those felt right. Julieta wanted to wow him, make him believe that keeping her was the right thing to do.

And then it hit her.

A Day of the Dead–themed tasting menu.

Pan de Muertos
Empanadas de Calabaza y Chorizo
Huitlacoche Soup
Pan-seared Dorado with Mole and Nopales
Chocolate Tamales

The course list made her salivate. The perfect blend of tradition and innovation. Just like her restaurant.

After the pumpkin was pureed, the spices were toasted, and the dough was kneaded, Julieta immersed herself in her work.

She was in the zone. Her feet tapped to the music Mamá played. Time flew by when she cooked. The freedom to create experiences from fresh ingredients made her spirit soar. She had been born to be a chef.

She put the finishing touches on all the prep work and glanced at her reflection in a shiny pot.

Sweat dripped down her face, her hair was frizzy, and her skin was blotchy.

She was a hot mess—ugh. She couldn't have a serious business meeting like this.

Julieta went into the bathroom and washed her face. She put on some moisturizer and lip gloss. That would have to do.

She left the bathroom. Mamá took one look at her and shook her head with disgust.

"What are you doing, mija?"

"I'm getting ready for Ramón. He will be here in an hour."

Mamá's eyes scanned Julieta from head to toe, and then she shook her head in disgust. "Go home, mi amor. Take a shower. Shave your legs. Wear a dress. Put on some lipstick. Get ready. Look nice for him."

"Ay, Amá. What are you talking about? This is not a date. And you don't even think this plan will work."

"I still don't, but you do, so I'll go along with the charade. And if El Banco is anything like his papá, you should look nice."

Julieta shook her head. "Well I'm not going to sleep with him to keep this restaurant, if that is what you are implying."

She should just sleep with him for fun instead. The thought of Ramón naked awakened feelings in her that she had repressed.

She hadn't stopped thinking about him since she had run out of his place last night. How his hands had strummed the guitarrón, how those same hands would feel caressing her breasts, clutching her waist, in between her legs, squeezing her ass.

Stop!

She couldn't sleep with him—not when he held her fate in his hands.

"Of course not. But that doesn't mean you shouldn't look pretty. Make him weak, Julieta. And wear some perfume, for God's sake."

"Perfume gives me headaches."

"You give me a headache. What kind of Mexican woman doesn't like to wear makeup? I have failed you as a mother. Ay, sometimes I wonder if you are my daughter. Maybe they switched you at the hospital."

Burn. Julieta hadn't inherited Mamá's love for bright red lipstick and heavy eye shadow. As a child, she'd preferred playing in the dirt with Tiburón to dressing up dolls with Rosa, much to Mamá's dismay.

Despite her attraction to him, Julieta didn't feel like she should have to look "nice" for any man, especially a man as blessed as Ramón. The last thing that he needed was an ego boost. Let's see— multimillionaire, *People en Español*'s Most Eligible Bachelor, Stanford and Harvard degrees, a musician, a great kisser. The dude drove a McLaren and lived in an oceanfront house. He seeped self-confidence. She was probably the only woman in all of San Diego to reject him, a fact that made her proud.

It also might make her stupid.

Even so, she gave in to Mamá. "Fine. I'll be right back."

She set off out the back door to walk the three blocks to her home just off Logan Avenue. She didn't just work in Barrio Logan; she lived here; she was raised here. These streets meant everything to Julieta.

She reached her bright yet tiny home on the corner and let herself in. Her dog, Taco, greeted her at the door and wagged his nubby tail.

He was a black and brown Min Pin that Julieta had found near a dumpster six months ago. He'd had mange and a cloudy eye. Mamá had at first refused to let her keep him, but Julieta had stood up to her and nursed him back to health.

Julieta wished she could move out someday and live in her own place. She'd had an apartment a few blocks away for a while, but once Papá passed away, she felt guilty that Mamá was alone and had moved back home like the dutiful daughter she was. Especially with Mamá's health issues, Julieta wanted to be close to her.

And now, with the impending closure of Las Pescas, even if she found another job, Mamá likely would not be able to. She'd be stuck—and Julieta couldn't leave her homeless.

Unless she could convince Ramón to keep it open.

She gave Taco his dinner of chicken, rice, and carrots, which he scarfed down. Then she took him out back and threw the ball with him for a bit. Her yard was small but enchanting. She had one raised garden bed where she grew chiles that she couldn't find in the local markets. There were some pots containing roses, dahlias, and agave. In the center was Julieta's favorite part of the house—a small Mexican-style fountain. Bees buzzed and the floral-scented air calmed her nerves. The only benefit that could possibly come out of losing the restaurant was the ability to spend more time sitting out here reading books while Taco sunbathed.

Julieta took a quick shower and then combed out her long black hair. The weather was surprisingly humid for San Diego. Her hair would probably look just like it did in the kitchen in about five minutes' time. Julieta slathered on some product, found Mamá's blow-dryer, blasted her hair, and then set it in rollers.

What should she even wear? Julieta's daily wardrobe consisted of baggy pants and clunky clogs—great for being a chef but definitely not what Mamá would consider looking nice.

She perused the back of the closet and found one outfit that she had worn to her prima's quinceañera. The bright red dress cut off at her thigh. It seemed a bit too sexy for the occasion, but since she didn't have any other options, it won.

Time to tackle the makeup. Moisturizer, primer, foundation, eye shadow, bronzer, blush, lip liner, lipstick, gloss, mascara. She even filled in her brows and curled her eyelashes. Mamá would be so proud.

She glanced in the mirror. Julieta looked pretty, beautiful, even— two words she had never used to describe herself. Ever.

Before heading back to the restaurant, Julieta took a moment to herself.

She sat on the sofa and lifted up Taco, who burrowed on her lap.

She had to ground herself before she saw Ramón. Just being in the same room as he was made her heart race.

Was it possible to keep it professional with him? Was she doing all this for nothing?

Possibly. Probably.

But Julieta had run out of options. She had to try.

CHAPTER ELEVEN

Ramón kept checking his watch. He didn't want to be too early or late. Why was he so nervous? He felt like he was on a first date, and he rarely dated.

But this wasn't a date. She had made that abundantly clear. Even so, Ramón wore his best suit, dabbed on his most expensive cologne, and shaved with a brand-new razor. He drove by a local flower stand and paused—should he get her flowers? He didn't want to come on too strong, but a beautiful bouquet of peonies caught his eye, and he purchased them anyway.

He pulled up in front of the restaurant, locked his car, and opened the front door.

People milled around, all generations, all cultures. Ramón had mistakenly assumed that she would have shut down the restaurant for him. How arrogant was he? Of course, she wouldn't. Her restaurant was a business; he doubted that she wanted to disappoint the customers.

He stood in the arch of the doorway. A different waitress than the one he had met earlier greeted him.

"Table for one?"

"No. I'm here to see Julieta."

Ramón stood near the entrance and studied the goings-on in the restaurant. There were around twenty or so tables of different sizes and configurations. Kids colored on paper menus, sweethearts stole kisses between sips of cocktails, families laughed at one another's stories. A chill ran through Ramón as he pictured this place transformed into a fast-food joint.

The kitchen door opened, and Julieta appeared.

Ramón gasped at the sight of her. The tight red dress she wore hugged her curves, worshipped them as if her body was a church. *I feel a religious experience coming on.*

When she approached him, he handed her the flowers. "You look gorgeous. These are for you."

She blushed. "Thank you, Ramón. You shouldn't have." She glared at him. "Really. Your table is in back. Follow me."

Didn't have to ask Ramón twice. She turned around, and he stared at her perfect ass as she led him to a private room in the back. The table was decorated with marigolds and candles.

But there was just one problem—it was a table for one.

"Won't you be joining me?"

She shook her head no. Ramón didn't want to press her, not yet.

He sat down and looked at the menu on the plate in front of him.

A Day of the Dead menu. Well, it was the second and final night of the holiday. Wow. All the dishes sounded incredible. And unique. Just like her.

"Julieta, can we talk?"

She shook her head. "No. We can have a discussion after dinner.

For now, I want you to enjoy yourself." She poured him a glass of wine, lit the candles, and then left the room.

Her rejection stung, but Ramón understood that she didn't want to spend time with him. He was rarely speechless, but Julieta took his breath away. Not just by her beauty, but by her actions. She was strong and decisive. She didn't wait for him to call the shots; she took control. Ramón was used to people fawning over him, telling him what they thought he wanted to hear, but never being real.

He doubted he would have that problem with Julieta.

She brought out the first course—small, golden empanadas.

He reached out and grabbed her hand. "Would you sit with me for a while? Please, Julieta."

She pursed her lips. He could almost see an invisible wall she had built up between them—one that hadn't been there last night. "Okay, but only for a bit. I have other courses to finish."

As much as he enjoyed the meal, he would rather spend the time with her. He craved her company. She sat across from him, and he took his first bite of the appetizer. The flaky dough concealed the spicy pumpkin and chorizo mixture. It was served with a tangy avocado salsa. Simply delicious.

"This is the best empanada I have ever had."

"Glad you like it."

"I love it." He reached across the table and took her hand. "Look, I'm really sorry about surprising you this morning. But you have to admit, it's like we were meant to meet again."

She withdrew her hand. "By that logic, then you must believe you were destined to buy my building?"

"No, of course not." Ramón leaned forward. "I'm really glad to find you. I had a great time last night. I have to ask you—why did you leave?"

Julieta's eyes widened, and she stood up from the table. "Break's over. Next course is coming up."

Ramón slunk back into his chair. This night was a bust.

At least each course was better than the last. The ingredients were fresh, everything was made from scratch, and she had also planned the perfect wine pairing. He had never had mole with fish, as it was usually served with chicken. And for the first time in his life, he actually enjoyed eating cactus, a feat that even some of the best chefs in the world who had cooked for him hadn't managed to accomplish.

Julieta was so talented. Why was she wasting her skills here when she could be at the helm of a Michelin-starred restaurant?

But just as that thought crossed his mind, he knew the answer.

Because she didn't want to. She was happy cooking her own creations, for her community.

How could he tell her that he intended to shut this place down?

And if he did that, there was no way he would ever see her again.

There had to be a way to allow her to keep her restaurant and make Papá happy.

He'd spent all afternoon trying to think of a solution, preparing for tonight, but nothing had come to mind.

Think, Ramón.

Then an idea hit him.

Yes! That could totally work.

She would hate it. Probably break another dish, this time quite possibly over his head, but he had to try.

She brought the final course—chocolate tamales drizzled with strawberry puree.

Finally, she sat down across from him. Ramón was distracted from his food.

"Julieta, this is incredible. You didn't have to cook for me."

"No, I didn't. But I wanted to show you what I'm capable of."

Ramón grinned. "Are we talking about your cooking?"

She licked her bottom lip. "Yes, of course. What else would I mean?"

Their eyes locked, and even though she was in a serious business mode, Ramón felt the fire between them. The chemistry from last night still sizzled.

"Listen, I'd like to propose something to you."

Did he say he wanted to propose to her?

"What?"

"I'd like to make you an offer."

Ah, propose something to her, not propose to her.

Clearly, she had heard wrong.

But she couldn't let him start on the business talk yet—not before she'd had a chance to state her case. To try to persuade him that Las Pescas staying open was the best option for both of them. "Before you tell me your plans, I have something to say."

Ramón leaned back in his chair and took a sip of wine. "Go ahead."

She took a deep breath and spoke as calmly as she could. "I know I have no control over this situation. I know you own the building now, and I'm merely a tenant. But Ramón, I beg of you. Please don't kick us out. You don't know what it means to me, what it means to my community. And people will hate you if you shut us down. They will—trust me. If you have a heart, you have to listen to me."

Ramón focused his gaze on Julieta. "Look, Julieta, your food is out of this world. I wish I could tell you that you could stay here. But the truth is even if I didn't buy the property, someone else would've. You have been paying below-market rent for years. You're a good businesswoman; you know that. I'm not the bad guy."

Yes, he was. So deliciously bad.

Ay, Julieta, focus!

Julieta bit her lip and forced the fantasy of Ramón talking dirty to her out of her head.

He was right about paying low rent, though she hated to admit it. But that didn't make the pain of potentially losing her restaurant any easier.

"Fine. You're right. But let's be real, Ramón. This isn't about rent. I know you want to put a Taco King in Barrio Logan. In this spot, which is the best location on the block. Admit it."

Ramón shifted uncomfortably in his seat. "Julieta, it's not that simple." His avoidance had answered her question. It was over. And just like the air in his chest that he let out, Julicta's dreams drifted away.

Her throat constricted, and she closed her eyes, trying to will back the tears that had already pooled in her lids.

"It's time for you to go."

"Wait, please. I have an offer for you."

Julieta crossed her arms. "And what is that?"

"Promise me you will keep an open mind."

Open mind, closed legs. Got it. But wouldn't it be nice if it could be the other way around? "Go ahead."

"Well, you are right—we plan to put a Taco King in here."

Julieta's last glimmer of hope faded as quickly as it had arrived. It was all over—this man was a snake. He had his mind made up about what he would do with this place from the second he purchased the block—nothing she could do would stop him. Not even an amazing-tasting meal could appeal to his soul. Hell, he didn't have a soul.

Nada.

It was hopeless.

An icy coolness spread through her body. She closed her eyes and imagined the restaurant that she had slaved over for years ruined. Taco King? They might as well be called Tacky King!

Visions filled her head of her hand-embroidered Otomi chairs replaced by gaudy orange plastic ones. Instead of her delicacies being served on ceramic dishes that were made in Mexico, the crap they called food would be thrown on flimsy paper plates picked up at Walmart. The fish in the tacos would be farm-raised tilapia instead of sustainable, wild-caught cod. Their bland salsa was made with canned tomatoes, which often weren't even ripe. And there were no jalapeños in the restaurant! Ever. What was sadder than Mexican food with no heat? How about gummy store-bought tortillas? She shuddered in horror. It was almost too much for Julieta to bear.

Rage boiled inside her. Julieta couldn't even stand to be in the same room as Ramón. "Then we are done here. I have nothing left to say to you. Not tonight—not ever. If you would please leave, I'd like to serve my customers before you poison them with your food, if you can call it that."

Julieta stood, clenching her fists. She would not fight with this guy, no matter what. Pride was all she had left.

Ramón got up from his seat. "Julieta, no, wait." He reached out to her and grabbed her wrist. She quickly pulled it back, but the electricity of his touch pulsed through her.

Ugh, why did he have to be so hot? And why couldn't she stop thinking about their kiss? The way she came alive against his mouth, the way his hard body reacted when she pressed against his chest, that way her soul sang when he played the guitar.

But that had been fake. It had been a moment. A simple flirtation and nothing more.

"No, Ramón, don't. There is nothing left to say. Please. Just leave. I don't want to ever see you again." In real life, that was. The memory of his kiss could linger in her dreams.

"Well, I do."

"That's too bad."

"Just hear me out."

Julieta gave Ramón the evil eye. She didn't trust this devilishly handsome rogue who clearly was only out for his own interests.

"Fine. Talk. I'll give you two minutes." She started the timer on her phone and tossed it on the table.

Ramón smirked when he glanced at the seconds ticking down. "Julieta, I want you to be the chef at the restaurant."

She straight-up laughed at him. "At Taco King? You must be high, Ramón. Do I look like a short-order cook to you?"

"No, of course not. This will be our flagship restaurant. We are going to reinvent the menu. All fresh ingredients. You will have a five-star staff and sous-chefs. Whatever you want. Unlimited budget."

Unlimited budget?

Julieta's interest piqued, but she was disgusted at herself for even listening to his degrading proposal.

"The answer is no, Ramón. That will never happen."

"Listen, Julieta. You are the best chef in Barrio Logan, and probably one of the top ones in San Diego. But the restaurant business is hard. You need funds and investors to succeed. Remember what happened during the pandemic?"

How could Julieta forget. Julieta had scraped by with help from the community, but all the mandatory shutdowns had almost ruined them. But that was the point—the people of Barrio Logan rallied behind them. She couldn't betray them now or ever.

"Of course I do, Ramón. But I'm not a sellout."

"I never said you were. You are the heart of this community. I know that. I'm not stupid. We need you. I need you."

"Well, you clearly don't know a thing about me. I would never consider working at your crappy chain restaurant. Ever. Now, you've wasted enough of my time tonight. Goodbye." Julieta turned again to walk out of the room.

"I'll pay you two hundred thousand dollars a year."

Julieta tripped on a Saltillo tile.

What did he say? Was he insane?

"I'm sorry, what? Are you mad?"

"No. I'm quite sane. I'll pay you a salary of two hundred thousand dollars to be our executive chef. That's a contract for one year. You will receive a signing bonus. And, of course, benefits including health insurance, stock options, life insurance, retirement, and paid leave. We even offer pet insurance."

Pet insurance? Did companies actually offer that? Taco needed a dental!

But the real motivation was health coverage. Private health insurance was so expensive, and if Las Pescas closed, she would have to find a new job. How could she pass this deal up?

And she could probably get Mamá on the plan. With her lupus, she needed insurance. Not that Mamá would ever agree to work at Taco King. Julieta wouldn't, either.

Would she?

Julieta felt woozy, and it wasn't from the shot of tequila she had downed while she made Ramón's dinner. Fine, two shots. Maybe three. Four, tops.

"That's ridiculous. It's way too much money."

He took a step closer to her. "You're worth it."

Don't give in to his flattery! "I can't accept it."

"My offer stands. You have forty-eight hours to make your decision. Either way, we are closing Las Pescas. Take it or leave it."

Julieta couldn't even fathom that kind of money and those kinds of benefits. Not now. Not thirty years from now.

That money could do so much good for her and her family. She could buy Mamá a new house, one with a bigger garden. She could take her on a vacation. She could pay off her own debts from culinary school. She could buy a car that ran.

But money wasn't the only thing in life. How could she, a chef who had worked at a Michelin-starred restaurant, ever agree to be employed at a Taco King? Especially since they'd stolen her family's own recipe.

All her credibility would be shot. Once he had stripped her restaurant of all its character, he would move on to the next starry-eyed ingenue that caught his fancy. And she would never have a career—in the culinary world or in Barrio Logan.

No. Julieta would not consider it under any circumstances. She couldn't, she wouldn't work at Taco King.

"I'm sorry, Ramón. The building was for sale but I'm not. You can let yourself out."

Ramón didn't move, so Julieta stormed out of the room. She would soon lose her restaurant and her income. But she had kept the one thing that she had always valued most.

Her foolish pride.

Chapter Twelve

Well, that didn't go as planned.

Ramón quietly left the restaurant, got into his car, and drove back to La Jolla.

He had to get Julieta to agree. Not just because he wanted to see her again, but because if she didn't work there, the new restaurant would never be a success. Ever.

Papá didn't understand the depth of the problem at all. In this day and age, you couldn't just take over a block in a historically ethnic area and expect acceptance. And you shouldn't even want to. Barrio Logan was special. His father should know that—Papá fought for the rights of this community once. This was part of the reason Papá wanted a location here. What was he now thinking? Ramón didn't want to hurt his culture; he wanted to celebrate it.

If Julieta would helm his restaurant, there was a chance it could be successful. But her accepting his proposal was very unlikely.

She should, though. It would be good for Julieta also. He had offered her an exorbitant salary, fifty thousand over the average income of an executive chef, to mitigate the pain of closing her down. And he was confident that the restaurant could easily turn a profit with her cooking skills and his marketing expertise. She could work there for a few years, save up, and open a new restaurant, either in Barrio Logan or elsewhere. Hell, Ramón would probably invest in it.

He just hoped she considered his offer.

Ramón drove home and parked in his garage. He had planned to go upstairs and work on Julieta's formal offer—he'd send it for consideration—but he needed a breather and to center himself.

He stripped in his garage, pulled on his wet suit, grabbed his longboard, and walked to the ocean.

He was so lucky to live steps from the beach. But what was the point of having an oceanfront residence if he was too busy to dip his feet in the sand and didn't have anyone to share it with?

Ramón paddled out in the ocean. The water was dark. Night surfing was an art in La Jolla. Sometimes there would even be a bioluminescent display in the water.

Tonight was one of those nights. The aqua glow mesmerized Ramón. Nature's own light show right outside his front door.

There were a few other surfers taking advantage of the calm conditions. Ramón dodged them by locating the glow sticks they had strapped to their wet suits. He didn't need a glow stick—he had a custom-built LED surfboard made for night surfing.

Ramón scanned the dark, fathomless ocean, searching for any ripples or the dark shadows of a fin. There were no signs of any sharks, but that didn't mean they weren't lurking nearby.

Paddling out to the moonless sea was complete bliss—no crowds to compete with for that perfect wave.

The frigid water washed over him, but warmth flooded Ramón's body. This was what he needed—to connect with the ocean, connect with his soul. It had been a while since he had given himself a real break. He hadn't even surfed in a few weeks because he had been so busy working on this deal.

He caught his first wave, a small but smooth ride. As he glided on the board, the wind blowing on his face, he was free. This was his form of meditation.

And out here, in the night, he made peace with his role in taking over Las Pescas. It was business, his business. And in the long run, investing into Barrio Logan and supporting a chef like Julieta could only bring more opportunities to the area. Change was never easy, but it was necessary.

An hour later, Ramón finally left the water, completely relaxed. He planted himself on the cool sand with his board splayed out beside him. He took a moment to appreciate his life. Ever since college, he had been driven and completely focused. He had lost touch with himself and what made him happy. He didn't know if his new feelings had anything to do with meeting Julieta, but he couldn't dismiss that theory entirely. He did know that he wanted to impress her, and the normal trick of money and nice cars didn't seem to have an effect on her.

Yet she had loved when he sang to her.

Maybe, just maybe, he could impress her with who he truly was deep inside, and not just with his money.

Ramón drove up the street the next morning to the La Jolla Country Club, one of the most exclusive clubs in San Diego. It cost one hundred thousand dollars to join, required two member recommendations to even apply, and there was a three-year waiting list. Not to mention the annual sixty thousand dollars in dues.

But Ramón had learned at Harvard that the majority of business was done on the ninth hole and not in the boardroom. Part of his job was to play golf with other business owners. Papá had been one of the first Hispanics to be allowed into this club, and Ramón had spent much of his youth there.

He pulled up to the driveway, and the valet took his car. His wasn't the only McLaren there that day. He checked out the Bentley SUV parked ahead of him—he had to get one of those. It wasn't a status thing—he loved cars. He wished his abuelo could see his McLaren. He would've loved the sleek design and the fast engine. But investing in the Bentley SUV would allow him to take more clients out, since only one other person could fit in the McLaren.

He signed in and sat in the dining room for breakfast.

"Ramón, what are you doing here?"

His mother's voice startled him—she didn't come here as often since the divorce.

He looked up. A group of women in their sixties, hair perfectly coiffed, lips in various shades of plastic pink, sat around one of the white tables on the patio. Mamá held court in the middle. She always was the queen bee.

Better play the good son.

"Good morning, Mamá. Good morning, ladies." He kissed Mamá on the cheek.

"Please, sit down." She pulled over an extra chair before a waiter rushed to help.

"Now, Ramón. I was just telling my friends about how I wanted to take a cruise to Italy this summer with you and your brothers."

Ramón bit his lip. The trip was news to him. "That sounds fun." He had always wanted to go on trips with her when he was young, though usually he was just left alone with his nannies. Even on his eighth birthday, a memory that Ramón never forgot.

"Oh, it will be." She leaned on his shoulder. Mamá was extra affectionate with him because she was in front of a crowd. She always wanted to pretend they had a good relationship, when in reality, she didn't know a thing about Ramón's life.

The uncomfortable stares from the ladies who all seemed to be sizing him up unnerved him. Ramón took control. "What are you all chatting about today?"

"We're discussing how we can help the homeless. Do you have any ideas, Ramón?"

Ramón had to physically stop himself from rolling his eyes. His mom always got herself involved in some cause to raise money, but it was more an excuse to plan a gala than to truly do charity work. "I don't, actually. Though in Texas they have a plan where they provide housing and pay them jobs to clean up the city that seems to work."

"Oh, that is interesting." Mrs. Camarillo's face was pulled so tight from her latest face-lift that she reminded him of a cat. She took a sip of her mango mimosa and narrowed her sights on Ramón. "Are you seeing anyone these days, Ramón? You know, Sarita just graduated from USC. Top of her class! She's training to be a real estate agent at Berkshire Hathaway. Maybe you could take her out sometime?"

Breathe, Ramón, breathe.

The last thing Ramón needed was to be set up with Mamá's friend's daughter. Sarita was pretty, but full of herself. She had a viral following online. If Ramón went out with her, every detail of their relationship would be set to music and captioned while tagging sponsored businesses.

Maybe he should set her up with Jaime.

"Tell her congratulations, Mrs. Camarillo. But I just met someone." That wasn't actually a lie—he *had* met Julieta. Too bad she told him she never wanted to see him again.

Mamá dramatically placed her hands on her face. "This is news to me, mijo. Who is the lucky lady?"

Great. Here we go. This was Ramón's fault—he shouldn't have tempted her.

Mrs. Alvarez piped in. "Yes, please tell us. Do we know her? Is it Mrs. Lopez's daughter? Her maid told my maid that she just broke up with her fiancé. He was a doctor, but supposedly he left her for his nurse! Can you imagine? Anyway, she's always had her eye on you."

Yeah, they were practically promised to each other by their parents after Ramón had been her chambelán at her quinceañera. "No, she isn't. The woman I met is a chef."

Mamá's eyebrow fought through the Botox and miraculously lifted. "Where, Ramón? Have I dined at her restaurant before?"

"I doubt you've been there. It's a sea-to-table taquería in Barrio Logan."

A look of horror flashed on Mamá's face. "Barrio Logan? How on earth did you meet this woman?"

Mamá was such a snob. Had she forgotten how she spent her youth picking garlic on the farms in Gilroy? "At the Day of the Dead event. She was cooking. Oh, and we finally closed that deal down there."

The other ladies nervously sipped their beverages and stared at Mamá, who scrunched her face. Ramón couldn't help but take pleasure in her misguided embarrassment.

"Ah. Now I see. It's that father of yours." She turned to her friends. "Arturo was always obsessed with getting a restaurant in Barrio Logan. I could never figure out why—it was probably because he used to hang out with those radicals in the Brown Berets when he was in college."

Ramón laughed and tried to imagine Papá, who spent his days off work playing golf here or sipping mint tea in his La Jolla mansion with a full staff of maids and gardeners, chanting about Brown Power and protesting in Chicano Park.

"Actually, I love Barrio Logan. And this chef is truly gifted."

Mamá dramatically fanned herself with her napkin. "Really, Ramón. Get ahold of yourself. You're in your late thirties. Your fun days sowing your oats with wild girls should be behind you. You should start thinking about your future. I would like grandchildren one day."

Why? To ignore them, too?

Time to go. "Well, nice seeing you all. I have to order before tee time."

He hugged Mamá and then waved goodbye to the ladies. Then he returned to his own table and ordered his breakfast.

Ramón checked his email on his phone, but he still didn't see any reply from Julieta. Would she change her mind? He couldn't blame her if she didn't, but he hoped that she would accept his offer and that he would have an excuse to see her soon.

His eggs arrived quickly. They were perfectly poached, but the hollandaise was bland. No originality in these Eggs Benedict and most definitely no heat. Ramón doused his with Cholula Hot Sauce, but that didn't fix the underlying issue. The dish was tasty, but he was certain that Julieta's version was better.

After he finished eating, he made his way to the golf course. He ran into a couple of buddies and joined up with them. As he teed off over the ocean, Ramón took a hard look at his privilege. He didn't want to end up like Papá, alone and miserable, and he definitely didn't want to end up like Mamá, bitter and pretentious.

He wanted what he had seen in Julieta's restaurant the other day. Authentic laughter and closeness.

But Ramón didn't have a clue how to get that.

Chapter Thirteen

The last customer finally left the restaurant, and Julieta couldn't help but blink back tears. How many more nights would Las Pescas be open? Would she be able to say a proper goodbye to her customers?

And what would she do once it closed?

She reread the email that she had received last night.

Julieta,

Here is your formal offer, including the list of benefits.
I'd also like to offer you a signing bonus of $75,000.

Please let me know if you have any questions.

I will await your answer.

Sincerely,
Ramón

Now he added a seventy-five-thousand-dollar bonus? Ramón gave out money the way Julieta gave out tortilla chips. Maybe Mamá wasn't too far off when she called him El Banco.

Julieta studied the PDF. There were paid holidays and generous benefits. She would be a fool not to accept this offer.

She lit a candle and sat down to try to figure out what she wanted to do. Many chefs took gigs at chain restaurants. They received great perks and salaries and were eventually able to save up and achieve their dreams.

Julieta was too prideful to work for a chain. The humiliation of being a sellout would be too much for her to bear. But what about the future? If Julieta worked at Taco King for two years, she would be able to do anything she wanted. She would be debt-free. She would be able to take over the mortgage on Mamá's home or possibly move the two of them into a bigger one. She would be able to save for and start a new restaurant—one even more epic than her current one.

Las Pescas had been her entire dream, but it was a small space. It didn't have a huge outdoor patio or a private garden. This money would be able to fund a dream of hers that was completely out of reach at the moment. To have the resources to start a restaurant that could possibly be one of the top restaurants in San Diego, if not the state. And she would have the funds to hire an experienced business manager who could monitor the financials. Visions of Michelin stars and Zagat reviews danced in her head. She'd always envied chefs who had come from money and had the ability to run the restaurant of their dreams without having to beg investors to fund their fantasies.

But it wasn't just the money that tempted her, it was the benefits.

Mamá's health-care costs were huge, and she had no emergency fund, nor any retirement money put aside. Mamá's idea of saving was stuffing extra cash every week under her mattress. And Mamá refused to talk about the future. Julieta's family had spent their entire life living paycheck to paycheck. All their money was tied up in Las Pescas—which was closing no matter what. It wasn't stable. It wasn't sustainable. How could she not take this job?

Mixed emotions consumed her.

She blew out the candle, grabbed a bucket of soapy water, and started scrubbing the floors. Her restaurant would be shut, no matter what. It was over.

But she could build something new.

Someday.

Ramón had said that she would have creative control and be able to source for ingredients. It wouldn't be Las Pescas, but it would be her restaurant. Well, kind of. Wasn't that better than closing it down completely? How could it not be?

And if she didn't do this, what were her options? It was unlikely she would be head chef, or even sous-chef, anywhere. She had no desire to play the politics to get a top job in a high-end restaurant. Been there, done that. She hated that world. And she didn't want to cross the bridge every day and cook for tourists in Coronado or commute to La Jolla and work at one of the restaurants on Prospect Street.

She wanted to stay in Barrio Logan and walk to work. She wanted to serve her people—however she could.

She had to seriously consider it.

The floor was clean, the bucket was dirty, and her soul was weary. Time to go home.

She put the supplies away, emptied the mucky water, and found Mamá in the kitchen.

"Amá, let's go."

Mamá pulled Julieta's hand. "Julieta, what happened with Ramón?"

"Nada."

Mamá shook her head. "Julieta, don't shut me out. Please, just tell me what Ramón said. You've been acting like a sullen teenager all day."

She still hadn't told Mamá about the offer. Julieta needed time to process it on her own before she listened to Mamá tell her she told her so.

"You were right. He's closing us down."

Julieta's mother cursed under her breath. "I told you so, mijita. That good-for-nothing son of a bitch. The nerve. Haven't they taken enough from us?"

"Stop, Amá. What his father did to you is awful, but it is in the past. If you had wanted to go after him for taking your recipe, you should've done that years ago. Then we might not be in this mess."

Mamá didn't respond.

Julieta locked up the shop. "What are we going to do?"

Mamá shook her head. "I do not know. I can take a job. And someone will hire you. We will be okay."

But Julieta didn't want to be just okay or take just some job. She wanted to keep what she had built. And more importantly, she didn't want Mamá to have to go get another job. Maybe she could retire and focus on her life. With Julieta's salary, Mamá wouldn't need to work.

And by putting Mamá on Julieta's health insurance, she could give Mamá all the medical care she needed.

They crossed the street and passed by some neighbors. The night was clear, and the stars were bright and mystical, but the glorious sky brought little joy to Julieta.

She took a deep breath and let it spill. "You're right. Someone will hire me—I got a job offer."

Mamá pinched Julieta's cheeks. "See? We will be fine. Which restaurant?"

Julieta lowered her voice to a whisper, hoping the freeway noise would drown out her words. "Taco King. Ramón asked me to work for him."

"That cabrón!" Julieta's mom shook her fist at the sky. "I hope you told him what he could do with his job."

"Oh, I did. But Amá, he offered me to be executive chef of the restaurant. For two hundred thousand dollars. And a seventy-five-thousand-dollar signing bonus."

Mamá dramatically clutched her chest. "Qué?"

"Yup. That's a lot of money. But I told him no, of course."

Mamá playfully smacked her daughter's hand. "Are you crazy? Two hundred seventy-five thousand dollars? Do you know how much money that is?"

"I do. It's a lot of money. But I can't work for the enemy." Sleep with the enemy, maybe, but working for him was definitely out of the question. Julieta had some standards.

Julieta's mother clasped her hands and said a quick prayer. Then she clutched Julieta's hand. "You will take the job."

"Amá! How can you say that? We hate him. He is closing our restaurant. His father stole from you. He can't be trusted."

"I didn't say you had to trust him—I said you had to take the job. That is final."

"Oh, that's funny. I thought that I was in charge of my life. I don't know what I was thinking."

Mamá shook Julieta's shoulders. "Ay, Julieta. This is a wonderful opportunity. You aren't married; you won't have a job soon. This kind of money will allow you to do anything you want. You can open another restaurant; you can make a future for yourself. You will never have an offer like that again."

That was true. "But it's a guilt offer for taking over our restaurant. Or because he wants to sleep with me. Or both."

"I'm sure he wants you, but you don't have to sleep with him. He is a wealthy businessman. He wouldn't offer the position to you if he didn't think that you could do a good job. He ate your food; he knows you are talented."

Mamá had a point. Why should Julieta let her foolish pride get in the way of her future? "But Amá, it doesn't feel right at all. I just don't think I can do it."

Julieta's mother shook her head. "Julieta, forty years ago when Arturo stole my recipe, I could've pitied myself. I could've wrapped myself up in a ball and wallowed in what could have been. When I read that he made millions on my tacos while I was still stuck in Mexico, I could've become bitter and ruined my life. But I didn't do that. Instead, I pulled myself together. I married your father and had you, which was the greatest blessing of my life."

They paused under a dim streetlight, cumbia music blaring from a house nearby. Julieta wanted to dance the night away and not have to make this decision. "You're so strong. I don't think I could've done that."

"Yes, you could've, and yes, you can. You are my daughter. But nothing in this life comes easy. When we moved to America, we had nothing. I cleaned houses when you were little, and your father would take any job he could get to put food on the table. But I had a dream. I started selling tacos from my home. I would make food at weddings. I would cater family events. But the most important thing was that I never gave up, and neither can you, mi amor. If cuisine is still your dream, you need to take that job. He is throwing you a lifeline. You need to take it."

Mamá was right. What other choice did she have? If she turned down this job, she would regret it.

Julieta pursed her lips. "I'll think about it."

Mamá pointed a long nail in Julieta's face. "But mija, whatever you do, don't get involved with him. I know he is handsome and rich, but you need to keep this professional."

"I know, Mamá." She didn't have to like him. Or sleep with him. Well, maybe just once. Twice, tops! Third time's a charm. She was in control. Right?

They arrived home. She loved the bright lime-and-tangerine-colored shingles on her roof. Julieta couldn't wait to decorate for Christmas—it was always her father's favorite holiday. But this year would be her first Nochebuena without him. She needed to make it special for Mamá.

And if she took this job, she would have the money to buy her family nice presents.

Julieta leashed up Taco and took him for a walk. As her dog dawdled, she glanced at her phone.

She shot off an email.

> Ramón,
>
> Thank you for the offer. I am pleased to let you know that I will accept this position under the provision that I get to hire my own staff, keep my current employees, and have full control over the menu. Please put that in writing.
>
> Sincerely,
> Julieta

She pressed send. Her stomach was in knots.

Julieta took her dog back inside and grabbed an old vintage bottle of tequila that she had been saving for a special occasion. It had been her father's. She needed the liquor to mask her uncertainty.

She filled two glasses and handed one to Mamá.

"I accepted."

Mamá embraced her, and they spent the next three hours empty-ing the bottle and cursing irresistible taco-thieving men. They even began looking at vacations and real estate. And for once all their lofty financial goals were within reach.

She checked her phone a final time before she went to bed.

There was another email from Ramón.

> Julieta,
>
> I'm thrilled that you have accepted. I am amenable to all your requirements and will happily put them in writing. I will come by on Monday morning to go over the details.
>
> I'm looking forward to working with you.
>
> Sincerely,
> Ramón

CHAPTER FOURTEEN

Ramón woke bright and early. Today was the first step in preparing the new restaurant. And he'd be working side by side with sexy chef Julieta.

Ramón had already read himself the riot act. Yes, he wanted her. No, he wouldn't hit on her. He was now her boss, and the last thing he needed was a sexual harassment lawsuit.

He gathered his briefcase. A flutter rose in his chest—was he nervous? Ramón was never, ever nervous.

He pushed aside that unfamiliar feeling and left for Barrio Logan.

The traffic was light today, but he wasn't a fan of this commute—or any commute, for that matter. If he was going to work in Barrio Logan daily—which he would be doing for this project for at least six months—maybe he should buy a place closer. Coronado was the obvious choice, just across the bridge.

Yup, that sounded like a plan. He placed a call to his real estate agent.

Gloria answered on the first ring. "Ramón, darling, how are you?"

She was a friend of his mother's, but he didn't hold that against her. She was the best real estate agent in San Diego. More importantly, he trusted her. "Hey, Gloria. I'll be working down in Barrio Logan opening a new restaurant with a hotshot chef. I may have to pop in a few times a day. I'd like to purchase a property in Coronado. I've always wanted a beach home there anyway." Yes, he lived on the beach in La Jolla, but Coronado had a different vibe. It was a small island with a historic hotel, the Navy SEAL base, and tree-lined streets. He had fond memories of spending his summers bicycling around the island with his brothers and learning to sail in the cays.

"Oh, that sounds like an excellent idea. And a great addition to your portfolio. What are you thinking price-wise?"

"I'd like to stay under three."

"Three million it is. Stand-alone? Condo? There are some beautiful oceanfront condos over by the Navy SEAL base."

The condo tempted him. Low-maintenance, secure. But after living with his brothers, he yearned for a bit more privacy. He'd like a small yard—Ramón had been considering getting a dog. Maybe a Great Dane or a Weimaraner.

"I'm thinking beach cottage with a yard."

"Well, that may be tight in that price point, but I'll see what I can do. We'll be in touch."

"Sounds great. Talk to you later."

He hung up the phone and exited into Barrio Logan. The street buzzed with life and laughter. The owner of the café next to Julieta's restaurant waved at him. He waved back as a knot formed in his stomach. He would enjoy her greeting while it lasted. Soon, no one on this block would greet him at all.

After Ramón parked, he walked down Logan Avenue. Before heading into Las Pescas, he strolled into the café next door.

Señora Flores greeted him with a smile and a concha. "Hola, Señor Montez. I made this one especially for you."

Ramón accepted the treat. "Hola, Señora Flores. Gracias."

Señora Flores came from behind the counter and stood next to Ramón. "I will make them for you every day; well, if we are still open."

Ramón pursed his lips. He wanted to say something to soothe her fears, he wanted to do right by her business, and he wanted to ensure a lifetime of conchas.

But he could offer her no such comfort. "Señora, I love your café. I hope you stay for many years."

Her eyes lifted, and Ramón's heart sank. He had given her a false ray of hope. He knew that Starbucks had already reached out to his father. Ramón was putting off the meeting, but he couldn't avoid the conversation forever.

"I have to run." Ramón quickly exited the café and opened the door of Las Pescas. Breakfast was in full swing. He spotted a younger couple feeding their toddler son eggs as he giggled.

The little boy waved at Ramón, and Ramón waved back.

He turned to see Julieta watching him. She smiled slightly. Then she pointed to a table, and Ramón sat obediently.

She motioned for him to wait and disappeared into the kitchen. *Okay, then.*

Ten minutes later, Julieta appeared carrying two plates.

She set one in front of Ramón and the other in front of an empty chair. "Here is your Carnitas Eggs Benedict with Chipotle Hollandaise. I still feel bad about dropping your food the other day."

He shook his head. "Don't apologize. You were shocked. I'm just grateful I can eat here every day now."

"Until you close it down."

Ouch. "Well, maybe we can add these to the menu."

Julieta rolled her eyes.

Man, she was tough.

She sat in the empty chair and motioned to the waitress. "Rosa, dos cafés, por favor." She turned her attention back to Ramón. "Every day? I didn't know you were involved in the day-to-day operations of opening a restaurant. I assumed you just dealt with numbers."

Ramón shoveled a bite into his mouth. His taste buds were on fire. The eggs were excellent—spicy and smoky but not overpowering. "These are great."

"I know."

Ha. He loved her confidence.

Rosa brought two coffees. "Ramón, this is my cousin, Rosa. Rosa, this is Ramón. He just bought the building."

Rosa's eyes widened, then her lashes fluttered. "Hi, Ramón. Mucho gusto." She covered her mouth and then tugged at Julieta's hair. Julieta shooed her away from the table.

Well, at least one member of Julieta's family didn't despise Ramón.

Julieta dug into her own plate of food. She was a chef—of course she liked to eat. Ramón was relieved. He loved eating out at nice restaurants—it would be nice to take Julieta with him. He was sure she would actually eat the food instead of just taking pictures of it for Instagram.

"So, what is the plan? When are you shutting me down?"

"Not for at least a couple of months, until the deal goes through escrow, and then it will be another three months until we open."

Her lips twisted. "Okay. But you are paying me now, even though it is still Las Pescas?"

Ramón nodded. "Yup. I will put you on salary now, and you will retain ownership and proceeds for the restaurant until you close. I will spend some time shadowing you to learn everything about your restaurant."

And you.

"Then we will discuss our vision of the place and plan different menus. After that, we will finalize any renovations that need to happen and schedule the grand opening."

"Well, at least I will have time to say goodbye to my customers."

Ramón gave Julieta a quizzical look. "I get they will be upset with the changes, but they will still be glad that you are the chef."

"You still don't get it Ramón, do you? Yes, I will be here. But many of my customers will no longer support the place if it's a corporate chain. Of course, you will get new customers, tourists from out of state and residents of the beach towns who think coming to Barrio Logan is some type of Mexican Disneyland, where they can buy churros and take selfies in front of Chicano murals. But many locals will avoid us like ICE. And there will be protesters, including members of my own family and my friends. I can guarantee that."

Ramón's throat tightened. "Julieta, you are from the community. And I'm no gringo—I'm Mexican, too."

"You're a coconut, Ramón. You may be technically Mexican, but you are not part of this community."

Ramón was painfully aware he would never be accepted. And he definitely had to figure out the best way to address the protester issue. Hopefully, by the time they opened, Julieta would be proud of what they'd built together. If the locals saw her supporting the restaurant, maybe they would, too.

Quizás.

Maybe not.

But he had to portray that air of confidence—that was what made business deals work. "I'm confident everything will work out."

"What about the other businesses on the street? Will you be shutting them down? Raising their rent?"

Ramón did not want to talk about that yet. "There have been no decisions made about the rest of the block. But once we get going on the transition here, we will be exploring all options."

"Okay." Julieta pursed her lips and twirled a single lock of hair. "So, I did want to thank you for the job opportunity. It will be life-changing for me."

He grinned. "De nada."

"And I wanted to apologize for everything that happened before. Storming out of your place on Day of the Dead, dropping your food, kicking you out of the restaurant. I was just overwhelmed."

"Apology accepted." Ramón took a sip of his coffee. It was smooth, and he tasted a hint of cinnamon and Mexican vanilla. He lowered his voice and gazed into her eyes. "But I have to ask, why did you leave my house that night? You couldn't have known I was planning to buy this building. The bids were secret."

She looked out the window. "Right. I didn't."

"What was it? I hope I didn't make you uncomfortable in any way."

"No. It wasn't that." Her eyes shifted over his head.

He waved his hand in front of her face. "Were you having a good time?"

She nodded yes.

Then dammit—why had she left? Ramón hated playing the guessing game.

"Julieta, dímelo."

She exhaled and took a sip of her own coffee. Her hand shook as she grasped the mug.

"I saw that picture of you and your dad and your brothers."

"And? You have something against Taco King? I know it's fast food, but is that why you left?"

"No. It isn't. It doesn't matter."

Ramón clenched his jaw. "If we are going to be working together Julieta, I need you to be honest with me. It's a requirement."

"Fine. I left because . . . because your father stole the fish taco recipe from my mom."

What? Ramón put down his coffee. "Why would you say such a thing?"

"Because it's the truth. They dated in the seventies. My mom worked at a taco stand. Your recipe, the beer-battered fish tacos, is my mom's."

Ramón rapidly blinked but remained speechless.

Well, this was awkward. But, of course, he wouldn't know that his own father was a thief, that his company's success was built on the back of her family's secret recipe.

He clearly didn't believe her, so she threw in more details.

"My family were taqueros in Mexico. For many generations. Your signature fish taco recipe is my mother's. Well, your original one anyway."

There. She had laid out all her cards. But maybe she shouldn't have said that. He could still fire her, and then she wouldn't have any job.

She couldn't work with him if he didn't know this. She always vowed to live her truth.

He ran his hands through his hair. "I don't know what to say, except I don't believe that is true."

"Well, it is. Ask your father about it."

"I will. But if that's the case, then why hasn't your mom tried to come after my dad? Or tried to sue?"

"Because Mamá isn't like that. At all. She's not vengeful. She decided to move on with her life. She married my papá, and they immigrated here. She didn't want to waste her energy on what could have been." Julieta threw him a lifeline. "And yes, she made that batter—and the sauce—but your father started the business here from scratch. The recipe is only a part of your success." The big part, but still.

Ramón shifted in his seat, and a vein bulged in his neck. "Lay it out for me, Julieta. Are you or your mom trying to blackmail us with this claim that she created our iconic fish tacos recipe?"

Julieta clenched her fist. How dare he accuse her of that?

She should throw him out of the restaurant again for even asking.

But after a few deep breaths, she calmed down. Ramón was a shrewd businessman—he was clearly just trying to protect his many assets and figure out what he was up against.

"No. Absolutely not. I just thought you should know exactly why my mother reacted that way to your father."

"Understood. Well, I'll ask him about that. And if what you said is true, I'll make it right by you and your mom. You have my word."

A lump settled in her throat. Julieta had imagined many ways this conversation could've gone before she blurted out those words. But never in her scenarios had she considered that Ramón would actually listen to her, and possibly believe her—or that he might want to do right by Mamá.

For now, she wouldn't get too hopeful about Ramón compensating Mamá for her recipe.

"I'm curious what your father will say."

Ramón smiled, his dimples deepening. "Me too, but Julieta, that's their problem, not ours."

The way Ramón said "ours" caused Julieta to pause. There was no Ramón and Julieta as a unit. They were completely separate, only bound together for this restaurant.

Time to change the subject.

"What is first on the agenda? For the record, all the recipes from Las Pescas are mine. But I suppose anything created for Taco King will be yours?"

Ramón nodded. "Yes, exactly. Any recipe you currently use will not be owned by our restaurant. But you will create new recipes that we can use in all our locations. You will be a sort of test kitchen. Is that okay with you?"

"Yes. That's fair. Would you like to discuss my ideas for the menu?"

"Not exactly." Ramón's eyes raked over her, dropping to her breasts. He gave her a mischievous smile.

Julieta's nerves tingled. But she hated her body for betraying the way she felt toward him.

After he finally looked away, he reached into his briefcase and pulled out a leather folder. He then took out a super expensive-looking pen and began to write notes.

"Then what?"

Ramón finally focused his attention back on Julieta. "Well, first, I'm going to watch you."

Julieta instinctively clasped her hand to her chest. Ramón made those words seem dirty. Julieta couldn't decide if he pissed her off or made her excited. She settled on both. "*Watch* me? Why?"

"I'm analyzing the output. I'm going to sit here and count how many customers come in, see what they order, how long they spend here, how much they spend here. It will help me formulate my business plan."

Julieta rolled her eyes. Boring. How could this ever work? He operated based on numbers; she was guided by her feelings.

"Is there a problem, Julieta?"

"Yes, Ramón, actually there is. You can't judge a restaurant by numbers and data alone. You have to experience it with all five senses." She pulled her chair closer to his. Without hesitating, she picked up his fork, shoved some food on it, and lifted it to his mouth. "Taste the food." He readily opened his lips, and she fed him. This moment felt intimate, yet scary.

She lifted a small bowl of salsa to his nostrils. "Smell the spices. Listen to the laughter of the patrons and the music over the speakers. Touch the embroidered place mats and chairs. See the art on the wall. This may be a business to you, but this place is my life. Mi vida."

Ramón paused for a moment and just stared at Julieta, grinning. He then slowly looked around the restaurant, his eyes lingering over the many details that Julieta had spent years cultivating.

He placed the cap on the pen and slid it into its holder in the folder, which he then closed and put into his briefcase. "Fine, you are right. Let me rephrase that question. Where should we start?"

Julieta beamed. "In the kitchen. I'll get you an apron."

CHAPTER FIFTEEN

Julieta threw Ramón an apron. He tied it on and walked over to the sink to wash his hands.

"Have you ever worked in a kitchen?" she asked.

Ramón rolled his eyes. "Yes, Chef, I have. I didn't just wake up one day and become the CEO of Montez Group. I spent my teen years working in Taco Kings. I was never that good at it, though. That was more my brother Enrique's thing—he wanted to be a chef for a while. He's still an excellent cook, but he's an artisan farmer now."

Julieta tilted her head, revealing her sexy neck. Ramón wanted to plant kisses on it. Keeping their interaction professional was easier said than done.

"Wow. Where is his farm?"

"He has a few acres out in Encinitas."

She took a step closer to him. "I'd love to visit it."

He cocked his head to the side. "That can be arranged. He grows some unique herbs and vegetables for our test kitchen."

"That is so cool. Honestly, one of the many reasons I considered your offer was because you said I'd have an unlimited budget. I have always wanted to experiment with new ingredients and have access to the finest gardens. But those things cost a lot, and I have always tried to keep my prices low."

"Well, you don't have to worry about that anymore. This will be our flagship, so we can splurge here. But in the main restaurants, that is why we used canned tomatoes and store-bought tortillas. I know you hate those items, and I'm not a fan of them, either, but they keep our costs low and our food accessible to people who may otherwise not afford it. We provide free lunch for many schoolchildren. We also give meals to the homeless."

Julieta swallowed, and Ramón almost felt her softening toward him. He hadn't wanted to brag about all of the charity work his company did, but he had to say something to change her perception of him. His group did many wonderful things—the profits they made allowed them to give back to the community. Ramón wasn't a monster.

"Wow. That's great. I had no idea you did all that." She paused. "Do all your employees get those benefits you offered me?"

Ramón nodded. "Yup. Even part-time employees."

Julieta pursed her lips. "That's really wonderful." She looked up, then at Ramón, and blinked nervously. "Actually, can I ask you a favor?"

"Anything."

"Well, my cousin, Tiburón, needs a job. He's a great guy. Could we hire him? Full-time?"

Ramón had to trust Julieta to hire who she wanted. "Sure. Have him come by, and I'll start him with the paperwork."

"Great. But, uh, he has a record. It's nothing really, just some trouble he got into as a teen. But he's a hard worker and really needs a break. I completely vouch for him."

Ramón frowned. "What kind of trouble, Julieta?"

She rubbed the back of her neck. "Uh—breaking and entering."

Dammit. It was against company policy to hire felons.

But he was the boss. He could override the rule. He was taking over Julieta's restaurant—he had to give her something she wanted.

Besides, everyone deserved a second chance in life.

She looked up at him eagerly. "Please? He's a hard worker."

He brushed a lock of hair out of her face. "I'll get HR to make an exception."

Julieta beamed. She wrapped her arms around his neck, her lips just inches from the side of Ramón's face. She quickly released him, but the damage was done. Julieta's hot body had been pressed up to his for long enough for him to be certain—he wanted Julieta.

"Thank you, Ramón. You don't know what this means to me. I promise you won't regret it." She took out her phone and began texting.

I better not.

"Don't mention it."

Her eyes were glued to her phone. She looked up. "Oh, sorry, I just told Tib. How can I repay you?"

Ramón had a few ideas.

He forced the fantasy of Julieta naked out of his head. "You don't have to. So, what are we doing in here?"

She turned and surveyed the kitchen. "Okay, we need to get ready for the lunch rush." She handed Ramón a bag of onions. "Let's see your knife skills."

He wanted to show her his other skills. Instead, he stood in front of the chopping board, grabbed the knife, peeled the onions, and began dicing.

Julieta turned on the radio. She began dashing throughout the kitchen, creating some type of braise for the meat. She sautéed, seasoned, and shaved various vegetables. He loved watching her work, joy radiating through her, spring in her step.

If only he could feel purpose in his work the way she did.

Julieta changed the music from Spanish rock to mariachi songs. He resisted the urge to sing along and instead focused on his prep work. He hadn't cooked in years. Even at home, his brother normally took care of the cooking, or they would get takeout from one of their restaurants or better ones in La Jolla.

There was something enjoyable about getting into the rhythm of chopping. But he couldn't help being distracted by Julieta. She managed her kitchen brilliantly, and the other few cooks in the kitchen seemed to respect her.

A while later, the kitchen door opened, and Julieta's mother walked in.

Great.

She took one look at Ramón and rolled her eyes. "What is El Banco doing here?" she asked, as if he were not in the room.

El Banco? Ramón laughed. That nickname was hilarious and not entirely untrue.

Julieta gave her mom a pointed stare. "*He* owns this place, Amá, remember? And his name is Ramón."

Linda looked from Ramón to her daughter, then back to Ramón again.

Would Linda say something rude to him?

After a few minutes of awkward silence, she opened her arms toward him.

Did she want Ramón to *hug* her?

He was confused, so he stood there and continued dicing.

Linda stepped closer to him. "Mijo, come here. Give me a hug."

Ramón put down his knife and awkwardly hugged Julieta's mother. She grabbed him tightly and then pushed him away to stare at him.

"Ramón, I can't help but look at you and see your papá. When he was your age, he was so handsome and full of dreams and hope. He wanted to change the world." Her tone was a bit tragic.

Ramón didn't know how to respond, especially because he had just learned about Linda's accusations. He needed to talk to Papá as soon as possible.

"Well, he has fond memories of you, as well." Ramón kept to himself the part of Papá's story when he had wanted to marry her but had seen her with another man. Did she even know that he'd gone back for her? It wasn't Ramón's story to tell.

"Well, Ramón, I must tell you the irony of this entire situation." A smug smile graced Linda's face. "When your father first tried my tacos, do you know what he liked about them?"

"He just told me he tried fish tacos during spring break, and that he met a beautiful señorita on the beach. He never said that they were your tacos."

She shook her head. "Well, ask him again. And if he still lies, bring him to me—let him lie to my face. Yes, they were *my* tacos. I had a stand on the beach, and he ordered two tacos and a beer."

He'd told Ramón this part of the story many times; he'd just never said that she had been the one to make the tacos. Then again, he had also left out the part about how he had stolen her recipe, if that was true.

"He loved the fresh fish."

Linda laughed. "No, that was not it at all. Yes, he did love the fish, and he had never had a fish taco. But he loved the fresh salsa. He loved the spicy batter. He loved the handmade tortillas. It's funny to me, because you have absolutely none of those elements left today in your tacos."

Linda's words struck Ramón deep in his chest. She was right. Ramón had heard the story so many times. And Papá *had* always talked about how fresh and delicious all the ingredients were, including the handmade tortillas.

Ramón looked at her. "I know. He told me the same thing."

Linda placed her hand on Ramón's arm. "Ironic, isn't it? He used to tell me a story about a girlfriend he had in college who had made him an awful taco with canned tomatoes, American cheese, and iceberg lettuce. That her taco was so awful, that he could never marry her. And now, that is exactly the type of taco that you serve in your restaurant."

Wow. She was absolutely right. The full reason that Papá had started Taco King was to bring authentic Mexican food to the college kids at San Diego. Somewhere along the line—due to business advisers who'd suggested cutting costs and replacing fresh tomatoes with canned, crumbled queso fresco with American cheese, and handmade tortillas with mass-produced hard shells—Papá had abandoned his vision.

"Well, hopefully, in this restaurant, we can bring it back."

Linda smiled and hugged Ramón again. She seemed to soften toward him once he'd admitted that she was correct. "Mijo, I'm going to make for you the exact tacos I made for your father that day."

Julieta looked at her mom. "No, Mamá. You don't need to do that. He already tasted my tacos at the Day of the Dead event."

Linda glared at her daughter. "So, that was who you gave your tacos to. You shouldn't be giving your tacos to strangers."

Ramón laughed.

"He wasn't a stranger, Amá. He had serenaded me in the garden."

Linda rolled her eyes. "Julieta, your tacos are amazing and innovative, but they are not traditional. Let me show Ramón where it all began."

Linda began grabbing ingredients out of the refrigerator. She demonstrated step-by-step exactly how to make the tacos. Julieta smirked as she playfully nudged her mamá.

"Ramón, you know, if your father had just come back for me, I would've given him the recipe."

Ramón pursed his lips and nodded. Papá *had* come back, but his father would have to tell Linda that himself.

Linda finished the tacos and presented them to Ramón.

Ramón examined the plate carefully and even lifted it to smell the tacos. There was no fishy scent at all—just a heavenly aroma of ocean mixed with heat. A crispy, yet not greasy, corn tortilla enveloped the fried and battered fish, garnished with lime, avocado, crema, cabbage, and pico de gallo, which was as fresh as his beloved abuela's salsa.

Ramón squeezed lime on the taco, raised it to his mouth, and took the first bite. The crunch of the cabbage contrasted with the soft avocado. But the real star was the fish. Crispy, spicy, and delicious. The buttery flesh melted in his mouth.

Ramón devoured both tacos in a matter of minutes.

Linda was right—they were nothing like the ones that were served daily in his restaurants.

"These are excellent, Señora Campos. Thank you."

"Oh, wait, I forgot something. It is meant to be paired with cerveza." Linda handed him a beer from the cooler.

Should he be drinking on the job? Well, just this once, to get the authentic taste.

When Julieta went into the freezer to grab some ingredients, Linda cornered Ramón in front of the island in the kitchen.

"Ramón, I want to thank you for giving Julieta this job. The money is great, and we are appreciative."

"Of course. I plan to hire you also."

She shook her head. "No need. I plan to take a break when the restaurant transitions. I can never work in a Taco King. I've told you why."

Ramón nodded. He had to talk to Papá.

"But I want you to stay away from Julieta. I know you two had a spark, but I would like to ask you not to pursue her. I don't want her to get hurt."

Ramón's mouth became bitter. He downed some more beer to cover the taste.

Ramón refused to make a promise he couldn't keep.

"I'm sorry, Linda. I'm not going to agree to that. I like your daughter."

She scowled at him. He needed to change the subject as quickly as possible. "These tacos are really great. Thanks again."

Ramón took his final bite as Julieta emerged from the freezer.

"Can we get back to work now?" She beckoned him over to the carnitas.

Break over.

He stirred the pork, and she placed her hand on top of his.

He was attracted to her, but now it wasn't just lust. He liked her. He liked her mother, even though she had told him to stay away from her, something no mother had ever asked him to do. Mothers were usually begging Ramón to date their daughters.

Julieta had been right. A restaurant was more than numbers and bottom lines; it was about emotions and feelings.

Ramón tried to ignore his own feelings about Julieta.

But he couldn't.

Chapter Sixteen

After leaving Las Pescas, Ramón was going to head straight home, but instead, he found his car veering toward his father's place.

He couldn't stop thinking about what Julieta had said. About how Papá had stolen the recipe from her mother.

It couldn't be true, could it?

He needed to find out.

Papá also lived in La Jolla, though unlike Ramón's beachfront bachelor pad, Arturo's home was a compound in Olde Muirlands. The place was like a castle, filled with haunted memories and a lonely childhood. His mom could've kept it in the divorce, but she decided she'd be happier in a modern mansion in the shores. Ramón hated returning home. Years of being alone in that house, waiting for Papá to come home from work, praying that Mamá would stop ignoring him, had taken a toll on him and his brothers.

And now, he worked as much as Papá did. Would Ramón end up like him?

He vowed not to, but sometimes he found himself with tunnel vision. It scared him.

Ramón pulled into the perfectly landscaped driveway, entered the code on the gate, and parked in front of his childhood casa. He let himself in and found Papá watching football on the sofa in the den, the screen dominating the wall space and casting the room in hues of green and blue.

"Ramón!" He got up to hug him. "What are you doing here? You usually call first."

"Yeah, sorry about that. I just wanted to see you."

"Anytime. Have a beer." Papá paged the maid. Maria appeared in the doorway. "Maria, get Ramón a beer."

"Sí, señor." She waved at Ramón.

Maria. He had been around her almost his entire life, but he didn't actually know anything about her, except that she had a daughter. That was about all.

Time to change that.

"Hola, Maria. ¿Cómo estás?"

"Bien, Ramón."

Before he asked her another question, she ran off and quickly returned with his beer, and then left again.

Ramón and Papá both reclined on the sofa.

"Apá, how long has Maria worked for you?"

"I don't know. Thirty years? Why?"

"Do you ever do anything nice for her? I mean, give her a big bonus or send her on vacation?"

Ramón's father rubbed his chin. "She gets a Christmas bonus. Why?"

"Because she works for you. She helped raise me and my brothers. Don't you think we owe her a bit more than an hourly wage?"

Papá stared at him. "What has gotten into you? What is this about? Now I don't treat my staff well?"

He shook his head. "No, it's not that at all. That's not what I'm saying." He took a swig of the beer to take the edge off his mood. "Hey, tell me again how you came up with the recipe for our fish tacos?"

Subtle, Ramón was not.

Ramón's father wiped his brow. "Why are you asking me this? Have you talked to Linda?"

Ramón narrowed his gaze at Papá. "Would it matter if I had? Tell me the truth, Apá."

Papá clasped his hands. "Fine. I will tell you. I have nothing to hide. I was surfing down in San Felipe. I ordered two fish tacos from a local stand. They were incredible. I had never had a fish taco before. And these tacos were delicious. Out of this world."

He had heard this part of the story. Many, many times. "Dad, did Linda make the tacos? Was it her stand?"

Papá slumped on the sofa. "Yes, Ramón, it was."

Ramón exhaled. Dammit. But that still didn't mean that Papá had stolen her recipe. Maybe he just made a similar recipe, though Ramón knew that Papá was hardly a chef. Ramón would reserve judgment until he finished.

"Go on."

"We spent every day for two weeks together. I was obsessed with her. Beautiful, kind, loving, unlike all the American girls I had met. She loved listening to me play guitar on the beach. I vowed that I would marry her, bring her to San Diego with me."

A lump grew in Ramón's throat. Had Apá ever loved Ramón's mother as much as he loved Linda? "So, what happened?"

"Well, I was still in college. So, I went home, graduated, and spent every minute working with your abuelo to save up to buy her a ring. I planned to ask her father for her hand in marriage."

He had planned on proposing to her? This was clearly not a spring fling.

Papá continued. "I had been writing her, and for a while, she had written back. But then her letters abruptly stopped. I figured she was just mad at me for taking so long to come back. I didn't want to give up on her until she told me to my face she wasn't interested."

Why had she stopped writing? She had made it seem that Papá had ghosted her.

Papá continued. "I had purchased a diamond ring. I couldn't wait to see her. But when I arrived, I saw her kissing another man on the beach." Papá clenched his fist. "I was so angry, Ramón. I wanted to kill him. I hadn't even looked at another woman since I had left her that spring break. I was about to propose. I had the ring in my pocket."

Ramón shook his head and took a sip of his beer. "I can't even imagine."

"That night, I got so drunk that I showed up at her house. I decided to beg her to take me back, forget about him. But I saw them in the window of her bedroom. Her parents were gone. The lights went out."

Wow. That was brutal. "You didn't try to talk to her?"

"No. I passed out in a shed on her property. I woke up the next morning, and they were gone. The house was empty." Papá looked away from Ramón. Then his voice dropped to almost a whisper. "So, I went into her kitchen and ripped out the recipe for the fish tacos from her cookbook."

Ramón's heart wrenched.

Julieta had told him the truth.

Ramón's hand shook. "So, you did steal her recipe? How could you do that?"

"Ramón! I went out of my mind with jealousy. Do you know what that's like?"

Ramón had never been crazy in love like that, but he had a jealous streak. What would it be like to see Julieta with another man? Watching another guy kiss her, grab her ass, fuck her.

Heat spread through his body. Nope—he didn't like that idea at all.

Ramón put his head in his hands. What a complete mess.

"Apá! I can't believe you did that! Do you know what kind of lawsuit you have opened yourself up to? Opened *us* up to? And even if she doesn't have a legal claim, it would be a PR nightmare. Especially since we are already considered sellouts. She could come after us. For everything."

Ramón's father hung his head low. "I know, I know. I never thought she would immigrate to the United States, let alone to San Diego. And I had no idea she lived in Barrio Logan. Her last name has changed."

"Well, of course her name is different. She was married. And more importantly, she is here. And even worse, we have bought her building. We have taken over her daughter's restaurant. And I hired her daughter to be the chef at that restaurant, so the locals won't hate us. We need a new plan, Apá."

"What are you saying, Ramón? Linda may have originated that recipe, but I made this company. And we don't even use her recipe anymore. I worked for two years to save up money to open the first location. I worked twelve-hour days with your abuelo in the scorching inland heat pulling weeds to open that tiny taco stand in Pacific Beach. Business was horrible; nobody came. I thought I would have to shut it down."

Papá stood up and began pacing around the room.

"I worked seven days a week, Ramón. I dressed up like a fish with a taco wrapped around it and would dance around in the heat to get customers to come in. She didn't do that—I did. This is my business. This is my legacy. Yes, that recipe was my inspiration, but we don't owe her anything. She has no rights to my hard work."

Ramón disagreed—they did owe Linda something, but he wasn't sure what.

But shutting down Linda's daughter's restaurant forty years after Papá had taken her mother's recipe didn't sit right with him. It seemed not only completely unfair, but also cruel.

Ramón got up to face his father. "We owe her something, Apá. She could sue us. And the press will destroy us. We have to be careful."

Papá put his hand on Ramón's shoulder. "Don't worry. I'll handle it. I can call legal tomorrow and get their advice."

Ramón's stomach hardened. How had he ever become involved in such a mess? Normally, their business acquisitions were clean and drama-free. He felt like he was trapped in one of those telenovelas his mom liked to watch.

"Look, I talked to Julieta. She told me that you stole the recipe."

"Ramón! What are you doing? Is this why you have come to me? Did she tell you this story to get you to keep her restaurant in that location?"

"No, she didn't. But she does know that you stole the recipe from her mom. We need to be careful here."

"What do you think we should do?"

Ramón exhaled. "I think we should let them stay in the location. I have hired her as chef, as we had discussed, but I think we should keep the venue as Las Pescas. We can find another place to put in a Taco King."

"Have you lost your mind? The only reason we bought the block was to put in a Taco King. This is a business, Ramón—not a charity."

"Nobody wants a fast-food restaurant in the heart of Barrio Logan. Have you even tried her tacos? They are incredible."

"No. I don't need to. I tried her mother's. But that is not the point."

"It is, actually."

Papá grunted.

Ramón rarely stood up to his father, but now he had no choice. Ramón knew right from wrong—he had to say something or he wouldn't be able to live with himself. "I don't agree with what we are doing to the community. We can find other ways to make money on this deal. I'm not going to be part of wrecking this street. I apologize for not bringing up my concerns sooner, but I clearly didn't do the correct research. And had I known that you had taken the recipe from Linda, I never would've agreed."

Papá's face reddened, and he pointed his finger at his son. "Ramón. I order you to open the Taco King there."

"Apá! You will do right by Linda. I'm calling our legal team tomorrow. It's just money—and we don't need any more of it."

"This is my company. I founded it. I'm still the chairman of the board. You can't tell me what to do."

Ramón threw his hands up. "You're right. I can't. So let me put it this way—if you don't agree to compensate Linda, I will quit."

Ramón's father stood in the middle of the den with his jaw open. Ramón didn't even bother to say goodbye.

And with a nod of apology to Maria, who was standing in the kitchen doorway with a horrified look on her face, Ramón walked out of his father's house.

On his way out of the neighborhood, he drove by the multimillion-dollar mansions with all the workers maintaining the properties. Some were blowing leaves, others were trimming hedges, all were working their asses off.

There would be no La Jolla without Mexicans. They were the gardeners, they were the cooks, they were the maids, and they were the nannies who raised the children of these millionaires—like his own nanny, Berta. They were important, and they had voices, and for years Ramón hadn't heard them. But today he listened to their words, loud and clear.

CHAPTER SEVENTEEN

The week had gone slowly. Ramón had texted Julieta that he needed to do some work on another deal so he wouldn't be able to come in for a while. As for the details on this business, Ramón had seemed tight-lipped when she asked for specifics. She had assumed that he would already have made a plan to start turning Las Pescas into a Taco King. His lack of action led Julieta to hold on to the fleeting hope that somehow, against all odds, she could still keep Las Pescas in its original incarnation. But she knew deep down that though the restaurant was outwardly still Las Pescas, it was technically already a Taco King.

And she had spent way too much time staring at her phone, waiting for a text from him that never came.

But more important than the text, Julieta received her first paycheck.

Seeing that number in her bank account blew her mind. She couldn't believe it wasn't an error. This was so much better than checking her balance multiple times a day to ensure that she had enough money not to overdraw it every time she paid bills.

Julieta splurged and actually went shopping. She bought a few dresses, some new lingerie, and even some makeup and skin care products. Julieta couldn't even remember the last time that she had pampered herself. Maybe Mamá's vanity had rubbed off on her.

Ramón had even kept his word about offering Tiburón a job. But Tiburón had, not shockingly, refused. As desperate as her cousin was for gainful employment, he was a man of loyalty. And his allegiance was to Barrio Logan. Still, Julieta knew how much Tiburón needed this position. She hoped he would change his mind.

Sunday evening, Ramón had texted her that he would be stopping by Monday morning and planned to take her to see the test garden. Julieta was ridiculously excited to see all the fresh crops. Though she normally never left the restaurant during the day, she made an exception. Las Pescas was closing soon anyway, so there was less pressure, and she had to admit it was nice to have the freedom to leave. Julieta made sure that she had enough staff to cover the place while she was gone.

Shortly after they opened, Ramón walked through the door with another super-hot guy, who had to be one of his brothers. He was as tall as Ramón, and both were in great shape. Ramón's hair was cut short, whereas the other man's hair was longer and carefree, like a surfer's.

Ramón's face lit up when he saw her. "Julieta, I would like to introduce you to my brother Enrique. He's going to show us around his farm today."

Julieta waved. "Hi, Enrique. Nice to meet you. I'm so excited to go to the farm."

Enrique extended his hand. "Nice to meet you, too." He grinned at Julieta. "I can't believe Ramón conned you into being a chef here."

Ramón just rolled his eyes.

Julieta laughed. "That makes two of us."

"Well, Ramón gets whatever he wants, but you probably know that already."

Ramón glared at him, and Enrique laughed. Julieta enjoyed the playful ribbing between the brothers. She yearned for that sibling relationship—fighting one moment, teasing each other the next. Ramón was lucky to have brothers.

"Well, have some breakfast before we head out. What would you like?"

The men placed their orders and sat at a small table in the back.

Tiburón walked through the door, and Julieta greeted him.

He embraced his cousin. "Hey. Now that you are rolling and all, can you lend me some cash?"

Julieta shook her head. "No, but you can get to work. I need a dishwasher—Cesar's house got raided by ICE. He's gone. They took him in the middle of the night."

"En serio? Those bastards. Poor Cesar."

Living in fear of Immigration and Customs Enforcement was part of the daily life in Barrio Logan. She was so helpless to do anything about the situation, but it weighed on her soul. "So, do you want the job?"

Tiburón sighed. "Nah, prima. I can't do that. I'm not going to work for the man."

Julieta admired Tiburón's resolve. But no one else was going to give him a job. Time for some tough love. "Well, you have perfect timing. You can meet 'the man' and decide for yourself. Ramón is here. Just give him a chance."

Tiburón's eyes narrowed toward the corner where Ramón and Enrique were sitting. "Why are you letting him eat here, cuz? He's going to steal another one of your recipes, like his father did Tía Linda dirty."

Julieta pressed her hand on his chest. "Stop it. He's not that bad. And he does own this place."

Tiburón made a kissy-face at her. "You just have the hots for him."

She pinched him. "Tib! Stop. Just behave. Please. You need this job."

"Fine, fine."

Julieta led Tiburón over to Ramón and Enrique.

"Ramón and Enrique, this is my cousin, Tiburón."

Ramón's gaze lasered in on Tiburón's tattoo. Julieta's throat tightened. She prayed Ramón wouldn't make a comment about the great white on his neck.

Ramón and Enrique stood up and extended their hands to him.

"Nice to meet you, Tiburón. Julieta told me you're a hard worker."

Tiburón shook both of their hands. "Nice to meet you, too. I am. And as long as you treat my cousin right, we won't have any problems."

Ah, fuck. Apparently, Tiburón was interviewing Ramón, not the other way around. This was why Tiburón couldn't keep a job.

Ramón didn't seem to be fazed by Tiburón's comment. "Then we will be good. Do you want the job, or not?"

"I do."

"Cool. I'll get all the paperwork together, and you can start tomorrow."

"Actually, he can start today. My dishwasher just got deported."

Ramón gulped. "Really? You didn't tell me that."

Julieta pursed her lips. "Why would I? You weren't paying his salary yet."

He gritted his teeth. "Julieta, you have to tell me these things."

Tiburón raised his voice. "What's it to you, rich boy? Like you care if one of us gets deported. You are destroying our community."

Julieta pointed her newly manicured nail in Tiburón's face. "¡Basta! Just go to the kitchen. Now." Tiburón sneered at Ramón and

Enrique, but then turned toward the kitchen, where he pushed the door.

A lump grew in Julieta's throat. "Sorry about that. I'll handle him."

Ramón ran his fingers through his hair. "It's okay. I get it."

This was already a nightmare. "I'm just going to set him up and be right back."

Ramón nodded.

Julieta chased after Tiburón and threw her hands up in his face. "What was that? Why can't you behave for once?"

"Why should I? He doesn't care for Barrio. Sure, he gave me a job, but he's going to destroy us. And you, too."

Julieta shook her head. "Maybe it will be okay."

"I doubt it. Look, I need the work. But be careful, cuz. They are not like us. Don't get involved with him." He picked up a Brillo pad and began scouring the pots.

Julieta couldn't swallow the sinking feeling that Tiburón was right. She hovered over the cook making Ramón's and Enrique's food, added some garnishes, and took the plates out and served them.

"I promise, he won't be a problem."

Ramón winked at her. "Don't worry about it. He cares about his community, and he's just protective over you, like he should be."

Julieta's heart fluttered. It had been a week—she'd expected the effect he had on her to wear off. But here she was, her heart hammering, her eyes glued to him all over again.

Enrique's eyes shifted from his brother's back to Julieta. "Sit with us." He smirked, pulled out a chair, and put it suspiciously close to Ramón.

Julieta sat next to Ramón, their knees touching. She was a grown woman—why did the quivers in her stomach make her feel like she was a tween with a crush? She turned her attention to Enrique. "Okay. So, tell me how you became interested in farming?"

"Well, I always helped out our grandfather with his work. He was a landscaper. And in the summers, I would go to our mom's brother's farm in Salinas. I loved it out there. My uncle taught me how to harvest lettuce, pick strawberries, and grow garlic. I wanted to help his farm grow, so I went to Cal Poly SLO and got my degree in agricultural science."

"That's so cool." Julieta was so impressed by Enrique and, of course it went without saying, Ramón. They were both so driven. She couldn't wait to meet Jaime.

After breakfast, they left the restaurant. Enrique was driving, so they piled into his Tesla SUV and headed to Encinitas.

The daylight sun shone through the SUV's window as Enrique drove along the coast. People were hiking along the beach and riding bicycles on the beach paths. Did anyone work in this city?

But as the warmth from the weather relaxed her, Julieta turned inward. Ramón had been flirty, but respectful. He was her boss—he'd probably decided not to make a move until she made a clear signal that she wanted him.

Did she?

Well, that was easy. Yes, she did. Of course she did.

But that wasn't the question. Should she?

Mamá and Tiburón were against it. They were convinced any relationship between Julieta and Ramón would implode.

But maybe they were wrong.

Rosa told her to go for it, but Rosa never thought about the consequences of her actions. She lived in the here and now and couldn't possibly realize the potential aftermath of a torrid love affair between Ramón and Julieta.

Forty minutes later, Enrique headed away from the beach. He finally turned into a driveway off the side of the road. They parked, and Enrique led them to the main garden.

Julieta's heart soared. There were rows and rows of crops. All the vegetables she created with were in front of her, fresh and vibrant. This farm alone was reason enough to take Ramón's job offer.

Enrique pointed to some plants. "Here we have our lettuces, hybrid tomatoes, chiles."

Julieta laughed, and then put her hand over her mouth.

Ramón touched her shoulder. "Is something funny?"

"Why do you grow chiles if you don't use them?"

Ramón playfully grabbed her hand. "Aren't you the comedian? We do use them in our test kitchen."

Enrique led them to another area. "And in this plot, I've even been growing some specialty Mexican herbs."

Julieta dropped Ramón's hand. She bent down and inhaled the hoja santa. She loved that herb, but it was so hard to find. It smelled like root beer, and its leaves could be used to wrap food like a tortilla. She could plan the most amazing menu with access to these plants.

Then Ramón pointed to a bare garden with fresh soil.

Julieta crinkled her face. "What is that?"

"That, Julieta, is your garden."

Her mouth flew open. She stood up to face him, her heart thumping in her chest. "Really? For me?"

"Yup. For the restaurant in Barrio. You can grow anything you like in here. And you can come here whenever you want."

Julieta couldn't believe his words. She had always wanted to grow some rare herbs and vegetable hybrids like other chefs did but had never dreamed that she would be in the position to do so.

She pressed up on her toes and wrapped her arms around Ramón's neck. She didn't care that his brother was standing beside them. Before she could stop herself, she tilted her head and kissed Ramón.

Ramón hesitated at first, a look of shock gracing his face, but when Julieta pulled him toward her, his mouth enveloped hers. Their lips met. First slowly, then with more hunger. Julieta ran her fingers through his hair as his hands drifted toward her bottom.

Enrique chuckled, and Julieta broke away from Ramón's mouth.

"Like I said, Ramón always gets what he wants."

Heat burned in her cheeks. She looked up at Ramón, who had a smug smile on his face, like he had just struck the big prize in the piñata.

This kiss was more dangerous than their first one at the graveyard.

Because back then, she only lusted after Ramón.

And now, she actually liked him.

Ugh, she was so doomed.

Chapter Eighteen

Working with Ramón in the restaurant had gone surprisingly well. Julieta had expected him to question her about each and every decision she had made in her place, but he didn't do that at all. He showed up on time every morning, immediately put on his apron, and went straight to the kitchen.

And he did a great job, also. His chopping skills were decent, and even the customers liked him when he brought their meals out to the table.

Granted, they were probably just drooling over how gorgeous he was, but honestly, who could blame them?

Julieta was in awe over him, too. His wardrobe had devolved from business suits to fitted T-shirts and jeans. His biceps bulged out of his sleeves, and Julieta found herself distracted multiple times a day, staring at him.

Ramón grabbed an apron, and Julieta put her hand on his chest. "What are you doing?"

"What does it look like I'm doing? I'm getting ready to cook."

Nope. Julieta didn't need or want Ramón in the kitchen. Ever since they'd kissed in the garden earlier this week, Julieta had been trying to keep her distance from Ramón. She had been caught up in the moment, and until his intentions were clear, she didn't want to risk her job over some hot sex.

Well, maybe she did. It was complicated.

"Ramón, I appreciate all your help in the kitchen, but maybe you should do your business stuff."

"Good idea. May I look over your books?"

By books, did he mean all the handwritten pages of notes she took daily? Did those qualify as books?

"Ah, sure. Let me get them."

Julieta went to the tiny office in the back room. He followed closely behind her.

She sat behind the desk and grabbed a bunch of papers in a tray.

The room was so small, and Ramón was so big. She could feel his magnetic energy beaming toward her. The door was still open—but she yearned to close it to be alone with him.

She stood up, straightened the papers out, and handed them to him.

Ramón took one look at the messy pile, then at Julieta, and then smirked. "You do know you can set up your systems on the computer, right?"

Julieta threw up her hands. "You lost me at systems."

"Julieta . . ."

The way he said her name, deep and soft, made her stomach quiver. "Yes, of course, silly, but I'm not that great with them. I'm better with my hands."

He stepped closer to her and grabbed her hand. The pressure built between them.

"You *are* great with your hands." He slammed the door and pressed her up against the wall, pinning her wrists above her head.

Ay, Dios mío.

Her breath faltered. His rock-hard body was crushed against her curvy one.

"I can't stop thinking about you," he whispered. "The way you taste. The way you make me feel."

He claimed her lips, and the kiss set her core on fire.

The clack of Mamá's clogs startled Julieta. She wiggled away from Ramón's arms.

"We should go," she managed to mutter.

They tumbled out of the office, Ramón right behind Julieta.

Mamá saw them and waggled a finger at Julieta. Julieta felt like she was a teenager again, hiding boys from her mom.

They walked out to the front of the restaurant. Ramón took Julieta's hand. "I'm sorry. I shouldn't have kissed you in there."

"Don't be sorry. I liked it."

"I did, too." He grinned, showing off his dimples.

Breathe, Julieta. She fanned herself with a napkin.

He sat at an empty table, reached into his briefcase, took out his computer, and opened a bunch of software and graphs and reports. All of it looked as foreign as Mayan symbols looked to her.

Though Julieta had been worried about her restaurant, she'd always operated with one key philosophy in mind: build it and they will come. Food was her focus—and if it was good, surely the customers would follow.

But Julieta was oddly intrigued about the potential of this new venture. With Julieta's cooking skills and Ramón's business acumen, the possibilities were endless.

J ulieta proudly waved to her last guest of the evening. "Adios, Señora Garcia. See you next week." Because there *would* be a next week.

Until the sign on the door changed from Las Pescas to Taco King, her regulars wouldn't know any different.

She locked the front door. Ramón stood up from his table, where he had been working, and walked over toward her.

He leaned in close to Julieta and spoke in almost a whisper. "Let's have some fun. Go on a date with me."

"No, I can't."

"Yes, you can."

Julieta pulled a lock of her hair. "I don't know."

"I do, though. If you say no, I won't mention it again. I don't want you to feel pressured to date me." He licked his lower lip. "But please, say yes."

Heat flooded Julieta. Why was he so intrigued by her? There were literally thousands of girls available just by the swipe of his phone who would be thrilled to hook up with him. Why her? Was it some game?

Julieta had two options. She could stop this flirtation before it ever got started. A few stolen kisses could easily be written off. That was what she would normally do—retreat from love before ever giving it a chance. It was safer that way. She would never get hurt.

Or, she could give in to her desires. Like she had tried to do on Day of the Dead.

But back then, it had just been about lust and forgetting her life. Now, she liked the guy and could see a future with him. And she was almost thirty, dammit. She desperately wanted children. Preferably ones with Ramón's dimples and her sass. Beautiful brown babies.

Ugh, she was so pathetic. Fantasizing about having a family with this millionaire playboy. He probably was a confirmed bachelor who didn't even want to have children.

"Why me? Why do you like me?"

Ramón gave her a sincere smile. "What do you mean? Why not you? You're gorgeous. Incredibly talented. Unique."

His words warmed her heart, but unfortunately, they weren't enough to put out the flame of doubt flickering inside of her. "Right. I am all of those things." She paused. "And many more. But that's not what I'm asking. Why are you interested in me, Ramón? You don't strike me as the type of man who wants to date a girl like me. I'm from the Barrio; you're from La Jolla. We can't possibly have anything in common."

"That's not true—we have plenty in common. We are both workaholics. We love the same type of music. Hell, our parents hooked up, which makes me supremely uncomfortable, but still. Clearly, there is a pull between us, don't you think?"

A pull wasn't enough for Julieta. She didn't want to be used and discarded by Ramón once he got his fix of slumming it with her.

It wasn't like he was proposing—just asking for a date. A date. No one had ever taken Julieta out on a date. Sure, there had been hookups galore, especially during her time as a chef in San Francisco. Then there had been meaningless after-hours sex on the bar counter, trysts in the pantry, a one-night stand in a walk-in refrigerator, but she'd never had time for proper dates.

None of those other men had made her feel like Ramón did right now. Her heart raced in his presence, but she didn't trust his intentions toward her at all. They could never have a future together. Though they were both Mexican, they came from two different worlds. And she liked hers—it was warm and full of love. It had heart. She had no desire to ever live in his life full of McLarens and maids.

There she went again, allowing her anxiety to make her decisions for her.

She closed her eyes and said a quick prayer.

She opened her eyes back up and stared right at him. His deep, dark eyes stared back at her with no deception visible—just adoration.

Maybe her life had changed for the better. A few weeks ago, she had little hope of keeping her restaurant or meeting anyone. And now, she had possibilities for both.

Was she okay with dating her boss? That was a bad decision, for sure. But if it didn't work out with them, he would probably just work on another deal and they would have little contact. She seriously doubted he planned to spend the rest of his life working in Las Pescas, aka the new Taco King.

"Sure. I'll have dinner with you. When?"

He reached over and took her hand. "Right now."

Julieta's hand began to sweat. She pulled back. "Tonight? I look like a mess. I've been working all day. Maybe some other time."

He touched her chin and pulled it up. "You look beautiful."

Ramón stood in front of her, sexy, confident, calm—basically, the exact opposite of her. He wanted something, and he went after it. She had never been pursued like this by a man. Especially a catch as great as Ramón. She'd be a fool not to say yes, yes, and oh yes.

"Okay. Where to?"

"Coronado."

"Well, let's go."

She followed him out to his McLaren. As he drove her over the Coronado Bridge to the ocean, Julieta exhaled. The stars shone over the bay and the lights lit up the Hotel Del in the distance. She was in a dream.

And, for the first time since her father had died, she believed that everything in her life would work out.

As great as growing up watching her parents' relationship was, in a way it had also prevented Julieta from seeking out a boyfriend. She would meet guys and like them, but if she couldn't see a future with them, she would just relegate them to a "friends with benefits" situation. She would emotionally shut herself off from any possibility of having a relationship.

So why on earth did she think that she could possibly have a relationship with Ramón, who was completely out of her league?

Julieta wanted to know more about Ramón's family. He had never mentioned his mom. What was her story? "Are you close to your mom?"

Ramón raised his brow. "Why do you ask?"

"Just curious. You never mention her."

"No, not at all. She didn't spend much time with me when I was a kid. I was raised by nannies."

Poor Ramón. She wanted to hug him. Even though he had all this wealth, he didn't seem that happy.

"But you're close to your dad?"

Ramón exhaled. "He was a neglectful parent also when I was growing up. It took me years of therapy to forgive him and my mom. But at least he and I have some things in common—business, surfing, and golf. And now our relationship is rocky at best."

Julieta was impressed that he admitted to going to therapy. Nothing was sexier than a man who wanted to work on himself.

"Why?"

"It's complicated. Let's just say that we have different views about the direction of the company. I'm sorry, but I can't really talk about it with you."

Whoa. Julieta didn't expect that answer. Ramón had been so open with her about, well, everything. Was his conflict with his father about Barrio Logan? She was hopeful that it was. Deep in her heart, she knew Ramón couldn't possibly want to destroy her community.

But he told her he couldn't talk about it. She wouldn't press it, at least not now.

"I understand. That's impressive that you went to therapy. I need to go." She wanted to deal with her grief about Papá, create better boundaries with Mamá, and learn how to achieve work-life balance.

"You should. It really helped me and my brothers."

"Enrique seems wonderful. What about your other brother?"

"Jaime is an Instagram influencer. He's cool, but he's a partier."

She laughed. "Really? He takes pictures for social media?"

"Yeah, he's great at it. He could do some innovative things for the Barrio location."

Julieta cringed hearing Ramón call her Las Pescas "the Barrio location." But she had to accept reality. That was what it was.

Just another Taco King.

CHAPTER NINETEEN

Ramón placed his hand on Julieta's thigh as he drove through downtown Coronado. Normally, if he wanted to impress a girl, he would take her to the finest restaurant in town, but that strategy wouldn't work with Julieta. First, he had already dined on the most delicious food in San Diego—hers. And Julieta didn't seem to care about his wealth; if anything, it was quite the opposite. Sure, she seemed to like his car and his house, but she had been most enamored with him when he sang to her.

"I love it here. Where are we going?" she said as they cruised along Orange Avenue.

"To the Del for drinks and appetizers on the beach."

Ramón chose the Hotel del Coronado, a historic beachfront resort. Many presidents had stayed there, and it was the filming location of Marilyn Monroe's *Some Like It Hot*. L. Frank Baum even based the Emerald City of Oz on it. It was perfect for a romantic date with the woman he wanted to woo.

"That sounds great."

He pulled up to the driveway at the hotel. Luckily for him, the valets kept the most expensive sports cars up front, so he didn't have to worry about his McLaren being dinged or scratched in the nearby lot.

He opened Julieta's car door, put his arm around her, and led her to the beach. Miles of sparkly, golden sand in a city that was warm even in November was one of the many reasons Coronado was always voted one of the best beaches in the world.

"Wow. It's gorgeous here. I live just across the bridge but don't ever go to the beach."

Ramón went to the beach every chance he got. "Why is that?"

She shrugged. "I work all the time. If I'm off, I usually just hang out with my family."

"You mean your mom?"

"I mean my cousins, aunts, and uncles. We are all super close."

"That's cool. I always wanted to spend more time with my aunt and uncle and cousins. You know, they live in Barrio Logan."

Julieta placed her hand over her mouth. "Really? Who? I know everyone there."

"Miguel and Rita Montez. They have four kids, Benicio, Adella, Elena, and Jose."

"I know Benicio! Tiburón is friends with him. How did I not know he was an actual Montez?"

Ramón shook his head. "Because he wants nothing to do with us. Neither does my uncle." Though they'd been close when he was younger, they had definitely grown apart. He'd been reminded of that when he had his run-in with Benicio on the Day of the Dead. It still bothered him—they were family. Benicio should have his back no matter what.

Though, now, Ramón was starting to understand Benicio's point.

Julieta gulped and then put a comforting hand on Ramón's shoulder. "I'm sorry, Ramón. That sucks. Maybe he will come around when he sees what you do with Barrio Logan."

Ramón cleared his throat. He couldn't tell if Julieta was being passive-aggressive or sincere. Was that a dig, or did she truly believe that Ramón was capable of changing Barrio Logan for the better? Was he?

The hostess seated Ramón and Julieta at a small table facing the ocean and handed them a drink menu. A few minutes later, the cocktail waitress came to take their order.

"I'll have a dirty martini, and the lady will have a paloma."

Julieta beamed. "You remembered."

"Of course I did. I remember everything about that night. How you looked, how you smelled." His voice lowered. "How you tasted."

Ramón leaned over the table and gazed into her eyes. Her lips parted, and he slowly kissed her, inhaling her scent, lost in her mouth.

She pulled away almost as soon as the kiss began.

"Ramón, I like you. I do. But I'm so overwhelmed with losing the restaurant and trying to figure out how I will deal with the community backlash." She paused, and tugged on her hair. "Are you looking for just a hookup? Because that is not what I want."

"What do you want?" He was her boss—he had to make sure that she didn't feel pressured into going out with him.

She rubbed his arm. "I want to date you."

Guau. The wind knocked out of him. Julieta had no problem expressing her feelings and being honest, which Ramón found surprisingly sexy. He hated playing the guessing game. He was direct and to the point.

"I'd like to date you, too. After the Day of the Dead event, I never thought I'd see you again. But here we are. Let's see where this goes."

Julieta's mouth broadened into a wide smile.

He leaned over, cupped her chin, and kissed her.

He was catching feelings. Real feelings.

And as excited as he was to get to know her outside of work, one thing still worried him. The fact that his father had stolen her mother's taco recipe. Their lawyers were investigating their liability, so Ramón had to stay tight-lipped about the situation.

But he wouldn't stress about it now. He would focus on getting to know Julieta. Then he would continue the talks with his legal counsel. He had made a promise to himself that Linda would be compensated, but until the details were finalized, he didn't want to make any false assurances. And if Papá refused to take care of it, Ramón would quit like he'd threatened.

The waitress brought their drinks.

Julieta brought her glass up to Ramón's. "Salud."

"Salud." Ramón took a drink.

"So, I hate to bring this up, but everyone has been asking me. What are your plans for the rest of the block? Are you going to raise everyone's rent?"

Rent. Ramón would have to increase the rent on Logan Avenue to make the venture profitable. Once the owners started panicking, the trouble would start for Julieta and him.

"We haven't decided yet." Ramón popped one of the olives from his drink into his mouth. He had to figure out what he wanted to do. Was he so infatuated with this woman that he now wanted to make unwise business decisions? Never in his life had he let his heart rule his head, or in this case, his dick rule his brain.

No. No. It wasn't that at all. Sure, Julieta was a part of this decision, but it was more than that. He had seen the community in Barrio Logan. He'd watched the people who owned the businesses. He wasn't ready to come in and tear the seam of their lives apart.

Yet.

He had to make a plan and make Papá see his point of view.

But for now, he wanted to focus on Julieta and not his mounting ethical issues with the development in Barrio Logan.

"Can I ask a favor? Could we not talk about business? Babe, you need to learn how to take a night off."

"That's fair. Okay. I'll try to be present. Focus on us."

Music played in the background. Julieta swayed to the beat. "So, when am I going to hear some more of your music? You are really great."

Ramón winked. "Next year on Day of the Dead."

Julieta giggled. "Ha, funny. But no, seriously. You are talented. We have an opening down at the restaurant for a resident guitarist. You should come play. I can't pay you, but you can put out a tip jar."

Now it was Ramón's turn to laugh. Back when he'd founded his first band in La Jolla with his friends in high school, they'd started playing covers: Metallica, Guns N' Roses, and Mötley Crüe. Then, they'd moved to harder stuff like Slayer, Megadeth, and Death Angel. Ramón had grown his hair long, much to the dismay of his mother. He'd tried his hand at songwriting. His group, the Taco Kings, started to get a lot of attention. Ramón wrote songs in Spanish, English, and Spanglish.

They had a steady following and booked some local gigs, and even released a couple of viral YouTube videos, which he prayed that Julieta wouldn't find.

But then Ramón was accepted into Stanford, and he'd focused on his studies. He'd briefly formed a rock group there but then was roped into trying mariachi music. Before college, he'd never really liked that style of songs, but at Stanford he was seduced by their beauty. He loved the sounds of the different instruments, and once he'd placed his hands on a beautiful guitarrón, there was no going back.

As a mariachi, he'd played all around the Bay Area—at Casa Zapata, the Latinx center at Stanford; at the opening of the *Zoot Suit* play; at Cinco de Mayo festivals; at weddings; and at other local events like the Gilroy Garlic Festival.

In that charro suit, no one ever judged Ramón for being the Taco King's son. He was just Ramón, a Mexican mariachi, and he couldn't have been happier.

Of course, work made him happy, too. It did. But now, it was nothing but stress. "I don't have time for music."

"Well, make time. You're so good. I could listen to you play all night."

"What would the point be? I'm not a musician; I'm a businessman."

She playfully punched his arm. "Does everything have to have a point? Sometimes you just do something because it makes you happy."

Happiness. Ramón used to think that all his possessions would make him happy—another car, another house, another yacht—but was he truly happy? Did he feel fulfilled in life? Was he proud of himself? Was it easy for him to go to sleep at night?

The answer to all of those questions was no.

Ramón shook his sadness off and focused back on Julieta. "What do you do to make yourself happy? Outside of work."

"I like to garden, but I guess that's tied to work. I love hanging out with my dog. He's a Min Pin. His name is Taco. I found him on the street, and he was in really bad shape, but I nursed him back to health. I like taking care of him."

"You are so sweet—do you know that? You truly like taking care of others."

"I do. But I have to admit, it's been nice having you around. Though I still don't want my restaurant to become a Taco King, I like not having to worry about payroll and just focusing on the food."

He smirked. "So, what you are trying to say is you are glad I bought your block?"

She pinched him. "No, silly. Definitely not that."

Ramón stared into her eyes. "In all seriousness, we make a good team."

She leaned in closer to him. She smelled like a watermelon margarita. "I don't know about that. We are too different. I'm not the kind of girl you normally date, am I?"

He touched her thigh. "I don't really date." His eyes followed a family of four who were making s'mores over a firepit. They all looked really happy. Could Ramón be happy as a husband? A father? How could he possibly become a good family man when he had never really had a role model? Even his abuelo had been a philanderer.

She pursed her lips. "Right."

He looked back at Julieta. An overwhelming urge came over him to protect her, take care of her. He could see a future with this glorious woman by his side. "We could be happy together, Julieta. I'm not playing you—I really like you. Give me a chance."

She smiled. "I'm here, aren't I?"

"Yes, you are. But though you are so confident in your cooking, you keep questioning why I'm into you." He gazed into her eyes and brushed a lock of her hair out of her face. "But trust me, I am."

She kissed him. "I am into you, too."

Ramón downed the rest of his drink and looked out on the sand. Lovers walked hand in hand along the beach; teens danced around a bonfire. All of them were carefree and enjoying the moment.

Being around Julieta rattled him. Through her, he saw a world outside his own privileged yet sheltered existence. It didn't *scare* him—nothing scared Ramón. But it forced him to examine the way he had been living his life.

And unfortunately, he didn't like what he saw.

Chapter Twenty

Julieta was woozy from the liquor and the lust. The salty ocean air mixed with the scent of s'mores roasting nearby. This night was perfect. And Julieta was, for once in her life, blissfully content.

She stared at the tourists dining at tables around her as she took her last bite of sashimi. What must it be like to travel and have money to stay in a place like this? She was sure Ramón knew. "Have you stayed here before?"

Ramón nodded. "Yeah. I love it here. And I belong to the country club."

Of course he did. The only time Julieta had ever been to a country club was when she'd worked at one, catering a wedding.

"I didn't know they had a club."

"Yeah, it's great. In the summer they have bonfires and exclusive parties with musicians. Last year, Tim McGraw played here. But they don't have golf," he said, with a disappointed tone.

Oh no, the horror! How could Ramón live without golf?

Julieta couldn't even believe she was having this conversation. "How often do you play golf?"

"All the time—mostly for business networking. I belong to the La Jolla Country Club also. They have the best course. It overlooks the ocean. Have you ever played?"

He belonged to two country clubs? Because one wasn't enough? Who did that?

Right, the dude with the McLaren.

"No. Never picked up a club. That's not true—I played mini golf once."

"Well, I need to teach you."

Julieta stifled a laugh. What a joke. Didn't golfers have to wear special shoes and bright outfits? She wouldn't have a clue what to do and would probably embarrass Ramón. "I think I'd rather stay here. I prefer concerts. And live music."

"You've never stayed here?"

Why on earth would she waste money staying at the Del when she lived five minutes away? "No, there was never a need. I live on the other side of the bridge." Make that the *wrong* side of the bridge.

Ay, Julieta. Scratch that thought.

She should flip that narrative—she lived on the right side of the bridge.

There was nothing wrong with Barrio Logan. She loved it there.

Even so, it would be nice to check into a resort like this and spend her days getting hot stone massages and her nights taking romantic sunset walks on the beach.

Ramón winked. "Well, let's stay here tonight."

What? *Tonight?*

She studied him. His face had an almost movie-star quality to it. He was ruggedly handsome, yet still a pretty boy, all wrapped up with those adorably deep dimples. And so far, in every interaction they'd had, he had been a perfect gentleman.

But was spending the night with him a wise move? Yes, she had gone home with him on the Day of the Dead, but that was when she never planned to see him again. That was her typical no-strings-attached hookup plan. She had intended to smash and dash. Now she knew his name, and they worked together. It felt more intimate; it felt scarier.

Don't do it, Julieta. Protect your heart. This won't end well. Just ask to go back home—

"I'd love to." Did she just say that?

She did say that. She wanted to get out of her head. Be guided by her heart and just go for it. She deserved it.

Ramón grinned. "Check, please!"

Her pulse raced. Ramón pulled her chair toward him. He kissed her again, starting on her lips, and making his way down to her neck. Julieta was on fire. Where was that waitress?

Finally, the waitress brought their check, he paid, and they left.

Ramón led her to the lobby.

They stood under a grand chandelier, and a bride and groom walked by. Her gown was so ornate—Julieta never dared dream about her wedding day, which would now be even more bittersweet since her father wouldn't be able to walk her down the aisle. It seemed like a foolish dream anyway because she had never even been in a serious relationship. But if she did ever get married, it would not be at a place like the Hotel Del. A wedding here must cost a fortune. Ramón squeezed her hand, and Julieta didn't know what to make of that.

Turning her attention away from the newlyweds, Julieta marveled at the opulent interior. There were already Christmas decorations up. A huge upside-down tree was in the middle of the lobby.

Garlands and lights hung from the balcony overhead. Julieta had never seen anything like it.

A ghost supposedly haunted the property. Her name was Kate Morgan, also known as the Lady in Black, and her body had been found on a staircase leading to the beach, with a gunshot wound in her head. Julieta didn't believe in ghosts, but she did a quick sign of the cross just in case.

Ramón walked over to the reception, and Julieta remained near the tree. Ramón returned a few minutes later, took her hand, and led her through the hotel.

He opened the door to their room, and she gasped.

She had stupidly assumed that he would get a normal room, not flaunt his wealth. He didn't need to impress her; she already knew that he was filthy rich. But this room was bigger than her entire house. It was on the beach, had a sitting room, a fireplace, a bedroom, and a private patio. Was this the honeymoon suite?

How much was this room a night? A thousand dollars—possibly more? She needed to stop being shocked every time Ramón spent his money like he was doling out candy, but she couldn't help herself.

"Wow! Look at this place! You didn't have to go all out. I would have been happy staying in the maid's quarters."

Ramón laughed. "You're funny. Do you know that?"

"I do."

Ramón opened the minibar and found a bottle of champagne. He poured two glasses. "Shall we toast?"

"To what?"

He pursed his lips—his eyes shifting. "Love and tacos."

Love? She studied him quizzically, lost in the depths of his chocolate eyes. Surely not. It was too soon. But what if . . . "Love?" she asked, her voice soft, her heart a whirl.

He blinked, and a cheeky smirk replaced his look of gravitas. The spell was broken. "Sex and tacos sounded weird. So, I went with love."

"Good call."

They clinked their glasses and sipped the champagne.

He set down his flute, wrapped his arms around her lower waist, and gazed into her eyes. "Julieta, I haven't stopped thinking about you since the Day of the Dead. I wanted you so badly that night." He took her glass out of her hand and placed it next to his. Then he cupped her face. "*'Thus with a kiss I die.'*"

Julieta didn't hold back. She kissed Ramón passionately. His mouth overtook hers, and their tongues danced an intimate ballet, from soft and slow to wild and uninhibited. She nibbled on his lower lip, and he let out a guttural groan. She ached for him. She had never been kissed like this and definitely never in a place as magical as this one.

Julieta couldn't wait any longer to undress him. Ever since she first met him, she'd been dying to see his naked body. She pulled off his T-shirt and stopped to marvel at the sight of his chest.

Ay, Dios mío. There were abs for days, and his dark skin high-lighted his muscle definition. Not a tattoo in sight. From his wide shoulders to his tapered waist, with that delicious happy trail point-ing downward—she could've stared at him all night.

Ramón took back control. He kissed behind her earlobe as his hands raked over her body, stopping on her breasts. He peeled off her shirt.

"You're so beautiful, Julieta. How did I get so lucky?"

She laughed. "It was the guitarrón. I'm a sucker for 'Abrázame.'"

He chuckled and began humming the song. Julieta moaned as he rubbed her tits through her bra. And just like magic, the bra popped off with a single touch of the hook between her cleavage. Yup. Ramón was definitely a player.

But she didn't care anymore. She *wanted* to be played, just like he strummed his instrument. At least he knew what he was doing. She was so sick of meaningless hookups where the men would get off and she'd be left unsatisfied. Ramón was good at everything he did—no doubt he was a king in bed. Time for her to have some fun and indulge in some heedless pleasure.

Ramón undid her pants and tossed them on the floor, leaving her standing there naked except for her new lace panties. Julieta was so glad she'd gone shopping.

"Julieta, do you know how sexy you are?"

That was a definite no, but she kept her mouth shut, afraid that she would not only say something stupid but also drool all over him.

He traced her tattoos with his finger, slowly drawing up her arm, each brush of his skin against hers making Julieta gasp.

He picked her up, took her into the bedroom, and placed her on the bed. Wow—it was like a floating cloud.

Ramón reclaimed her lips before his mouth left hers to blaze a path down her body. Heat pooled in her belly as he made his descent. He leaned in to lavish attention on her right nipple, licking around in a circle before sucking on it, and then her left. Julieta moaned as he worked his magic. Her buds hardened against the softness of his tongue. She came alive under his mouth, writhing beneath. This entire night seemed like such a fantasy, and it was only going to get better.

His hand caressed her body, and he cupped her ass. She ran her hands through his thick black hair as he guided his mouth down to her panties. Julieta's core throbbed for him.

The sight of his wide shoulders and strong back was almost enough to put her over the edge. She couldn't wait to ravage him—kiss down his chest, pleasure him, but Ramón was in control, and he was focused only on her.

He kissed her belly and settled in between her legs. His lips pressed against her black lace panties, the heat of his mouth igniting her fire. He planted more kisses on her, focusing now on her thighs. Julieta was out of her mind with lust.

"Stop teasing me."

She wanted Ramón's mouth on her, and she wanted it now. She began to remove her panties, but Ramón quickly got the hint and took them off.

He looked up at her, and a devilish grin graced his face. "Tell me what you want, babe."

"Cómeme."

"My pleasure." He began to lick her, starting with her thighs, before lapping in between her lips. Slow and sweet, deep and dirty. Julieta wanted all of him.

Ramón's tongue pressed against her clit, and she gasped, a flash of pleasure overtaking her. "Ah, Ramón."

"You taste so sweet." He hummed against her, and she ran her fingers through his hair, holding him as his tongue worked its magic.

She cried out, desperate for release. Julieta wanted this moment—not just the intimacy, but the night—to last forever. Ramón was every fantasy she had ever had wrapped up into one—strong, sexy, sweet, and oh so skilled.

His deep voice, his capable hands, his delicious mouth. *Perfection.*

She completely surrendered to him.

"Ramón." She couldn't hold back any longer, as he edged her over the top. One final lick and a wave of ecstasy crashed through her followed by shivers of joy radiating through her entire body.

Ramón planted another kiss in between her thighs and pulled up by her side.

She turned to him, stroking his chest, reaching between his legs. "My turn."

Ramón shook his head. "No, baby. Let's have something to look forward to. This isn't a one-night stand. Tonight is just the first of many nights we will spend together."

Julieta didn't even know how to react to that statement. His talk of the future completely overwhelmed her.

"Okay." Ugh, was that the best she could do?

Julieta curled up under his arms and rested her head against his chest.

Chapter Twenty-One

Ramón gazed at the moon from the patio in his beach suite. He glanced at Julieta sleeping inside, her long black hair spread around her head. She looked like an angel.

After they had been intimate, they had talked for a bit. Julieta took a bath, and they had climbed back into bed. He had kissed her good night and held her as she fell asleep. He hadn't even tried to fuck her—what was wrong with him?

He didn't even know why he hadn't tried. But after some soul-searching, he believed it was because in the past he had sex with so many women and they meant nothing to him. He cared for Julieta. He liked her. He wanted sex with her to actually mean something.

He had lost his edge. Just a few weeks ago, he'd been a driven businessman whose sole focus had been closing the deal, whether that deal was a real estate acquisition or a one-night stand with a sexy woman.

And now his head was filled with crazy thoughts, like what would be best for the community, what would be best for Julieta, and, even worse, what would be best for his own emotional well-being.

No one cared about how Ramón felt inside. Certainly not Mamá, who could write the book on detachment parenting. Almost from birth, he had been pawned off on nannies, gardeners, maids, or anyone else who was around. And it wasn't because Mamá had a job . . . unless you considered sleeping with her personal trainer and her tennis instructor as "work."

Papá had been too busy working to even notice.

As a little boy, Ramón would watch the stands at his soccer games, praying that his parents would show up to root for him, only to be heartbroken when they never appeared.

Dammit. Maybe he needed to go back to therapy. He had struggled in his twenties but had stopped seeking professional help once he graduated from business school. Mental health was not something that was talked about in his family. Accomplishments were awarded; emotional growth was not.

He would probably fuck up whatever he had going on with Julieta because he wasn't capable of creating an emotional connection. He never had been.

His only college girlfriend had been a competitive swimmer— she'd been focused on winning. Sometimes, Ramón had almost felt used by her, which was ridiculous. He'd wanted sex as much as she did. But he wanted her to want more from him than his body. Just like his parents, his ex-girlfriend had never shown up to his open mic nights or his music shows.

And here Julieta was, begging him to play more music, even inviting him to play at her restaurant. Should he?

No, no. That would be ridiculous. He was a businessman, not a rock star. He had better things to do with his time than play guitar for Taco Tuesday.

But he wanted her to look at him again the way she had looked at him on Day of the Dead . . . when he'd been playing the guitarrón.

Ramón climbed back into bed and wrapped his arms around Julieta. How lucky was he to spend the night with this glorious woman?

The next morning, Ramón woke early and ordered breakfast for them in bed. He had the staff set it up on the patio of their beach villa.

Julieta finally woke up and stretched. A big smile widened across her face. "I slept better than ever. I wish I could stay here longer."

His eyes glinted. "Well, I could rent it for a while. It could be our secret getaway."

Her mouth twisted. "That's ridiculous and completely wasteful. In case you have forgotten, you own an oceanfront mansion. In La Jolla, no less."

"True. But my brothers live there with me. I have no privacy."

"I hear that. I live with my mother."

Ramón's eyes bulged. "You do? You have a successful restaurant."

"Had a successful restaurant." She glared at him. "It won't be mine much longer."

Ouch. Ramón chose not to comment.

"I did live in an apartment by myself. But after my dad passed away, my mom didn't want to be alone. So, I moved in."

Yeah, that definitely wasn't going to work. Her mom had warmed to him, but she'd also read him the riot act about staying away from Julieta.

Not that he had listened.

He sat next to her. "Let's just make this our hideaway. I will be spending a lot of time in Barrio Logan anyway with the business. It's more convenient for me to be in Coronado. In fact, I even called my real estate agent about purchasing a new place last week."

Her jaw dropped. "You would just buy another place because you don't want to drive thirty minutes to work? That's crazy. I mean, do what you like, but it's ridiculous to stay in a hotel. And honestly, if I visit you, I won't feel comfortable being waited on by maids."

Well, he guessed his place in La Jolla was out, too. "Why?"

"I don't know. I just don't like people doing for me what I can do myself."

"I understand that, but it's not worth an hour of my time to clean my house when I could be putting together another acquisition. But I see your point about living in a hotel. I'll just buy."

She threw up her hands. "You're insane, do you know that?"

"It would be an investment."

"Whatever you've got to tell yourself, Ramón. My idea of an investment is a lottery ticket."

He considered mentioning the probability of winning the lottery, but then decided against it.

They got dressed and dined on fresh berries, pastries, and a Maine lobster and chorizo scramble.

Ramón took a bite. "This is great, but the eggs you make are a thousand times better."

"Thanks."

Ramón didn't want this date to end. "Do you want to hang out today? Rent some bikes?"

She looked at her feet. "No. I can't. I have to see my mamá."

"Just tell her you want to spend the day in Coronado."

"Yeah, she won't be too happy if she knows I'm with you."

"Well, then don't tell her."

She hesitated, and Ramón was sure she would say no, but she finally grabbed her phone and dialed.

Before Julieta spoke another word, Ramón heard the angry torrent of Spanish flowing down the line at her.

"Amá, no, I'm fine."

"Look, I'll be home later."

"Yes, with Ramón. I know he's my boss. Stop it, Amá."

Her fist clenched. "No, he's not."

"I'm not listening to you."

"I'm hanging up now."

"Bye, Amá!" She angrily tossed her phone in her purse.

Well, that had gone well. Ramón was glad that he didn't have to check in with anyone. "See? Everything worked out." Ramón joked.

Julieta rolled her eyes. "My mother thinks I'm twelve. But it's fine."

Ramón paused. Should he tell her what Linda had asked of him? He had to. "Well, she did forbid me to get involved with you."

Julieta covered her face with her hands. "Please tell me she didn't."

"She did."

A scowl claimed Julieta's face. "Ay! I'm a grown adult. I can't believe her."

Ramón took her hand. "She's just watching out for you."

"Clearly, you didn't listen to her."

"Nope, I didn't. I also told her that I couldn't promise her that."

"Good, I'm glad." She sat in his lap.

Ramón brushed a lock of hair out of her face. "So how about that bike ride?"

Julieta looked down at her work clothes. "Let's just hang out here. I don't have sporty clothes."

Ramón shook his head. "Let's just get clothes in the shops below the hotel."

"Ramón. No. It's fine. We can go bike riding some other time."

He placed his hands on her shoulders. "Please. It's not a big deal. I just want to show you around Coronado. You can bike around the entire island."

Julieta threw her hands up. "Okay."

Ramón took her hand, and they left the beach room. They went down to the shops. Julieta picked out a shirt, some shorts, and some tennis shoes, and so did Ramón.

They left the shops and walked toward downtown Coronado. Older couples strolled by the beach, and children were building sandcastles. Coronado had such a different vibe than La Jolla. Coronado was one of the last amazing small towns in America. Between the Navy SEAL base, miles of beach, and the famous Fourth of July parade, living in Coronado was idyllic. It would be a great place to raise children.

Why was he thinking about children? He blamed his errant musings on the little boy with long, dark bangs in front of him clutching his ice cream cone.

Ramón and Julieta strolled down the street hand in hand window-shopping. She stopped to read the menu at the Henry as he rubbed her back. They passed by Bay Books, and an ice cream store, and finally arrived at Holland's Bicycles. Ramón had a mountain bike and an electric bike back at his house, but he'd never owned a beach cruiser. It seemed kind of touristy but would be a fun way to spend the day.

Julieta stood in front of a bike in the corner of the store, her eyes wide. "Oh my God, Ramón. Look at this bike!"

Ramón's mouth dropped.

A Día de los Muertos bike. It was a gorgeous Electra beach cruiser that was painted with colorful sugar skulls and had bright green-and-white wall tires. It couldn't be more perfect for Julieta.

She looked at the price tag and grimaced. "Oh, but it's almost a thousand dollars. I could never afford that."

But Ramón could. He really wanted to make her happy.

"It's a beautiful bike. Let me buy it for you."

Julieta shook her head no. "Nope. No way. That's ridiculous."

Ramón smirked.

She blushed, which Ramón found adorable. She pulled his arm. "I'm serious. I wouldn't feel comfortable."

"Do you own a bike?"

She shook her head. "I did, but it got stolen."

"You should have a bike."

"Ramón, seriously. We can just rent a bike."

"Consider it a gift. You will never see this bike again, and you will regret it."

He signaled the attendant, who was kneeling and pumping up a tire. "I'd like to purchase the bike."

The blond young man stood up and walked over to the register. "Right on, man. I love this bike."

Ramón picked for himself a beach cruiser in a Hawaiian tiki pattern, slapped his credit card down, and bought the bikes.

Julieta stood there with a shocked look on her face. Eventually, she kissed him. "Thank you."

"Don't mention it. Let's just have a good time."

They climbed on their bikes, and off they went.

Coronado was the most beautiful island, with the view of both the ocean and the bay. The historic homes included grand colonials, Spanish casas draped in bougainvillea, and classic Craftsmen. They headed on the path near the lush tree-lined streets. They passed American flags and ice cream trucks and finally made it to the golf course. Julieta pedaled slowly, her eyes constantly glancing up at the towering buildings across the water.

They rode around the bay and stopped at the ferry landing to get ice cream.

"Let's lock our bikes and go inside."

Julieta laughed. "You can get the ice cream; I'll stay here. I'm not leaving my bike alone—it's worth more than my car."

Ramón let out an uncomfortable laugh. Was her car safe if it wasn't worth a grand? Was it mechanically sound? He'd have to ask to see it. He didn't want her in danger.

"Ramón? Are you okay?"

"Sorry. Just thinking." He shook his head. He should be in the now—that was what time spent with Julieta was all about. "Okay, what flavor do you want?"

"Rocky Road."

Ramón went inside to order the ice cream cones. When he came out, he watched Julieta sitting next to her bicycle. She caressed the frame with the hand-painted sugar skulls and took a picture of the bright green tires with her phone.

Ramón pulled her in for a kiss. "I'm having an incredible day. Thank you."

"Me too."

Ramón looked around at the kids playing on the beach.

A cute little girl in pigtails ran up to her father. "Daddy! I found a sand crab!"

Julieta turned to Ramón. "This place is paradise. I'd love to have kids and bring them here."

Ramón also wanted to have children at some point later in his life, but how late? He had plotted out every detail of his professional life, but had left his personal future up to chance. "It does seem like a pretty amazing place to raise kids."

Julieta beamed and her chest lifted. "Do you want kids? I want a huge family. I was so lonely growing up. Five children, at least."

Ramón laughed. "That's a lot of children."

"Not really. My mom is the second eldest of five. She wanted more, but after she gave birth to me, she was unable to carry another child."

"That's too bad. I think my mom always wanted a girl."

"Well, she was lucky to have three boys."

After they finished their ice cream, they got on the bikes and headed around the bay back to the Del.

Julieta stopped in front of the bike path and stared across the bay to Barrio Logan. "Did you know Barrio Logan used to include the beach, before the Navy took it? The government kept pushing our community inland, confining us under the bridge."

"Yeah, I did." Barrio Logan had so many refugees after the Mexican Revolution. They lived in Logan Heights, across the bay from Coronado, and since barrio means neighborhood in Spanish, the name stuck.

"It's so different to be on this side of the water. We're just across the bay, but we are worlds away from these mansions and tree-lined streets."

A lump grew in his throat. He had been on this side of the island so many times, and he had never once thought what it would've been like to live under the freeway on the other side of the bay.

Chapter Twenty-Two

After a glorious afternoon with Ramón, Julieta had to return to reality. He drove her across the bridge.

"You can drop me at the restaurant," she said.

He gave her a knowing look. "I can take you home."

She shook her head, no. Julieta didn't want him to see where she lived and pity her. It was so hard running a business in California. She had invested everything into her restaurant and spent what remainder she had on her parents' medical bills.

If she were being honest with herself, it would be a relief not to worry about the financials of her restaurant and just focus on the food.

Maybe Ramón could truly help the entire neighborhood, without robbing it of its character. Update the buildings, invest in more advertising, bring more customers to her beloved town. He swore he still planned to transform Las Pescas into a Taco King, but Julieta clung to the sliver of hope that she would get him to change his mind.

Were his intentions good? Did he have a hidden agenda?

"I have to grab something in the restaurant anyway."

Ramón sighed and dropped her in front of the building. She attempted to open her door, but Ramón got out and opened it for her.

"When can I see you again?" he asked.

"Silly, tomorrow at work."

"That's not what I meant. When can I take you on another date?"

Julieta didn't want to make herself completely available, but she did want to hang out with him as soon as possible.

"Next weekend?"

"Okay. Friday? Can you get off early?"

She could arrange it, but Mamá would have to agree. "Sure."

A crowd had already gathered and was staring at his car, which over the past few weeks had become a welcome sight in the neighborhood.

Tiburón walked out of the restaurant; his eyes became wide, and Julieta could've sworn he was drooling. He stroked the McLaren. "Nice car, man. Let me take it for a spin."

Julieta tugged Tiburón's sleeve. "Tib, stop." She turned to Ramón. "Ignore him."

Ramón winked at Julieta and tossed Tiburón the keys. "Go for it, bro."

Julieta grinned, but not half as big as Tiburón did.

"Seriously? Thanks, homie."

Tiburón climbed into the seat and stretched out on the tan leather. Then he took a selfie. And then another flashing a peace sign. He finally revved the engine, blasted some musica, and drove down the street, waving at the passersby, as if he was the king of the Barrio.

Julieta turned to Ramón. "You didn't have to let him drive it."

"I know. I wanted to. It's not a big deal. He's your cousin."

Ramón cupped her face with his hands and kissed her in broad daylight for the whole block to see.

Julieta didn't care. She kissed him back and wrapped her arms around his neck. She couldn't wait to be with him again. To spend the night with him. Everything so far had just been an appetizer. But she was ravenous toward him. She wanted to feel him deep inside her, to please him, to ride him.

Señora Flores walked out of the café, and Julieta pulled away from Ramón. Her eyes shifted from Ramón to Julieta, back to Ramón. Julieta's stomach clenched.

Señora Flores waved at Ramón and smiled. "Hola, Señor Montez. I brought you a concha and a café de olla." She handed him the goodies, which he readily accepted.

"Gracias, Señora Flores. You look beautiful today."

She visibly blushed and shrugged her shoulders. With his Latin lover movie-star looks and dimples for days, Ramón was a hit amongst the ladies on the street. So far, they had been intrigued by his presence and, though worried about the future of their businesses, were hopeful that he would just invest in the community. Guilt swept over Julieta. She was kissing him in the calle, giving him some sort of seal of approval, knowing full well she had already accepted the position as chef at Taco King. Once the vendors found out, they would never forgive her.

"Where's my coffee and concha?" Julieta asked.

Señora Flores shook her head. "You, mija, can come by later. I need to talk to you."

Great. Now Julieta had to worry about Mamá *and* Señora Flores.

A few minutes later, Tiburón returned.

He stopped the car in the middle of the street, hopped out, and gave Ramón the keys. "Thanks, man. Hey, do you want to bring it back Wednesday evening for the car cruise?"

Julieta's throat constricted. Had her cousin invited Ramón to La Vuelta? The sacred lowrider event in the Barrio?

Please say yes, Ramón. Por favor.

Ramón slapped Tiburón's hand in some weird handshake, which for some reason, Tiburón instinctively knew. Men. "Of course. I'd be honored."

"Awesome. Be here at five. I'll drive."

Julieta burst out laughing.

Tiburón cocked his eyebrow. "Something funny, prima?"

"Nope. Just glad you two are getting along." She turned to Ramón. "I should go inside and deal with my mom."

"Got it." He waved goodbye to Tiburón, gave Julieta a kiss, and hopped back in his ride. "Bye, bella."

Julieta melted when he called her beautiful. "Adiós. Oh, let me know when my bike gets delivered to your place." The bikes couldn't fit in or on the McLaren, so Ramón had arranged to have them delivered to his home. Julieta figured the bike would be safer in Ramón's garage in La Jolla.

"I will." He waved and drove down the street.

Julieta exhaled. It was time to face the music.

But first, she needed some sustenance. A woman should never face a firing squad on an empty stomach. She ordered a horchata cold brew and a chorizo bolillo from Señora Flores's café.

Señora Flores served Julieta and then sat next to her under a mural of La Virgen de Guadalupe. Like Julieta needed more guilt. She should probably go to confession soon to admit all her sinful thoughts about Ramón.

"So, dímelo. What are your novio's plans for our business?"

Julieta stuffed a bite of the chorizo on the soft white bread in her mouth.

"No sé." Julieta shrugged. It wasn't a lie. She didn't know what Ramón was going to do. "And he's not my boyfriend. But we are dating." Was he? They hadn't had the talk yet.

"Be careful with him, mija." Señora Flores squeezed Julieta's shoulder. "And, when you find out what he's going to do with this block, you tell me."

"Will do."

Julieta wasn't hooking up with Ramón just because she hoped he would do the right thing by Barrio Logan, but she *was* hopeful that spending time with her and in her community, like at the lowrider cruise, would make him want to strengthen and support the street instead of ripping its seams apart.

Once she was satiated, she walked inside her own restaurant. Mamá stood at the back, a scowl across her face.

Great.

"Julieta! Kitchen!" Mamá stormed into the kitchen.

Julieta looked at Tiburón, hoping he would save her, but he continued to wipe down the menus.

She pinched him. "Tib! Help me!"

He finally spoke. "Hey, don't ask me. I think Ramón's cool—for a pocho."

Julieta rolled her eyes. "He's not a pocho. He doesn't act white."

"Whatever, cuz. I'm not insulting him. It's the truth. But we're cool. If I were him, though, I'd be scared of Tía Linda."

Good point. "Thanks, Tib."

Julieta took the walk of shame into the kitchen, with Tiburón following behind her. He could never resist watching a train wreck.

"How could you spend the night with the man who is seeking to destroy us?"

"This isn't a Metallica song, Mom. He has a name. It's Ramón."

Mamá rolled her eyes. "Ay! How can you be so foolish? I told you to take the job, not sleep with him. He owns the building, mija. He owns the business. He can fire you. Do you think just because you cooked dinner for him and had sex with him, he will change his mind and let you keep this restaurant as Las Pescas?"

Uh, maybe? But that wasn't why Julieta did it. She lusted after Ramón. It was quite simple, really.

And, technically, she didn't have sex with him, at least by the Clintonian definition. But she wanted to. Desperately. And she definitely would the next time she saw him. Julieta counted down the days.

Tiburón glared at her, the vein in his neck popping, which made his shark tattoo look even more menacing. "She's right, prima. I like the dude, but I don't want you to get hurt."

"I'm not going to get hurt. And who are you to talk? Driving his car and inviting him to La Vuelta."

Mamá pointed at Tiburón. "You invited El Banco to La Vuelta? Are you mad?"

Tiburón shrugged. "I like his car. What can I say?"

Mamá shook her head. "Ay, Tiburón." She clutched Julieta's shoulders. "You will not date him anymore. That is final."

Julieta had had it with Mamá. Her life already revolved around her. But she was an adult. She could make her own decisions. "No, it's not final. I like him. He's a good man. You don't even know him." She turned to Mamá. "He's not like his papá."

"Yes, he is. He is exactly like his father. You don't think that Arturo promised me the world? The sun, the moon, the stars, and the sky? He was handsome and seductive, just like that son of his."

She took a deep breath. "I know you love me and don't want me to get hurt. I see where you are coming from. But I have spent some time with Ramón. He's really deep. If you got to know him, you would see that."

Mamá shook her head. "I don't want you to date him, Julieta. And he's not welcome in our home. And for that matter, as long as you are still dating him, you're not welcome, either."

Wow. "Are you serious right now, Mamá? You are kicking me out of the house?"

"Yes, I am. You have chosen this traitor over your own family. After everything his father did to us, what he is still doing to us. How could you sleep with the enemy?"

Rage seethed inside Julieta. She understood Mamá's concern— Julieta was playing with fire. But she didn't care. She would risk it all— even getting burned.

"Fine. I'll crash with Rosa." Her prima would always welcome her. "Just remember, Amá. Ramón isn't Arturo."

"He's worse. Arturo was poor. Ramón is rich and thinks he can buy everyone. Including you."

Tiburón grabbed some salsa and chips and began eating. Julieta glared at him—he had no shame.

"I don't get you, Amá. You make absolutely no sense. One day you are hugging him, making him tacos, calling him mijo, telling him about his father, and now today you don't want me seeing him."

"I make perfect sense, Julieta. He is your boss. I was nice to him because he is putting food on the table. He is allowing us to pay our bills. And I will stay working here until they change the name on the marquee. Everyone still thinks that the restaurant is Las Pescas. Once it says Taco King, I'm gone."

Mamá had a point. Julieta still couldn't wrap her head around the reality of showing up to work, crossing the protesters, and working at Taco King. She'd rather stand naked in Chicano Park. *The shame.*

"That has nothing to do with me dating him." Or spending the night with him, more accurately.

"I don't approve of you dating him. I don't want you to get hurt."

"How do you know I'm gonna get hurt? Maybe it will work out. Who knows? We may fall in love and get married and give you grandbabies. It's so new now, though, I'm not stressing. I'm an adult. I'm allowed to have a life."

Mamá laughed loudly. "You are kidding yourself, mija. You are already in love with him. I can see it. I'm your mother."

Julieta wanted to deny that she had any feelings for him, but Mamá would see right through her.

"You're a beautiful girl and a very talented chef, but we don't fit in with their world."

Julieta paused. He belonged to not one, but two separate country clubs. He'd bought her a thousand-dollar bike and didn't even flinch when he put down the credit card. And in order to be closer to Barrio Logan for the next few months, he planned to purchase a home in Coronado. It was mind-blowing.

Mamá was right. They were very different. But when they were together Julieta felt comfortable with him. She didn't feel like he was just using her. He hadn't even tried to have sex with her.

Julieta should cut him off now and save her heart, but she wanted to enjoy this ride as long as it lasted. "I'm going to keep seeing him."

Mamá stormed out of the restaurant. Julieta didn't have the time or energy to go after her. Mamá would calm down, and eventually, she would learn to trust Ramón.

Since she had nowhere to go, she stayed in the kitchen and began preparing her tomatillos for tomorrow's special. Tiburón stood next to her.

She threw her hand up like a stop sign. "Don't start. I don't want to hear it."

"Julieta, I get that you had no choice about the restaurant. You have to eat. That money is life-changing. But don't date him. He can never make you happy. He's not one of us; he will never be. You should date Pablo. He's a good guy."

She groaned in frustration and shooed him out. "Tiburón. Just go." She grabbed her tomatillos and threw them on the comal to roast.

"Prima, just don't fall in love with him."

Julieta ignored her cousin and drowned herself in her salsa.

As happy as she had been that morning, doubt seeped back. There were no good outcomes for this romance. He would either dump her and leave her brokenhearted, or they would fall madly in love and be torn apart by their families. Her family saw his as the enemy, and Julieta was certain that his family would never accept her.

And Julieta didn't want tension. She never wanted to be in a relationship where she had to choose between her family and her man.

She should end it now with her dignity intact.

But she couldn't reason with her stubborn heart.

Chapter Twenty-Three

Ramón called out to his brothers. "Let's go. I don't want to be late."
He couldn't wait for the car cruise. Why had he never gone to one?
Ramón never missed the yearly La Jolla Concours d'Elegance, a luxury
and classic car event in his hometown, but La Vuelta had never even
been on his radar. Even his cousin Benicio had never invited him.

But Tiburón had. And dammit, Ramón was going to go and soak
up every bit of his culture until he was deemed a traitor and banned
from Barrio Logan forever.

Enrique and Jaime followed Ramón to the garage. Ramón ran his
fingers over the lime-green McLaren.

Enrique slid next to Ramón. "You gonna hop in that car or just
feel her up?"

Smart-ass. "You jealous?"

Enrique shook his head. "No, but let me take her. You can take
Abuelo's Mustang."

That was actually a great idea. Ramón never drove that car anymore. "Sounds like a plan." He tossed Enrique the keys.

"Can we go?" Jaime rolled his eyes as he started his Lambo. Ramón and Enrique followed him out of the garage.

Ramón had become used to his regular drive to Barrio Logan, but the journey felt different driving Abuelo's car. His grandfather would be so proud of him for all his accomplishments. He stroked the tan leather on the seat and blasted the music as he looked out over Mission Bay.

By the time they arrived in Barrio Logan, the evening was already in full swing. Candy-colored lowriders were parked along the side streets, displayed for the crowds to enjoy. Hoods were popped open to show off the shiny engines. There were lifted cars and low cars, old cars and new cars, expensive cars and beaters. And every one of them was glorious.

Ramón and his brothers parked diagonally in front of Las Pescas in three spaces Julieta had reserved for them.

Jaime walked to Ramón's door. "Man, this place is sick." He pulled out his phone to start taking a video. "Why haven't we ever been to this event?"

Ramón threw up his hands. "No clue. We're idiots. I didn't even know about it."

Enrique joined them. "I'm in heaven. Benicio is a punk for never inviting us."

Ramón agreed. Julieta was so close to her cousins. Why weren't Ramón and his brothers close to theirs?

"Maybe he's here." Ramón took out his phone and shot off a text to Benicio.

Ramón was staring at his phone, hoping for a reply from Benicio, when Julieta and Rosa appeared in the doorway in front of Las Pescas.

Guau. Heat flooded Ramón. Julieta looked fantastic. Her hair was curled, and there was a red rose pinned behind her ear. She wore a low-cut white top, a skintight pencil skirt that hugged her incredible ass, and super high black heels.

"Damn, you're a knockout." Ramón couldn't help himself. He moved toward Julieta, cradled her cheek in his hand, and planted a possessive kiss on her bright pink lips.

"Thanks. So glad you came. These are my cousin Rosa's clothes, actually. She's great with hair and makeup."

Enrique waved at Julieta and Rosa.

Ramón said hi to Rosa, whose hair was in a pompadour. She was dressed in a fifties pinup-style vintage dress with bright red cherries on it. "Julieta and Rosa, I'd like you to meet my brother Jaime."

Rosa licked her bottom lip and dramatically stuck out her hand. "Hello, Jaime."

Jaime's eyes raked over Rosa. He took her hand and kissed it. "Nice to meet you, Rosa. I like your cherries. You're beautiful just like your cousin."

Rosa giggled. "And you're hot as hell, just like your brothers."

Nope. Definitely not. Jaime was a playboy. Ramón glared at his baby brother and then elbowed him in the rib cage. The last thing Ramón needed was Jaime romancing Julieta's cousin and then ghosting her.

Jaime smirked at Ramón. "What?"

"Excuse us for a second. I forgot something in my car." Ramón pulled Jaime to the car, leaving Enrique with Julieta and Rosa.

Ramón glared at Jaime. "Whatever you are thinking, you can forget it. Rosa is off-limits."

Jaime laughed. "I'm just having fun. She's a smokeshow. Did you see that ass?"

Ramón wanted to smack him. "Jaime, I mean it. I actually like Julieta. A lot. Their family already hates us. Please don't make this harder for me. I haven't dated anyone in years."

Jaime's brow raised. "Is she your girlfriend?"

Was she? Ramón hadn't made it official with Julieta yet, but he planned to. Soon. Maybe tonight. "She will be. Come on, I'm begging you."

Jaime gave a smug grin. "Maybe I can fall for Rosa, too. We can all be one happy family. What makes you think I can't be serious about anyone?"

"Because I know you—I live with you, remember? You're a man whore."

Jaime pointed at Ramón. "Pot, kettle. You're no better than me."

Jaime's words stung Ramón, but he knew he was right. Ramón hadn't been serious about anyone since college. He always figured that at some point in his life he would decide it was time to settle down and then go find the perfect wife. He never thought that a chance meeting with a masked señorita in the moonlight on Day of the Dead would change his path and turn him into a better man, worthy of a woman like Julieta.

"Fair. But I'm serious about Julieta. We already have so much against us. I don't want to fuck this up. Just please, don't hook up with Rosa."

Jaime huffed. "Okay. I won't. But you owe me." Jaime looked around the event. "I'm going to make my own way. Later." He took off on the blaring bass path and disappeared into the crush.

A lump grew in Ramón's throat. He had been harsh with Jaime.

He checked his phone. Still no word from Benicio. Ramón walked back over to Julieta, Enrique, and Rosa.

Rosa's eyes scanned behind Ramón. "Where did Jaime go?"

"He went to check out the music."

She frowned and twirled her hair. "Oh, okay. I'll catch you all later." She walked toward the crowd, probably to find Jaime. Ramón felt like a jerk.

Tiburón came out of Las Pescas. Ramón exchanged a handshake with him and then showed him his abuelo's Mustang.

"Nice! Is that a '66? Who did the paint job?"

"It's a '67. Some shop up in Oceanside."

"It's sick." Tiburón looked at Jaime's Lamborghini. "How many cars do you all have?"

"Enough. Come to La Jolla and I'll show you our collection."

"Thanks, man."

Tiburón and Enrique started chatting and walked toward some other cars. Julieta tugged on Ramón's hand. "I'm so glad you came."

Now that they were alone and hidden near the awning, Ramón caressed Julieta's face. "I haven't been able to stop thinking about you." Ramón's hand slipped to her ass, careful that no one was watching.

They shared a quick kiss, and Ramón placed his arm around her waist.

"I can't believe I've never been here. This is incredible."

"Let me show you around."

Julieta led Ramón down the street. They strolled through the food trucks, craft tents, and DJs.

Julieta gestured at a tall woman wearing a bright pink pantsuit. "Ramón, this is Yesenia." Yesenia waved hi. Her hair was pulled in a tight bun that contrasted with the loose scarf wrapped around her neck. "She owns Barrio Books. Have you stopped in yet? It has so many Spanish books, and she even hosts a bilingual story time for the kids."

Ramón's throat tightened. He had said hi to her in passing but hadn't formally met her. "Nice to meet you."

She gave a generous smile. "I'll admit it, I was scared when Señor Gomez sold the street, but I just love how you are truly getting involved in our town."

Ramón's skin burned. "Thanks. Everyone has been so kind to me." And he was going to stab them in the back.

"Stop in anytime! I'd love to talk to you about a literacy program I'm developing."

Ugh, a literacy program? How could he force her out? "I will."

"Bye, Yessi!" Julieta waved.

Could Ramón turn this around? For once, with Julieta on his arm, Ramón felt like he belonged in his community.

For now.

But he didn't want to *feel* like he belonged in this community—he wanted to actually belong. He exhaled. He had to talk to Julieta.

He bought her a coconut paleta, which she devoured. Then they sat on a bench and watched the cars cruise by.

He brushed a lock of hair out of her face. "Julieta, what do you want to happen?"

Her face contorted. "With us?"

He grinned. "Sure, but I was asking about the business." He considered asking her to be his girlfriend right then but wanted to wait for a more romantic moment. "I can't promise you anything because it's not just up to me, but I really want to hear your ideas."

Her eyes sparkled. "Really? Well, in a perfect world, I would keep Las Pescas as Las Pescas, but with the new salary and budget and garden. And the other businesses would be able to stay. If you needed to raise the rent, that would be understandable, but it would have to be within reason. You could still make a profit."

A honk rang out, and she turned her head. A brilliant smile lit her face. She waved to a car of teenagers cruising, then she turned back to him, her dark eyes serious. "We could have big events and bring more people into the community. You could work with the other owners to maximize revenue. And it would be a win-win for everyone."

"That's a good idea. I'll consider it." She leaned on his chest, and Ramón stroked her hair.

There was no way Papá would agree to that.

None.

But Ramón could figure something out. He had to.

Not because he was falling for Julieta, but because Ramón could never live with himself if he didn't.

CHAPTER TWENTY-FOUR

The week dragged on. Julieta had barely said a word to Mamá; she'd been staying with Tía Adriana, Rosa, and Rosa's younger siblings. Julieta had enough money to get her own place now, but she didn't want to sign a new lease until she was certain that she had the guts to work at the restaurant when it became Taco King.

Friday finally rolled around. Ramón had wanted to take her somewhere downtown. But Julieta had told him she wanted to make the plans.

He'd happily agreed, which was nice. She didn't want to date a man who always needed to be in control. She wanted a partner.

Julieta considered picking him up but changed her mind—she doubted he would want to be seen in her crappy car.

Ramón arrived at Las Pescas at eight. He wore a polo shirt that showed off his muscular arms and nice slacks. He looked sexy as all hell.

Julieta kissed him as he handed her a dozen red roses.

"Ah, thanks!"

"Don't mention it. Where are we going?"

"It's a surprise. Just drive."

She directed him up the coast to Leucadia. Julieta was friends with a chef at a cool Spanish restaurant and bar up there.

And, more importantly, they had an open mic night.

As they drove along the coast, the wind blowing through her hair, a handsome man by her side, a sense of peace and calm overtook her. This was nice—living her life instead of serving people who were living theirs.

"So, how's business?" she asked.

"It's rough. I had a bad week."

Oh no. "Oh, I'm sorry. Do you want to talk about it?"

"Not really."

Gotcha. Being with Ramón was still so new. She didn't know when to push and when to let go. Did his bad week have anything to do with her telling him her vision for Barrio Logan? Not that anything she had said was new. And she could tell that Ramón had truly enjoyed himself at La Vuelta. He'd been smiling and laughing and carefree. She still held out hope that she would never have to close Las Pescas. Either way, she hoped that this night would make him feel better.

Julieta directed him down the road.

When they arrived, she had him park in front of the restaurant. It was dimly lit and romantic. Small tables on an outdoor patio with Christmas lights hung around the building.

"I know the owner here. We used to work together."

"Cool. This place looks great."

Julieta greeted Carlos when they entered. He sat them at a table in front of the stage. A group of ladies talked animatedly to their left, and a family with young children dined on their right. After Ramón ordered some wine and tapas, Julieta let him in on her little secret.

"Look at that chair over there."

"On the stage? Why? Is a cool band coming tonight?"

"Well, not a band, but a talented musician." She batted her eyelashes at him.

"Julieta, you didn't . . ."

"I did!"

Ramón shook his head. "Julieta, no. I don't play in public. I don't even have my guitar."

"The owner has one you can play."

He scrunched his fingers in a fist and then released them. "No. I haven't played in years."

"That's not true. You played for me in Old Town. And you were glorious. I can't stop thinking about it." Julieta whispered in Ramón's ear, "You turned me on so much that night. I love hearing you sing."

Ramón's eyes darted at her and then at the stage and then at the restaurant patrons. "Fine. I'll do it for you."

"Yay!" She kissed Ramón on the lips. "Go now."

Ramón glared at her, then walked over to the stage. Carlos was standing by the stage and handed Ramón a guitar.

Ramón spoke into the microphone. "Hi, everyone. I'm Ramón. I have to admit, I haven't played much in years, but a beautiful woman asked me to play her a few songs. Julieta, this one is for you."

Swoon. Julieta beamed.

Ramón began to strum the guitar. He sounded just as great as he had on the guitarrón and even played a complicated riff, which impressed Julieta. A lock of his hair hung in his face, accentuating his strong bone structure.

He sang "Mi Vida Sin Tu Amor" by Cristian Castro. Julieta loved that song. She and Ramón seemed to have the same musical taste. How could she have so much in common with this man but at the same time be so different?

Julieta had resisted trying to think about the future all week, but she couldn't help herself. They would be good together. And their children would be adorable. Why couldn't it work?

She turned her attention back to Ramón. The crowd swayed with the music, and honestly, he sounded like a professional. His eyes lit up; his deep voice belted out the notes. He was so sexy and passionate. He should've never stopped playing.

He played a few more songs, mostly old Spanish classics. He even received a few dollars' worth of tips in the jar. Ha, if only these people knew how rich he was.

"Thank you, everyone. I appreciate the support." He walked back over to Julieta, sat down, and then pulled her into his lap.

"You were amazing! I'm your biggest fan."

"I can't believe you did that for me. It was such a blast." He grinned from ear to ear and then downed a glass of water.

"I just wanted you to have a good time. The best things in life don't cost money."

He kissed her, sending shivers throughout her body.

"Julieta, that's the nicest thing anyone has ever done for me."

Warmth flooded her chest. He gazed at Julieta, and she felt that he could truly see into her soul.

They dined on paella and then listened to a flamenco guitarist. It was a perfect night.

Julieta watched the guitarist, and then touched Ramón's thigh. "This is a silly question, and I'm sure the answer is yes, but have you ever been to Spain?"

"Yeah. I've been all over that country. I love it there. The people are so warm."

"I've always wanted to go to Seville. But I'd be happy to go anywhere. I've never even been to Cabo. I hear it's beautiful."

Ramón hesitated and chose his words wisely. "It is." He didn't want to keep promising Julieta the world if he wasn't going to deliver, but he was completely serious about her.

He wanted to give her everything. He wanted to look toward the future and plan trips with her to Spain and Mexico.

But everything was happening so fast. Ramón had always been cautious in love. Papá had warned him about women using him for his money, but he didn't feel that Julieta was like that. She didn't seem to care about his wealth. Ramón had a suspicion that if he lost every penny, Julieta would still like him, even if he was a bum on the beach with a guitar. Ha, she would probably like him even more.

His heart sang. He hadn't felt this alive in years. Was it being with Julieta? Or the fact that she had brought music back into his life? Or feeling more connected to his culture? Or a combination of all?

After dinner, they walked on the beach in Encinitas. The town had a different vibe than Coronado or La Jolla. There were a bunch of bropreneurs and boss babes living here, and the residents were very health conscious. There were many New Age shops and vegan restaurants, too.

Maybe he should open a vegan Taco King here.

"Julieta, have you cooked a lot of vegan food?"

She shook her head. "I mean, I always have vegan options on the menu, no matter what. But I love meat. Why?"

"I just had an idea of making our Taco King here vegan."

"That's a great idea! The residents would love it."

"Really? You think so?"

"Absolutely." She paused. "Once we figure out what's happening in Barrio Logan, I would love to try my hand at creating a vegan menu. I mean, if you wanted me to. It seems like a great challenge. I do make vegan carnitas with jackfruit. There are so many things you can do! Rajas, nopales, elotes. As a chef, you don't want to get complacent—you always want to learn and grow. Plus, now that I have access to the garden, it would be easy."

Ramón squeezed her hand. The Montez Group needed Julieta. She was so innovative and forward-thinking. Restaurants had to grow and change to be competitive. With Julieta creating cutting-edge cuisine for them, they would be unstoppable.

They finished their walk on the beach and then took a leisurely drive back to La Jolla.

Jaime was out of town for an event, and Enrique was out with some friends and wouldn't be home until tomorrow—which wasn't a coincidence. Ramón had told his brothers not to come home tonight.

Julieta stepped out onto the balcony, as the waves crashed against the rocks below. "I was so excited that night you brought me here that I never got to really take in the view."

"Well, make yourself at home."

She looked at him. "Don't say that. I may never leave."

"You can stay here anytime you like."

She pursed her lips. "You might regret that offer. I moved out of my mom's house."

"*What?* Why? When?"

She looked away from Ramón. "Last week."

Ramón heard her nonanswer loud and clear. "Was it because of me?"

She shrugged. "Yeah, kind of."

A stab of guilt startled him. "I'm so sorry. I'm kind of in the same boat."

She laughed. "Really? You're homeless?"

Damn. Ramón didn't mean to be so thoughtless. "No, I didn't mean that. My father is mad at me, too. The day you told me about my dad stealing your mom's recipe, I confronted him." Should he tell her this?

She scowled at him. "Really? What did he say?"

Fuck it. He wanted to be honest with her.

"He said it's true."

Julieta clasped her hands together. "Oh my God, really? He admitted it?"

"Yup." Ramón paused. He didn't want to tell her all the details of his conversation with his father—that Ramón had told his dad that she should keep her restaurant. He didn't want to get her hopes up. "We got into a huge fight, so I threatened to quit."

Julieta's jaw literally dropped. "So, you don't have a job? I hear there's an opening for a guitarist in the restaurant."

Ramón chuckled. "Very funny."

"Is this something you normally do? Fight with your father and then threaten to leave your job?"

"Not since I was sixteen."

Her face fell. "I hope I'm not a bad influence on you."

"Why would you even say that?"

"Because I'm causing you to fight with your father. I can't believe that you stood up for my mother."

"Well, you got kicked out of your house because of me."

"That's different. I have nothing to lose."

Ramón's heart ached for her, and he realized that if he quit his job now, he would jeopardize Julieta's job security. He couldn't let that happen. "Julieta, of course I asked my dad. I wanted to know if it was true or not. And it is. We do owe your mom something. I'm not sure what, and I don't want to get into any legal battles, but I'm hoping we can work something out that makes everyone happy. When your mom made those tacos for me, I finally got it. I finally understood what this was all about."

She walked over to him, her eyes locked on his. "I appreciate you doing that for me. For my family."

"It was the right thing to do."

"I know. But sometimes it's hard to do the right thing."

Ramón made her a paloma, and they relaxed on the sofa, gazing at the ocean. Julieta pointed at the bare Christmas tree in the corner.

"Why don't you have any ornaments on it?"

"Oh, Lupe will decorate it tomorrow."

"Lupe?"

"My maid."

Julieta rolled her eyes. She stood up. "Where are the decorations?"

Ramón got off the sofa, excited to prepare for the holidays with Julieta. What should he get her? He needed to plan something soon. "I'll get them."

He went to the garage and grabbed his box of Christmas ornaments and brought them upstairs.

Julieta was popping kernels in his popcorn maker.

"Popcorn?"

"Yes, silly, to string on the tree."

"I've never done that."

"Well, I'm sure you had lights or diamonds. But it's fun. Do you have thread?"

Ramón did have some that Lupe had stashed for alterations. He found her kit and sat at the kitchen table with Julieta.

They talked and laughed.

"Decorating is half the fun of Christmas. Didn't you put ornaments on the tree as a kid?"

Ramón shook his head no.

"Well, we did every year. We never had many presents, but we spent the whole month celebrating. Just being in the moment. Together."

Ramón never did things like decorate the tree or make snow angels at their house in Lake Tahoe. As a child, he was to be seen and not heard. Maybe he had carried much of that into his adult life.

After Julieta strung the last strand of popcorn on the tree, she leaned into Ramón.

Julieta kissed him and pressed her soft body against his chest. Her hands glided down his body and landed on his cock.

Yes. Ramón cupped her face and kissed her again.

Julieta pulled away and dropped to her knees in front of him.

"Yeah, baby."

Her hands squeezed his ass, and she pulled down his pants and his boxer briefs. Ramón had been fantasizing about this since he'd met her.

He was already so hard. He couldn't wait to feel her mouth around him.

She kissed around the base of his cock and licked the tip.

"Stop teasing me."

She licked down his length and spat on her hand before she grasped him. Ah, that felt so good.

A few more kisses on the head, and he was dying with anticipation. She finally took him in her mouth.

He exhaled, enjoying the moment of pleasure. Having her eyes locked on his was almost enough to send him over the edge. Her mouth was so hot. The pressure built in his balls.

"That's it, baby. Don't stop. Just like that."

Her head bobbed up and down, taking him deep. She created a seal with her lips.

Ramón took control. He held her right where he wanted as he fucked her mouth. He thrust deeper. He was right on the edge.

"I'm going to come, baby."

He tried to pull away, but she wouldn't let him. She sucked him so hard, so deep. He finally let go, and she swallowed.

That was epic. Ramón took a second to recover before pulling up his boxers.

He raised her up to him, and he kissed her forehead. She excused herself to the bathroom and then came back to sit next to him on the sofa.

"I see you took the picture down. Of you and your brothers and dad."

Ramón smirked. "I didn't want you to run off again."

She laughed.

He stroked her hair. He wanted this. Not just the sexy times, but the intimacy. He wanted a life with Julieta. "Julieta, you know how I said I just wanted to see where this goes?"

She nodded, pursing her lips, which now turned into a frown.

"About that. I lied. I'm crazy about you. Will you be my girl-friend?"

CHAPTER TWENTY-FIVE

After double shifts at work, Julieta collapsed on her aunt's sofa. But she had a wonderful week basking in Ramón's words. He asked her to be his girlfriend, and of course, she said yes, but she still couldn't believe it was real.

Her phone pinged with a text.

Ramón: Can I see you tonight?

Julieta: No, it's Lotería night at my aunt's house.

Ramón: Sounds fun. Can I come?

Julieta shuddered. That was a horrible idea. What a nightmare it would be. First off, Mamá wasn't even talking to her. And Mamá hated Ramón. Add in her crazy aunts, her weird cousins, all drunk... what could possibly go wrong?

Julieta: Sure, come on over.

This was the only way for Mamá to change her opinion about Ramón. If she spent some time with him, she would see that he wasn't a cocky, rich gentefier.

Okay, maybe he was. But he was trying to grow as a person. And to do that, he needed to be surrounded by people who cared about more than his wallet.

Ugh, but her aunts were crazy. Absolutely batshit. There was Tía Eva, Tiburón's mom, who had been married more times than J. Lo and currently had a boy toy who was younger than Ramón; Tía Adriana, Rosa's mother, who was a mean drunk; Tía Gabriella, who was a born-again Christian when the rest of the family was all Catholics; and Tía Juanita, who liked to bargain everywhere she went, including at Target. Tía Juanita was Julieta's favorite aunt. She loved to collect old dolls, and her house always smelled like cumin.

Julieta was about to text Ramón the address and then considered telling him to take an Uber instead of his McLaren. She didn't want to be responsible for it getting stripped for parts and ending up in Tijuana. Maybe she should pick him up instead? But her beater needed a new transmission.

He had other cars. He could take one of those.

She texted him the address and told him not to bring the McLaren or the Mustang.

Though Julieta had been cooking all day, she always made food for Lotería night. On tonight's menu was enchiladas verdes and tres leches cake. And tequila. Gallons of it. Julieta should start drinking now.

Julieta began to prepare the food for the party. She roasted the chiles de árbol and the garlic, ground the spices with the temolote, and boiled chicken. Cooking at a home was different from cooking at the restaurant. As much as her family got on her nerves, Julieta enjoyed the sounds of laughter and the loud voices booming through the room. She especially loved watching her younger cousins running in the backyard, dirty and messy. That was the kind of family life she wanted.

Ramón's life wasn't messy. His sleek, modern oceanfront mansion, his spotless sports car, his pressed silk suits. Would he ever want this type of life?

But he had already seemed to change. He had a great time at La Vuelta and even enjoyed decorating the tree with her.

She would see how he fit in tonight.

Ramón texted her that he had arrived. She rushed to the door and noticed he'd brought his Jeep. Good choice.

He carried six bouquets of sunflowers. He handed her one.

"The rest are for your mother and for your aunts."

Nice move, Ramón.

He was dressed as casually as Julieta had ever seen him. He wore a T-shirt and board shorts. He almost looked like a surfer instead of a millionaire businessman.

Tía Eva didn't miss a beat. Her bleached blond hair and heavy makeup hid her natural beauty. She pushed her way through the rest of the crowd to the front of the house.

"And you must be Ramón. Julieta has told me so much about you. And your family," she hissed. All of Julieta's aunties were well aware that Ramón's father had stolen their family's taco recipe. Julieta prayed they wouldn't hold it against Ramón.

Tía Eva squeezed Ramón's bicep and then tried to give Julieta a high five. Julieta left her hanging.

Ramón presented Tía Eva with the flowers. "Mucho gusto. These are for you."

Tía Eva dramatically grabbed the bouquet and clutched it to her chest. This would be a long night.

"Hey, Tib."

"Hey, Ramón."

Ever since Ramón had let Tiburón drive his car, they had been cool. Julieta never expected them to be best friends or anything, but at least being civil was a start.

Mamá emerged from the backyard. She checked out Ramón from head to toe, then ignored him.

But Ramón didn't give up. "Señora Campos. Here. These are for you."

Mamá accepted the flowers but quickly handed them off to Julieta. "Let's eat."

Ramón gave out the rest of the flowers. The aunts gathered around the dining room table along with Rosa, Tiburón, and some other cousins. Julieta had snacks and drinks lined up. She poured herself a shot of tequila. She needed it.

Tía Juanita was first up to interrogate Ramón. Her jet-black hair was pulled tight against her face. "So, Ramón, Julieta tells me that you own a McLaren and a beachfront house."

Julieta rolled her eyes.

"I'm just saying! I've never met a multimillionaire before."

This was such a bad idea. Ramón should leave now.

It was Tía Eva's turn. "How's your father? When I was a little girl, I would look out the window all night, waiting for him and Linda to return so I could see them kiss. I was jealous."

Mamá smacked Tía Eva. Lord. Julieta wanted to crawl under the covers. Tía Eva always wanted to get a rise out of Julieta's mother.

For some reason, Ramón was still there. "He's good. He's still pretty hands-on with the business. I'm hoping he will be able to retire and take a break soon."

Tía Eva leaned in closer. "What I mean, Ramón—is your father single?"

Julieta's cheeks burned. "Oh my God, Tía Eva. Just stop."

She gave an evil smile. "Oh, I'm sorry, I forgot. Linda still has a crush on him. My bad."

Ramón gave a nervous laugh.

Mamá spoke up. "Don't mind Eva. All she thinks about is sex."

Julieta was officially mortified. "Jesus, Mamá!" she yelled.

What on earth had Julieta been thinking, inviting Ramón over? He would never ever want to come back here again.

Tía Gabriella glared at Julieta. Her kind, almond-shaped eyes exuded warmth. "Please don't take the Lord's name in vain."

Rosa saved the day by bringing in a platter of food. "Dinner!"

Julieta prayed they would all behave.

Tía Gabriella blessed the food.

Julieta and Rosa served everyone enchiladas, arroz rojo, refried beans, and a side salad. Simple, classic recipes with fresh ingredients. Sometimes, even Julieta wanted comfort food. She dug her fork into the cheesy enchiladas and took a bite.

Ramón devoured his food, and all of her aunts watched him eat like he was some kind of caged animal.

Tía Juanita cozied up to him. She wore a big cardigan despite it being eighty degrees in the house. "Do you like the food, Ramón?"

Tía Adriana knocked back a shot. "Of course he loves it. She's the best cook."

Tía Eva chimed in. "Yes, she is. She will make a great wife, don't you think?"

Julieta wanted to drown in the tequila. "You all are so embarrassing. This is why we can't invite anyone over. Can you just behave and act normal? For once?"

Her tías remained quiet. The answer was no. This *was* normal for them.

"I'm here to play Lotería. Let's get started?" Julieta set out pinto beans as markers.

Tía Juanita smiled at Ramón. "So, Ramón, have you ever played Lotería?"

"Not a lot. I played a few times with my tía."

Tía Eva scooped up a handful of beans. "Maybe Ramón should play with cash?"

"Or diamonds." Tía Adriana laughed and took a swig of tequila. From the bottle.

It would be a long night.

Play the game once and you can leave.

Julieta gave Ramón a handful of beans. "Pinto beans will be fine. Who's going to call?"

"I will," Tía Gabriella volunteered.

Julieta handed Ramón a tabla.

Tía Gabriella clasped her hands. "Let's say a prayer."

Tía Eva pinched her sister. "Gabi, we already prayed once tonight."

Julieta cringed. Ramón would never want to date her after this night. "Can we just begin?"

Tía Gabriella began calling out the riddles. She always went so fast; it was hard to keep up.

"El borracho!"

"Tía Adriana!" Tía Eva yelled out. Julieta rolled her eyes. Sure, Tía Adriana drank too much, but did Tía Eva have to tell Ramón?

"El valiente!"

Ramón yelled out, "Ese soy yo!"

Everyone laughed. Tía Eva touched Ramón's arm. "Yes, you are brave. And handsome."

Kill me now.

"La mano!"

Julieta's mother blurted out, "La mano de un criminal. Arturo Montez!"

Fuck. Did she just call Ramón's father a criminal?

Julieta had had enough. Julieta had barely spoken to Mamá since she'd kicked her out. And of course, Mamá had every right to be angry at Ramón's dad for stealing from her. But Julieta was now Ramón's girlfriend. He was not his father.

Julieta stood and turned to Ramón. "Let's go."

Ramón crossed his arms. "I'm fine. Let's just finish this."

"No, I want to go."

"Let me handle this." Ramón turned to Julieta's mother. "Look, I know what my father did. He admitted it to me. I'm sorry. I want to make it right by you and your daughter."

Julieta's mother glared at him. "He told you he stole from me?"

"Yes, he did. And I'm going to figure something out. For both of you."

Julieta's mother's face lit up but then fell as quickly as it had risen. "We will see, Ramón."

They resumed the game of Lotería and kept the insult hurling to a minimum.

"Who wants dessert?" Julieta went to the kitchen, and Mamá followed her.

"Julieta, I was wrong. I'm sorry."

"About what?"

"Being rude to Ramón. I still don't believe his father will do right by me, by us, but I think Ramón really likes you."

Julieta wanted to open up and confess to Mamá how she felt for Ramón. Emotion bottled inside of her.

Mamá hugged her. "What's wrong, mijita?"

"I'm falling for him. I am. And I think he really cares about me. He even asked me to be his girlfriend."

"Then why are you crying?"

"Everything is wrong. I don't know if I can work at Taco King. I'm still so embarrassed. He is so rich, and we are so poor. Well, not actually poor, but comparatively. I'm just afraid he's going to leave me, Mamá. For someone better. And I don't know if I'll ever get over it."

Mamá held her as Julieta cried. "Mija, you know there's a chance he won't leave you. That you will be very happy and rich and give me plenty of grandchildren. But no matter what, if he leaves you, you will be okay. You are smart and beautiful, and honestly, Ramón would be incredibly lucky to have you. He's a smart man."

Julieta needed to believe that she was worthy of Ramón, but it was hard for her. She pulled herself together. She walked back out to the family room with her head held high.

"Tres leches cake, anyone?"

Ramón grinned and walked over to help her serve it.

He whispered in her ear, "How did I get so lucky to find you?"

She confidently flipped her hair back and grinned widely. He was lucky. And maybe he was just as afraid of losing her as she was of losing him.

And for once, she didn't doubt his words.

CHAPTER TWENTY-SIX

Ramón kissed Julieta goodbye and left her aunt's house full of liquor and laughter. After he apologized to her mother, she'd relaxed, and Ramón had felt right at home. His family never had fun like that. Ever. Maybe part of that was because he had two younger brothers, and all three of them could beat one another up one minute and be best friends the next.

Even so, he missed his brothers. With the exception of going to college, Ramón had been around them daily his whole life. They'd moved into his place right after they'd graduated from college. But lately, he had been spending so much time with Julieta and working in the restaurant that he hadn't really hung out with them.

He texted Jaime.

Ramón: Hey. I'm heading back to La Jolla. You around?

Jaime: No. I'm out. But I'll be home later.

Ramón: Want to play soccer tomorrow?

Jaime: Do you remember how?

Smart-ass.

Ramón: Yes, asshole. See you in the morning.

Ramón drove back home guided by the stars and finally opened his garage and parked his Jeep. Back inside, he sat on the sofa. He wasn't tired. He flipped through some channels, but nothing captured his attention. Normally, he would read a book, always nonfiction, usually about business, and then go to sleep.

But tonight, he did something different.

He grabbed his guitar off the wall.

Ramón ran through a playlist. From Spanish classics to Mexican rock to American hair metal, Ramón played it all. His fingers burned a bit at the lack of calluses from years of not playing. Why had he quit?

The guitar had been his refuge when he was a boy. When his parents argued, he would lock himself in his bedroom and spend hours learning songs by playing along to his iPod. When he found out his best friend was talking shit behind his back, Ramón drowned himself in the solace of his strings. He used to write songs, too, but lyrics eluded him now.

As he gazed out to the ocean at night, he was truly grateful that he had met Julieta—not just because of how sexy she was, or how she made him feel like a man, but because she had done something no one had in years.

She had brought music back into his life.

The next morning when he rolled out of bed, he found his brothers in the kitchen.

Enrique handed Ramón a green smoothie.

Ramón quickly downed it and grabbed a soccer ball. "Let's go."

The three brothers walked out of their place and to Calumet Park, which overlooked the ocean. This was how they bonded best—no words, just a competitive game of soccer and the view of the ocean to unite them. The park was empty this morning, with only a woman doing yoga by herself and a mother playing with her toddler.

Did Julieta play soccer? What did she like to do for fun?

She really needed a vacation. No one worked as hard as she did. When he was done with soccer, he would book them that trip to Cabo. He couldn't wait to spend some time with her outside of San Diego. He wanted to teach her how to surf, take her snorkeling, treat her to a spa, and take her to Lover's Beach.

Ramón and his brothers attacked the ball. They took turns playing one-on-one while the third played goalie. Jaime was the best of the three—he had been a Division One player in college and could've probably turned professional. Ramón had been more focused on music than sports. Enrique had been a surfing champion, but surfing wasn't about winning, it was about simply being.

An hour later, Ramón and his brothers stopped playing. They sat on a bench and gazed at the water.

"So, what's up with you and Julieta?" Enrique asked.

"She's my girlfriend."

Jaime smirked. "Are you whipped?"

"No," Ramón lied. "But I'm crazy about her."

Enrique patted Ramón on the shoulder. "That's cool."

"Thanks. Hey, did you know Papá stole the fish taco recipe from Julieta's mom?"

Jaime shook his head. "No. Who told you that?"

"Julieta. I didn't believe it, either. But I asked Dad, and he said it was true."

Enrique glared at him. "It doesn't matter, though. That was forty years ago. Papá built an empire."

"True. She doesn't get all the credit. That's still fucked-up, though, don't you think?"

Jaime brushed grass off his shorts. "It *is* fucked-up. But man, don't get all crazy with this chick and her family. She knows you have money. Don't go promising her the world and talking about what we owe them. This is a business. *Our business*."

"Since when do you care about the business?"

"I care plenty. We don't need a scandal."

"I thought scandals were good for business. Impressions, views, likes."

Jaime huffed at Ramón. "You don't show me any respect, do you? You think my job is a joke."

"I didn't say that."

"It's not that easy, Ramón. There's a lot that goes into the perfect post, the perfect hashtags."

Ramón *was* always giving Jaime a hard time. "I'm sorry. I don't think your job is a joke."

"Whatever. You're just like dad. Your idea of success is the numbers, the bottom line. But you don't appreciate all the things that go into growing a successful media presence. I'm sick of you acting like I don't contribute shit."

"I'm really sorry. It won't happen again. For what it's worth, I know you are great at your job."

Jaime didn't respond.

Enrique broke the silence. "I'm starving. Let's get some food."

The brothers grabbed breakfast burritos down the street and then went back to their home. Ramón played video games with his brothers, and they ended up taking the entire day off.

Ramón moved his guitar from the sofa back to the wall. "Guess what? I'm playing music again."

Enrique smiled. "What? Really? I used to love hearing you play. Why'd you stop?"

"Dad wanted me to go to Stanford and Harvard and take over the business."

"Just be happy, bro. I mean, look. You could quit Taco King tomorrow and have enough money to live on for the rest of your life. You don't have to work. I plan to forge my own path soon."

Enrique's words hit Ramón like a surfboard to the head. His brother was right—Ramón didn't have to do anything he didn't want to. He could walk away from everything and still have enough money to do what was right, until he figured out his next step. Hell, that was what he'd threatened to do anyway. The freedom paved by his privilege and earned through his hard work could allow him to live a more fulfilled life for himself, but more importantly, to give back to his community.

But Ramón did enjoy the work, and the thrill of closing a deal. Was he ready to give it up? He wasn't sure.

Jaime sat down on the sofa.

"How about you, Jaime? Are you happy doing social media? And no, I'm not giving you a hard time."

Jaime shrugged. "I'm kind of over it."

"What do you want to do now?"

"I don't know. I just want to be part of creating something instead of just promoting Dad's business."

Ramón was grateful to be surrounded by his brothers. Though they fought, these built-in best friends for life were the only good things that had come from their parents' marriage.

For years, their father's crushing expectations had almost suffocated them. For Ramón, it had turned him into a workaholic; for Enrique, it had turned him into a slacker; and for Jaime, it had turned him into a drifter. But now they were no longer boys, and it was time for them all to take responsibility for their actions and stop blaming their parents for everything wrong in their lives.

They all needed to be happy.

Ramón could literally do anything he wanted. It was time for him to become his own man.

And he wanted to get serious with Julieta.

He wanted to spoil her, pamper her, tell her how he really felt about her. What better place to do that than in Mexico?

He called his travel agent and booked a trip for the two of them to Cabo.

Chapter Twenty-Seven

Seeing Ramón with her family finally gave Julieta the confidence she needed. She would no longer hold back her heart from him.

Though they had spent a few nights together, they still hadn't had sex. Ramón hadn't even pursued it. Why?

Maybe he had been extra careful with her because she worked for him. He probably didn't want things to get messy if they didn't work out.

But that was the thing. For the first time in Julieta's life, she was pretty sure that things would work out.

That scared and excited her.

Ramón showed up at Las Pescas before it opened for the day.

"Hi. Are you ready to get back to work?"

"No. Hey, let's talk."

Julieta's heart dropped.

Did he want to have *the* talk? The one where he ended things with her?

Maybe Ramón had finally woken up and come to his senses, realized that he could never have a serious relationship with a girl from the wrong part of San Diego. Or maybe he'd fallen for some beautiful rich Latina girl with the pedigree to match his. Maybe because her family was completely crazy at Lotería night, he had decided he was done with her.

What was he going to tell her now?

"We're going to Cabo."

Julieta's jaw literally dropped. Okay, maybe she was wrong. Cabo was the exact opposite of breaking up. Julieta hated herself for doubting him, even just for a minute. What was wrong with her that she couldn't possibly believe he would be serious about her?

"What are you talking about? When?"

"Now. The plane leaves in four hours. Everything is arranged."

This guy was unreal. He should've asked her before he bought plane tickets. Who just dropped everything in the middle of the week and headed off to Mexico?

Crazy, rich Mexicans. That was who.

But Julieta wasn't one. She had to be responsible.

"I can't just go to Cabo. I have a restaurant to run."

"Oh, don't worry. I already cleared it with your mom. And she has Tiburón and Rosa. My brothers are on call if anyone needs anything."

Mamá waved smugly from the kitchen.

"I can't just go. I'm sorry. There's too much to do here."

"Julieta, relax. I got it under control—the restaurant will be here when we get back. Let's just go have fun."

"This seems very impulsive. You don't strike me as the type of guy who just flies to Cabo on a whim. You wouldn't be successful if you just ran off every time you wanted to take a vacation."

"You're right. I don't normally do this. But spending time with you made me realize that I need to be happy. I really, really need a vacation, and I'd like you to come with me. Please say yes."

Dammit. What if the place fell apart? In the four years since she'd opened it, she had never been away from her restaurant for more than a day.

But it wasn't her restaurant anymore, was it?

"Okay. I'm in!" She kissed Ramón.

Oh my God! I'm going to Cabo!

Julieta had never been. She'd only been to San Felipe to see her grandparents, to Tijuana to party when she was younger, and to Ensenada to dine on lobster, but that was really about it.

She couldn't wait!

And she couldn't wait to be alone with Ramón again.

"Let me go home to pack."

After the Lotería night, Julieta had been staying with Mamá again. But their relationship was still fragile.

Julieta's stomach quivered as she directed Ramón to her home. She loved her little casa, with its bright colors and sunny porch, but compared to Ramón's place, it was a shack.

But Ramón didn't judge her. He pointed to a painting of a low-rider in the family room. "Nice art."

"Oh, thanks. Tiburón painted that."

"Really?"

"Yeah, he's good, isn't he?"

"Definitely. He's talented."

Julieta needed to encourage Tiburón to spend more time on his art. Maybe one day he could have a little gallery.

Julieta packed her clothes. "I don't have a swimsuit. Can we stop by Walmart?"

"We can get one at the resort."

"Oh, I know, but they are so expensive there. I'd prefer to buy one here."

Ramón nodded and didn't push. "Sure, but we need to go now, or we will miss the flight."

Ramón drove her to the Walmart, and she rushed in and grabbed a suit. And then they were off to the airport.

Security went pretty fast, and they even had time to stop for a drink at the bar. Julieta definitely needed some liquor to take the edge off.

They boarded their flight. First class, of course. Julieta was in a dream.

"I'm so excited to go to Cabo," she confessed.

"Oh, Mexico is so beautiful. I need to take you everywhere."

Julieta hung on his words. "Everywhere? Where have you been?"

"Mexico City, to see the art. They have the most incredible tacos. I mean, nothing like yours, but different types: birria, cochinita, canasta."

"Oh, I love tacos de canasta. I can't believe I haven't been to Mexico City. They have a great culinary scene there."

"Yeah, they do. I spent a summer in Cuernavaca at a language school. I lived with a host family. It was so lush. It rained there every single night, and the flowers always bloomed."

How amazing! Julieta wanted to travel and see the world, too.

"Where else?"

"I've been diving in Cancún and seen the pyramids in Teotihuacan." He looked at her and stroked her hair. "I'll take you with me next time."

Julieta hung on the words "next time."

Two hours later, the plane finally landed. Ramón grabbed their bags, and a limousine took them to the hotel.

They necked in the ride like teenagers.

Nerves tingled through her body as they drove. Julieta hadn't had sex in a really long time. Basically, she had been married to her restaurant, and living with Mamá hadn't allowed her much in the way of freedom. And the thought of being with Ramón drove her crazy with anticipation. His hands and mouth had already brought her to ecstasy, but it was more than that. It was the way he looked at her. As if she wasn't just another girl. As if he was in awe of her.

Their suite in Cabo was breathtaking, but completely different from the one in Coronado. The backdrop of the sunset and the warm Mexican weather was all-encompassing.

Julieta marveled at the view as he slowly unzipped the back of her dress.

Ramón kissed her neck as her clothes fell to the floor. "You're perfect, you know that? I've been wanting to do this since the first time I laid eyes on you."

"Me too." She stopped and pulled away. "I'm nervous, Ramón."

Great, Julieta. Nervous is the opposite of feeling turned on.

He turned her around and gazed into her eyes. "Why? We're just going to enjoy ourselves. But we don't have to have sex, if you don't want to. You're worth the wait."

Those words washed away Julieta's anxiety.

"No, I want to."

The air around them was electric. His face tilted toward her, and his kiss sent a bolt of passion through her body. His tongue danced with hers, and her nerves were shattered by his desire. His lips were hard, but his kiss was gentle, and Julieta was all in.

He clutched her by the waist and pressed his body into hers, shoving her ass against the counter of their kitchenette. His hands rubbed her nipples through her dress. She could feel his huge cock, and her core ached for him.

Julieta couldn't get enough of Ramón. She stroked his length through his clothes, desperate to feel him inside her. He unhooked her bra, and then before she could react, his fingers slipped into her panties, which he then pulled off.

He lifted her dress off over her head and took a step back.

"You have the most insane body."

Julieta was glad she found a man who thought her curves were attractive.

He picked her up and carried her to the bed.

He kissed her neck, the scruff from his chin scraping against her skin.

She removed his clothes. Now it was her turn to stare. His chiseled body was like a dream. He was hard where she was soft.

Ramón pressed her back against the bed and lowered his body on top of hers. Julieta writhed under him. She was already so wet in anticipation of him.

He cupped one of her breasts and sucked on her nipple, as Julieta stroked his cock.

Ramón kissed slowly down her body. His touch was gentle, but the teasing was unbearable. Julieta was going to explode. He spread her legs wide and licked her as pleasure throbbed through her. She thrashed around on the bed as he drove her out of her mind with delight.

She was almost there when he stopped, leaving her breathless. She caught the hungry look in his eye.

She pulled him up and knelt in front of him. She couldn't wait to suck his cock.

She gripped the base and took him deep.

Ramón groaned but nudged her head off him. "I want you."

Julieta's body was on fire.

Ramón was so gorgeous naked. His dark skin accentuated every muscle. He was an Aztec god. And she couldn't wait for him to conquer her.

He grabbed a condom and rolled it on.

She lay back, and he kissed her neck as she welcomed him deep into her soul.

"Oh, Ramón."

His hard body pressed against hers as his rhythm quickened. She screamed in ecstasy.

Ramón kissed her neck and then slid out slowly. Julieta ached without him. He sat up on the bed.

"Ride me."

Julieta slowly lowered herself onto him, inch by inch. She gasped. He filled her perfectly.

"Let me look at you," he said.

She smiled and then he smiled. And they both laughed. They kissed, and she started rubbing her clit against him, the tension sending pulses of pleasure through her brain.

He sucked on her nipples, and Julieta was almost over the edge of ecstasy. His hands clutched her bottom as he guided her rhythm. She threw her head back in abandon.

Julieta never wanted this moment to end. She was so close.

"Ay, Ramón!"

He held her close, and she came harder than she ever had as he grunted in pleasure.

He brushed back her hair and looked at her. "Te amo, Julieta."

He loved her? And as she thrust against him and he cried out her name, coming inside her, she answered.

"Te amo, Ramón."

CHAPTER TWENTY-EIGHT

R amón woke up before Julieta.

What an incredible night. He couldn't believe he'd actually told her that he loved her. Even crazier, he'd actually meant it.

And he felt that she did, too.

Ramón didn't feel fearful. He was ecstatic.

He gazed out at the ocean. He was excited to surf today.

After ordering room service, he quickly checked his phone.

There was an email from his father. Wonderful.

Ramón,

It has come to my attention that you have not issued any of the rent increases to the tenants on Logan Avenue. Due to your reluctance to do your job, I have taken it upon myself to draft the letters. Please send these by the end of the day. I understand your

concerns, but we cannot continue to lose money on
the block. I would also like a timeline for the grand
opening of Barrio Logan's Taco King.

Please let me know your thoughts.

Love always,
Papá

Dammit! Ramón's gut twisted. He did not want to deal with this today. Not when he was actually happy.

Papá wouldn't ruin his bliss. He would speak with him when he returned.

He sent a standard out-of-office reply, knowing that it would infuriate his father.

Julieta finally woke, her hair wild and dark against the stark white sheets.

"Good morning, beautiful," he said.

"Good morning."

They fed each other fresh fruit, yogurt, and eggs. Ramón had been here before with his brothers and his friends, but it was definitely better being here with Julieta.

After breakfast, they made love again.

"What did you want to do today?" he asked as their breathing slowed. The scent of sex hung in the air between them.

Julieta stretched in the bed. "I'm happy to just do nothing and stay here forever."

She was clearly joking, but staying in Mexico and never returning to San Diego to face Papá crossed Ramón's mind. He kept it to himself. He did not want to tell Julieta about the email. He wanted to enjoy the trip before they went back.

"Staying here forever would be nice, but I think I'd miss the McLaren too much." He laughed, then paused, met her beautiful gaze. "And Las Pescas. It's starting to feel like home to me."

She linked fingers with his. "That means a lot. But by Las Pescas, you mean the Taco King, right?"

He bit his lip. It was as if she could sense that Papá had sent him the letter. "Give me time, babe."

"I will." She glowed, and there wasn't a hint of sarcasm in her tone. She trusted him. Ramón had to make sure he was worthy of that trust.

He pressed a kiss to her forehead then smiled. "But seriously, what do you want to do today?"

"I don't know. I've never been here."

"I was thinking we could take a tour of the tequila distillery, maybe go shopping downtown? We could try one of the local taco stands."

She laughed. "Why? Are you looking for a new recipe?"

"Ha. Very funny. I always like to try regional cuisine. It's *you* I should be worried about. Next thing I know, you will be serving octopus tacos."

"It is a possibility. Okay, let's go."

They spent the day strolling through the town. Julieta purchased necklaces for her mom and Rosa, and a ceramic shark for Tiburón. After sampling a bunch of tequilas, they found a cozy seafood restaurant where they dined on ceviche. That night, they listened to music on the beach.

The next morning, they woke early to snorkel.

Ramón had booked a private tour. The boat waves made Julieta a little seasick, but she grinned through it. The tour guide finally parked the boat near a cove.

"They call this place Lover's Beach."

Ramón applied suntan lotion to her body. Ramón was drunk on her curves. She had the most perfect ass he'd ever seen and incredible breasts.

Once their gear was fitted, Ramón and Julieta descended into the water.

Gliding through the ocean, Ramón swam among the tropical fish. Their bright, beautiful colors painted the ocean. Though he spent a lot of time above the water surfing, he loved exploring its beauty beneath. He was dive certified. Maybe Julieta would like to learn how to dive with him? He held her hand as they continued to snorkel.

When they got back on the boat, Julieta was giddy with delight.

"That was so awesome! Seeing all those fish in their natural habitat, all the shades of the ocean—I feel so inspired."

They suntanned on the deck. This was the life.

The next day, Ramón had a goal: to teach Julieta how to surf.

The Cabo waves were better than the San Diego ones. And the water was so warm that even in winter, Ramón didn't feel the need to wear a wet suit.

He rented the boards while Julieta sat on the beach, reading a book.

He ran up beside her. "Come in."

She crinkled her face. "No. I don't surf. I like reading."

"Come on, try. It's fun. I'll teach you."

"I liked snorkeling yesterday, but water is not my thing. I mean, fish are in the water, and I love to cook and eat them, but surfing, not so much."

"How would you know if you never tried?"

Julieta tossed down her book. "Okay. If I drown, though, promise to take care of my family."

"Deal."

Ramón taught her a few techniques on the board while it was on the sand. Then he guided her into the ocean.

Julieta stumbled at first but became braver by the minute. She paddled slowly with him right beside her on his own board.

Julieta crouched on the deck and slowly stood up.

"That's it, babe. Get up! You can do it."

She stayed upright for a full minute before she fell back down.

"You did great."

"That was so much fun! Can I try again?"

"Of course."

Ramón and Julieta surfed together for the next hour. Julieta seemed to actually enjoy it.

After they surfed, they relaxed in the beach chairs. Julieta grabbed her book and began to read again, and Ramón lay in the sun. The waiter brought them strawberry margaritas.

Julieta sipped her drink as she gazed at Ramón. "I've never been happier in my life."

"Me either."

Julieta paused. "So, what does that mean? Clearly, we both should bring some of this vacation life back home. For me, I realize that I work too much."

He rubbed her arm. "I do, also."

"Well, I'm going to change. I'm going to start taking one day a week off."

"Sounds like a plan. Let's do that." He grinned, imagining the two of them exploring the many hikes in San Diego, followed by romantic dinners at the hottest restaurants. "Let's go back to the room."

Julieta grabbed her book, and they raced back into the hotel.

The second Ramón closed the door, he pushed Julieta against the wall.

His hands gripped her waist, and he pulled off her bikini bottoms.

He loved eating her pussy.

"Ramón!"

She was so wet. She moaned as he devoured her. Once she was right where he wanted her, Ramón stopped.

He grabbed a condom, slipped it over his cock, and turned her around so her hands were against the wall.

He removed her bikini top, then squeezed her incredible ass. She was naked except for her mesh coverup, which was the sexiest thing he had ever seen.

He rubbed her pussy again, and she was so wet, so ready for him.

Ramón teased her with the tip of his cock.

"Please, just fuck me."

He slowly slid it in and reached around and rubbed her clit. She moaned as she pressed her ass back against him.

Ramón was in heaven inside her. He fucked her harder and harder, and she was so loud.

"Ay, Dios mío. Don't stop."

He squeezed her nipple while working her clit, until her pussy clamped around him. She came, and Ramón did, too.

He turned her around, her face sweaty.

"Do we have to go back home?" she panted.

He kissed her on the forehead. "Yes. But we can come back whenever you want."

CHAPTER TWENTY-NINE

After a great few days in Cabo, Julieta had to return home.
Reality was much less bright than their cocoon in Cabo.
What a glorious time they'd had—sun, sex, snorkeling, surfing.

And they had even said they loved each other. Julieta couldn't believe it.

She *knew* he loved her. And she loved him, too.

But back home, Julieta started getting nervous about the opening of Taco King. Ramón told her that his father wanted to close Las Pescas at the end of the month. Julieta still hadn't told anyone on the street that her restaurant was about to become a Taco King. When Ramón told her they would need to start going over the menus, her heart raced.

Julieta would become a pariah, and her community would turn its back on her. She was already seen by some as a traitor for sleeping with the enemy. It was all heartbreaking.

And she didn't know if she would have it in her to pass the protesters every day and continue to work in the restaurant. If it was any other business, *she* would be the one protesting.

Julieta herself had organized a protest when the last remaining gallery closed in Barrio Logan. She'd stood there side by side with Tiburón, holding signs. She'd fed the protesters. Now, she would be on the other side of the fight. She would be called a Coconut Barbie. She would be ostracized from her community.

Ugh. Julieta couldn't think about that now.

Tonight, Ramón had invited her over to a place he'd rented in Coronado, since he still hadn't found a new home he liked enough to purchase.

The Uber dropped her off, and the doorman let Julieta into Ramón's building.

Ramón grinned. "Wow, you look nice. Too bad we aren't going out."

She bit her bottom lip. "I thought you said you were taking me to dinner. Did you eat? We can go to the store, and I can cook something really quick."

Ramón laughed. "No, I'm playing with you. It's my turn to spoil you. I'm cooking."

Julieta pulled on his arm. "Are you sure about that? Do you know what you're doing?"

Ramón picked her up and placed her on the kitchen counter. She wanted him to throw her up against the wall and fuck her right then and there. Who needed to eat, anyway?

"Yes, I make a mean steak. Relax and make yourself at home. Dinner will be done in twenty minutes." He pushed a glass toward her. "Your paloma is ready."

Julieta beamed. Ramón was just so incredible.

This condo also had a view of the beach, which clearly must be a requirement for all places Ramón lived in. Hey, her place had a view of the freeway.

The furniture was modern and masculine, which suited him perfectly.

"So, what's on the menu tonight, Chef Ramón?"

"A salad with goat cheese, a New York strip steak with a beurre blanc glaze, sautéed asparagus, and roasted potatoes. For dessert, I made a chocolate cake."

"That sounds great. Where did you get the recipes?"

He laughed. "YouTube."

"That's where most people learn how to cook now."

"You should get a channel. Jaime could hook you up. You would make a killing."

"Yeah, I don't have time for that." Though she might soon if she quit Taco King. "But I do think it's a great way to make cooking accessible to so many people."

"Right." He paused, a worried look cast over his face. "Julieta, I need to talk to you about something."

Julieta's nerves spiked. "What?"

"Well, my father's going to start raising the rent on all the places on the block."

Her heart raced. "How much? I know Señora Flores can only pay a little bit more. That café is so essential to the community. She even found a village in Mexico to grow the coffee beans. And she sources them all from there."

He touched his forehead. He seemed so confused. Julieta almost felt bad for him. "Great. Now my company is going to devastate an entire village of people?"

"I don't know, is it? How much are you raising the rent?"

"It will be substantial."

She pursed her lips and looked away from him.

"Julieta, talk to me. What are you thinking?"

"I don't understand why you still have to do that. And frankly, and I know I work for you, and it's completely self-serving for me to say this, but I still don't see why you have to change Las Pescas. We could just keep it like it is now and you will turn a profit. I'm telling you, no matter what, a Taco King won't be accepted. There is nothing you nor I can do about that."

"Julieta, you know I don't have a choice. This was always the plan."

"Of course you have a choice. Everyone has a choice. You can choose to do what you want. You are not your father, just like I am not my mother. I'll tell you what—if I was my mom, I would've sued your father. Because yes, he started the business, and yes, he was inspired, but he gave us no credit at all. She struggled so much when she first came over from Mexico. My mom cleaned toilets. My father worked in the fields, and meanwhile you were being raised in La Jolla."

"I get it, Julieta. I'm working on it. I can quit, but that won't solve anything. It will just make it worse because my father will have no voice of reason. I'm trying. I need you to trust me."

"Fine." Julieta dropped it for now.

His voice lowered. "How bad do you think the protesters are going to be?"

"Bad. Especially if you raise the rent elsewhere."

"Julieta," he pleaded. "When we open the restaurant, I need you by my side."

She cringed. "I don't know if I can cross the protester lines. I don't know if I can betray my community." Julieta's heart sank. She dreaded this. Images of people blocking her path, yelling out "traitor," flashed in her head. Everyone would turn on her. Was she doing the right thing?

"I need to get ahead of it. Plead with the community."

"And how do you plan to do that? It's complicated, Ramón."

"I know that. I think maybe we should have a town hall meeting and discuss it."

"That's a bad idea. Ramón, nothing you can do will prevent them from protesting and boycotting you. They will come after you, come after me. I thought you knew this?"

"I did. I do. What should we do?"

Julieta couldn't answer that question. And no matter how much she loved Ramón and all the amazing opportunities that came with the new job, she was discovering she would never turn her back on her community.

Ramón drizzled the glaze on the steak and plated the vegetables. "Dinner."

The mood was somber. Julieta took the first bite of the meat. It was surprisingly tender and well seasoned. She was very impressed with her man's cooking abilities, and even more flattered that he'd taken the time to feed her instead of the other way around. But still, her lackluster mood prevailed. What would she do?

After they finished dinner, Ramón served her a slice of a gooey chocolate cake.

She took a big bite, the chocolate sauce melting in her mouth. "Oh, this is scrumptious."

Ramón must have sensed her mood. "Let's have some fun tonight."

"What did you have in mind?"

Ramón turned on a Mexican waltz song. "May I have this dance?"

"Ah! 'Tiempo de Vals'! I love this song. I didn't know you danced. Aren't you the Renaissance man? Shakespeare, musician, chef, and now dancer?"

He smiled. "My mom put me in cotillion classes. I had to take etiquette classes, dress in suits, and learn how to greet people. I was also a chambelán at many quinceañeras."

"Oh."

"Did you have a quinceañera?"

Julieta shook her head. "No. We couldn't afford it."

Julieta had wanted to have a quinceañera more than anything. She'd spent months looking at an absolutely gorgeous, huge pink dress with a bunch of tulle under it. She'd dreamt of having her chambelánes, her damas, the dancing, the music, and the food. Celebrating becoming a woman. She choked up. It was even more bittersweet because she could've danced with Papá then. And now, she would never dance with her father at her wedding.

Julieta didn't want to talk about it anymore.

Ramón turned up the music, grabbed her hand, and put his arms around her.

Lord, there was no place else she'd rather be—but how long would this last? How could they work when an entire neighborhood was about to turn against them?

"Remind me why you think this could really work out."

Ramón loudly exhaled. "What do you mean?"

"I mean, you took cotillion classes; you belong to two country clubs. I'm never going to feel comfortable around your world."

"I don't care about any of that. I care about *you*."

Julieta rested her head against his chest. He wrapped his arms around her, and they danced in the moonlight on the deck. Julieta didn't even know how to dance, but he guided her, his hand around her lower waist, her arms around his neck.

"Close your eyes. Just follow me."

And Julieta did exactly that, as if she were blindfolded, which it felt like she was. She was so in love. She would follow Ramón to the ends of the earth.

But she would not go against Barrio Logan.

CHAPTER THIRTY

Ramón wanted to blow off work all day and keep Julieta in bed, but his phone pinged.

He reached over. A text from his father.

Papá: We need to talk. Come to the office.

Great. Just what Ramón needed—Papá to ruin his day. Ramón couldn't avoid him much longer. But he didn't want to meet him in the office.

Ramón: Fine, meet me on the beach.

Papá: I'm serious, Ramón.

Ramón: Me too. See you at Windansea.

Ramón made coffee for Julieta. He considered making her breakfast, but whatever she could whip together was far superior to anything he could.

He didn't want to leave with her still asleep. That would be awkward. So, he took a shower, threw on his board shorts, and sat at the edge of the bed. He brushed her hair out of her face and kissed her. "Babe, I have to go meet my dad."

She rolled over and stretched. "Really? Now?"

"Yes, unfortunately. Look, I really want you to stay here with me. Please, make yourself at home."

"I mean, of course I would rather stay here. I just didn't want to impose. It's all so new and—"

"Julieta, stop. I'm crazy about you. I want you to stay." He kissed her on the forehead. "I'll be back in a few hours. I'll stop by Wayfarer and get some pastries and coffee."

"Oh, I love that place. Okay. See you later. Love you." She said it naturally, as if she had been saying it for a lifetime.

Her words filled Ramón with joy. "Love you, too." Ramón went to the garage and got in his car. He headed for La Jolla.

The traffic was light this morning. Ramón was grateful that he never had much in the way of a commute.

He finally arrived back at his place, parked in his own garage, retrieved his board, and then walked to the beach.

Papá stood under a palapa in the sand, clutching his own board.

"Ramón, we need to talk."

Ramón shook his head. "We can talk after we surf. Let's go."

Father and son ran to the water. The surf was calm, and the water was warm for this winter day.

As the waves crashed on him, Ramón marveled that the company that had provided him with such wealth and opportunity had started on Papá's surfing trip.

They finally exited the water and parked their boards in the sand. They both sat on the beach.

"Fine, Papá. Let's talk."

"Ramón, I know you are crazy about this girl. And I'm happy for you. But I'm not going to allow you to run my business into the ground."

"I thought it was *our* business? I mean, what more do you want?

We are wealthy beyond our wildest imagination when so many people struggle. Julieta and her family work so hard for everything. They save each penny they make. And you want to put them out of business? Why, Papá?"

Papá sighed. "It's not about the money, Ramón—it's about respect. And the land. That street has value. We can't just give it away for free."

"Apá. Why won't you listen to me? There is another way. We don't have to do this."

"What are you talking about? What is the other option?"

"We can invest in the stores. Her restaurant can be operated by us, but it doesn't have to be a Taco King. We can help the community with business plans. We can take a percentage of the profits. We can grow our portfolio. We have enough money—we don't need any more. Why is it so important to you? You have everything including restaurants throughout the United States. Why do you need this one?"

"Because that is the Chicano area of the city. You don't get it. In the seventies, when they created the murals, that was the place that we could go to be safe. I fought for Chicano Park. Brown Power."

Papá made no sense. Did he realize how ridiculous he sounded?

"So what? Now you want to tear the community down? The culture you claim to love so much? That you fought for? Do you not remember what it was like to taste Linda's tacos? How fresh the fish was, how you never had anything like that, how you wanted to bring that experience to the people in San Diego? You told me about your ex-girlfriend Penny. About how she made those god-awful tacos with American cheese and hard-shell tortillas, and she used tomatoes from the can. News flash—that's what *we* use now. Don't you get it? We are making all these disgusting tacos that you hated, which is the exact opposite reason why you started this business in the first place."

"I'm not going to discuss this anymore with you, Ramón."

Ramón didn't know where he could go from here. He didn't see a future as part of Taco King. But he couldn't quit now. If he did, Papá would fire Julieta and ruin the street even more.

"Fine. We'll open the restaurant. But after that, I'm done."

Ramón walked away from his father. He gazed toward the sky, which was as clear as his conscience.

CHAPTER THIRTY-ONE

Julieta turned the bathwater on and filled up the tub with warm water. Staying at this place was like staying at a hotel. Even so, she was grateful there wasn't a maid service.

That would make her feel very uncomfortable.

As the bubbles surrounded her, she tried to stay present in the moment and not worry about the future.

She got out of the bathtub, made herself an espresso, and sat on the balcony of the condo. She sipped her coffee while the Navy SEALs trained below. She was mesmerized. These young men were facing their fears, running through the water with waves crashing over them. Seeing the BUD/S candidates gave her a great sense of peace and hope. They were from all walks of life and all races. It didn't matter if they had college degrees, or high school educations, if they were rich or poor, black, brown, or white—the only thing that mattered in Navy SEALs selection training was who refused to never give up. It was their grit. None of them had it handed to them. It was so refreshing to be watching them up close.

Julieta found a new resolve. Instead of constantly wondering about what would happen with Ramón and the community, she would try to take life day by day. Just work as hard as she could.

Her phone rang. It was Tiburón.

"Hey, what's up?"

"Where are you?"

"Oh, I'm at Ramón's."

Tiburón grunted.

"What, Tib? He's wonderful. I'm crazy about him. You need to stop talking shit."

"Really, Julieta? Well, why don't you talk to Señora Flores, and she can tell you how great he is."

"Why? What happened to Señora Flores?"

"You don't even know, do you? You are too wrapped up in your delusional world with your millionaire boyfriend. I don't care how strung out you are on him, the guy's a fucking Coconut Ken doll."

"He's not. He's just as Mexican as we are."

Tiburón cackled like the coyotes Julieta often heard running around at night through her neighborhood. "Whatever you have to tell yourself, prima."

"What are you talking about?" Was this about the rent?

"Why don't you ask him?" Tiburón hung up.

Julieta looked around the room. She considered calling Ramón but didn't want to interrupt his meeting. She wanted to figure out what Tiburón meant on her own.

She quickly got dressed and wrote a note for Ramón. She was grateful that his front door automatically locked since she didn't have a key.

She went to the lobby, called an Uber, and headed back to Barrio Logan.

But instead of getting dropped off at her place, she went straight for the café next door.

There, she found Señora Flores.

"Señora Flores—what happened? Tiburón said—"

Señora Flores scowled at her. "Like you didn't know. You and that pendejo boyfriend of yours."

"Señora, I don't. Please tell me."

Señora wiped the tears from her eyes. "The rent. He raised it."

"How much?"

"Triple."

The wind was knocked out of Julieta. Clearly, that must have been a mistake.

There was no way Ramón would do that.

But it wasn't up to Ramón. It was up to his father.

"Triple the rent?"

"Sí. Six thousand a month. You know I can't pay that. None of us can. We will all close."

Yes, they would. Mari's panadería, Señor Pérez's pharmacy, and even Yesenia's bookstore.

Julieta loved Barrio Books. That place was one of a handful of bilingual bookstores left in the country. They had story time for kids and taught SAT classes on the weekends. There was even a romance section that Mamá loved. What was he going to put there?

She had to talk to Ramón.

And she didn't have the heart to tell Señora Flores that she had chosen to take the job at Taco King.

Señora Flores narrowed her gaze at Julieta. "Did he raise your rent?"

"No, not exactly." Deep breath. "He wants to put a Taco King here."

There it was—her painful secret was now out in the world for everyone to hear. Julieta hung her head in shame.

"¿Qué?"

"He offered me a job. He's turning it into a Taco King and said that I could stay and be the chef."

Señora Flores's mouth dropped, and her skin became so pale. "And you accepted it?"

"No, not at first. I told him no. I said there was absolutely no way I would ever even consider it."

She paused. She didn't want to throw Mamá under the bus, but she also didn't want to lie. "But I didn't have a choice. I didn't have another job."

"And you knew he was going to do this all along?"

She shook her head. "No. He said he was working on a solution. Señora Flores, what options do we have? We have no control. We do not own this land. Señor Gomez was selling this block, and if he hadn't sold it to the Montez Group, he would've sold it to somebody else. There were four other offers, and I doubt any of them would have left the rent as it was. No matter what, we would not have been able to stay here."

"But that's not right! This is our community. My father founded this café. We came here when there was nothing. You don't know—you were too young to remember. Do you even know the history of the barrios? We were here because we had nowhere to go. They took our land. We were segregated. They didn't want us in their schools. This is our home. And now that it's cool, they want to take it over. It's not right."

Julieta agreed with everything that Señora Flores said, but she still had no solution. "You're right. It's not okay, but there's nothing we can do about it. Changes keep coming, and we have a choice to be part of them or be left behind." Julieta couldn't believe her words. She was a traitor to her community.

"So, you expect me to be the manager of the Starbucks that will come in here?"

"I don't know. I can't speak for you or tell you what to do. But hope is not all lost."

"You are mad. There is no hope—he's raised the rent on the entire block. Las Pescas is about to be a Taco King. How can you possibly say that, Julieta?"

"Because I know Ramón, and he's a good man. I still believe that he can fix this." Julieta's voice broke, and she began to tremble.

Señora Flores placed her arm around Julieta's shoulders. "I have known you since you were a little girl. I used to watch you when your mom would work. You were the cutest niña, with the bright eyes and long braids. I love you, Julieta. But you will be dead to me if you work at Taco King."

"I understand."

Was this the last time that Julieta would ever hug Señora Flores? That Julieta would ever be a part of her community again? The minute the word got out to the rest of the owners, they would all agree with Señora Flores, but what was the solution? What did Julieta expect Ramón to do? Buy the land and not raise her rent? That was unrealistic. And as much as Julieta loved that fantasy, it would never be a reality.

There was a choice ahead—a fork in the road.

Ramón called her phone, but she turned it off, took a walk to Chicano Park, and prayed.

CHAPTER THIRTY-TWO

Ramón called Julieta, but she didn't answer. That was weird. She couldn't possibly know what his father had said to him, or what Papá's plans were.

Ramón stopped by the bakery and picked up a few pastries.

The shopgirl smiled at him. "Hi, Ramón. I haven't seen you in a while. Where have you been hiding out?"

Tamara was sweet. They had hooked up a few times. But that was way before he'd met Julieta. "Oh, I've been working on a deal in Barrio Logan. Spending a lot of time with my girlfriend down there."

Hurt flickered in her eyes, and she gave a forced smile. Ramón hated disappointing women, but he didn't want to screw up his relationship with Julieta.

"Oh right, I got it. Totally." She handed him a bag with two pastries in it. "She must be a special woman for you to fall for her."

"She is. Bye, Tamara."

Ramón took his coffees and his Danishes, left the store, and ran into Mateo, who sat on the patio.

"Hey, man. What are you up to?" Mateo asked after a bro hug.

"Not much. Heading back to my rental condo in Coronado where my girlfriend is waiting for me."

Mateo's head shifted back. "Nice. Congrats. You have a girl-friend?"

"Yeah, I'm as shocked as anyone. But Julieta's really great. I'm happy."

"Cool, man. I'd like to meet her."

"Do you want to come with me?"

"Yeah, I'll come. I was looking for a place to co-work for the day. I have a new house design I'm working on."

"Awesome. We can work at my place."

"Sounds good."

Mateo got into Ramón's car, and they took off for Coronado.

When they arrived at the condo, Julieta wasn't there, but Ramón did find a note.

> Hey, Ramón,
>
> I had to go into work. I'll call you later.
>
> Besos,
> Julieta

Ramón called her again, but she didn't pick up. She was probably busy.

Ramón and Mateo hung out for a bit, then they both got to work, tapping away on their laptops with complete focus. Two hours later, Ramón's stomach grumbled. "Want to stop for a break? We can go to Julieta's place for lunch. She's a chef."

"Sounds good. I can't wait."

Ramón opened his email, and there was a copy of the lease agreement for the café from his father.

Oh, fuck.

He quickly opened the PDF and scanned the letter.

Triple the rent.

He looked at the email one more time, hoping, praying that it was merely a draft.

Please, Papá, tell me that you didn't send that out.

But Ramón had only received it as a blind copy.

Papá had gone behind his back and raised the rent.

Dammit.

He had to get to Julieta before she found out. If she hadn't already.

Ramón stepped out on the deck to make a call. He called Julieta, but it went straight to voice mail. He then called Papá.

"Papá, did you send that email to everybody on the street?"

"Yes, Ramón," he said snidely.

A sinking feeling settled in Ramón's stomach. "So, you didn't listen to a word I said today."

"I did, but I don't agree with you. I didn't hire you because you are my son. I hired you because you were fearless. You've always been, even when you were a little boy. You were never scared of anything, but lately, you've changed."

"I've changed? I don't even know who you are anymore."

"Stop it, Ramón."

"No. I won't. What we are doing isn't right. It's not just about us. It's not always about what makes the most sense financially."

"I don't have time for this today, Ramón." Papá hung up.

Dammit. His father wasn't even mature enough to have a discussion about this.

The backlash would be swift. Julieta shouldn't be facing it alone.

"Hey, Mateo, I have an emergency in Barrio. Do you mind if we go now?"

"Nope, not at all. What's up?"

"We bought a block there, and my dad raised the rent on all the businesses to a price that they can't pay. I told him not to do it, but he didn't listen to me. I threatened to quit, but then he will just force everyone out anyway. I'm trying to fix this mess."

Mateo put his hand on Ramón's shoulder. "Wow, that sucks. But take a deep breath. You are a great businessman. You will figure something out."

"Thanks, man." Ramón took a big calming breath.

"Don't worry about it. Let's go."

Ramón got into his car and drove to Barrio Logan as his heart raced.

He pulled up, and Julieta must have seen him, because she came out of Las Pescas. Her eyes were blazing, and her hair was wild.

Ramón spoke to Mateo. "Stay in the car for a second."

Mateo nodded.

Ramón got out and faced the woman he loved.

"I didn't think you would show up," she said.

"Well, you didn't return my calls."

"I just need some space."

He took her hand and pleaded with her eyes. "Julieta, I didn't know he sent the email. We have been fighting about this for weeks."

"I know, Ramón." She looked away from him and spoke in a whisper. "I just don't know if I can go through with this."

"What are you talking about?"

"This restaurant. You, me, us—all of it. You're tearing up my neighborhood. I just think we need some space."

No.

"Julieta, please calm down. Nothing has changed. I'm the same guy who you fell in love with. I love you. What we have together has nothing to do with Barrio Logan."

Her lip trembled. "And I'm the same girl. A bird can fall in love with a fish, but where can they live? I live here. With my people. I'm the fish. I'm drowning, Ramón. I'm drowning in you. I'm drowning in this restaurant, in my community. Everything was so clear to me before you came along. Now I don't know what's up or down. I'm traveling to Cabo, riding thousand-dollar bikes, staying in Coronado and La Jolla. It was beautiful, but it is a fantasy. It's not reality. I don't want that life. I want simplicity. I want to work hard and enjoy my family. I don't want any tension. I just want to be happy."

Julieta's shoulders hunched; an anguished sob burst from her mouth.

Ramón wiped the tears off her cheeks.

Then he looked up. Tiburón was walking toward them, an angry scowl on his face.

"What the fuck are you doing here, rich boy? Why don't you go back home? You've caused enough trouble. We don't want you here. Oh, by the way. I quit."

"I'm trying to fix this, Tiburón."

"We don't need your help. I strongly suggest you leave before I bash in that car window." He pointed at the McLaren.

Julieta stood in between them. "Tiburón. Stop."

"No, I won't. Your father stole my tía's recipe, you seduced my cousin, pushed her out of her restaurant, and now you are destroying my street."

Mateo hopped out of the car.

Tiburón got in his face. "Get the fuck back in the car, boy."

"I'll go wherever I want," Mateo roared.

Tiburón walked around the side and bashed in Ramón's window with his foot.

Oh, hell no.

Mateo charged him, but Ramón held him back. "Let's leave, man. It's not worth the trouble."

"That's right. Fucking leave."

Mateo pushed Ramón out of the way, and then tackled Tiburón, who proceeded to punch Mateo in the face.

Holy fuck.

Ramón raced down and kicked Tiburón in the balls.

Tiburón keeled over, clutching his jewels.

Julieta screamed. "Stop fighting! This won't solve anything!" She turned to Ramón, her entire body shaking. "Ramón. Get out of Barrio Logan. And don't come back."

His shoulders hunched. "Julieta, please."

"Just go!"

Ramón sneered at Tiburón, and Ramón and Mateo got in the car and left.

Ramón needed to fix this fast, before he lost Julieta and Barrio Logan forever.

CHAPTER THIRTY-THREE

I t had been a few days since Ramón's father raised the rent on Señora Flores. After their fight, Julieta still hadn't returned Ramón's calls. Ramón understood she was angry but didn't appreciate her ignoring him. The people who supposedly loved him always shut him out.

Ramón met up at a bar with Enrique, Jaime, and Benicio, who shockingly showed up.

Enrique took one look at Ramón. "You look like shit, dude. Have you heard from her?"

Ramón shook his head no and downed some tequila.

Jaime put his hand on Ramón's shoulder. "I hate to say this, bro, but do you think she used you?"

"No. Why would you say that?"

"Because she was all too happy to be with you when you gave her a cushy job all the while knowing you were going to close the restaurant and make it a Taco King. But once her community found out, she dumped you."

Jaime's words hit Ramón in the gut. Julieta was nothing like the other girls he'd met, but maybe she *did* only want him as long as he did what she wanted.

That wasn't a healthy relationship.

"I don't know, man. All I know is I miss her. I don't know what to do."

"Well, she has to understand this isn't your decision alone. It *is* still Papá's company—he has the final say. He can do what he wants. And we can choose to work for him or not."

"Right. I don't even know what she expects me to do. We weren't the only bidders on the block. Whoever bought those buildings would've raised the rent. I'm at least trying to help."

Benicio turned to me. "You still don't get it, dude."

"What? What don't I get?"

"It's not about the fact that some other guy would be doing it anyway. It's about the fact that people in our community are being priced out. They can't afford to live and work in the areas we have grown up in. We can't compete with you people. Were the other bidders Mexican?"

"No."

"Right. So that makes it even worse. You are destroying your own community."

"I get that, I do. But the end result is the same."

Benicio threw his hands up and pushed back from the table. "Whatever you say."

Ramón stood. "Hey, Beni, wait."

"No, man. I'm going to bounce."

Enrique pulled Ramón back to the table. "Let him go, dude. You will just make it worse."

"I just don't know how to fix it."

"Well, sometimes you can't. Maybe you have to face the fact that you and Julieta aren't right for each other." He clapped Ramón on the back. "Tell you what. Let's go out tonight."

All Ramón wanted to do was forget about his troubles, about Papá, and about the hurt tightening his chest whenever he thought of the woman he loved. "Where?"

"There is this wedding we got invited to. It's going to be dope."

"Fine." Ramón had to get his mind off Julieta.

Ramón arrived at the wedding, which was held at the Fairmont Grand Del Mar resort. The place was incredibly opulent—ice sculptures galore, crystals cascading down from the heavens. This was a La Jolla society wedding if there ever was one.

But his world of the wealthy did seem a little less bright.

Mateo walked up to him. His lip was still busted up, but it did look better.

"Hey, man. Sorry about that again."

"No worries. The girls dig it."

Ramón laughed. "Still, I'm sorry."

"Don't mention it. What are you doing for the holidays? Aspen? Deer Valley? Tahoe?"

Ramón couldn't think of going anywhere without thinking about Julieta.

"I'm going to stay local this year."

Ramón saw his mom standing near a massive Christmas tree, sipping champagne with her boyfriend.

Great. Just what Ramón needed.

Two other women were with them—Mrs. Camarillo and her daughter.

"Ramón!" His mom acted like she was thrilled to see him. She walked over and kissed him on the cheek, with Mrs. Camarillo and Sarita trailing behind her. At least his mom's boyfriend didn't bother to greet Ramón.

"You remember Sarita?"

Ramón nodded. Sarita was pretty and proper and prim. "Hey, Sarita, how are you?"

"Good, Ramón. You look handsome."

"Thanks. You look nice, too." Ramón needed a drink. "Good night, ladies."

His mom attempted to make a worried expression. She ran after him.

"Ramón, don't leave in a huff. You could've asked Sarita to dance."

"I'm not interested."

His mom huffed. "You aren't still serious about that chef, are you? I looked her up. She has tattoos, Ramón. All over her arms. She's trash."

Rage boiled through Ramón. "No, Mom. She's not trash. *You* are."

Her mouth gaped.

Ramón was tired of the noise and went out to get some fresh air. He ran smack into someone carrying a big tray of food.

Smoked salmon tartlets slipped to the ground. The tray clattered and bounced. Ramón looked up . . .

"Julieta?" Why was she here?

Julieta wiped her shirt down, shaking her head. "I'm catering the event, Ramón. I need to work. Don't you see? That's the difference between us. These events are basic to you, and for me, the only way I'll ever gain entry is through the door marked employees only."

"Stop. Don't be ridiculous. Besides, you were still working for me a few days ago. When did you take this job?"

"The restaurant was booked for this party months ago, before I met you. Do you know how hard it is to get a caterer at the last minute? I would never flake on someone just because I got a better offer."

"Got it." Ramón felt like a jerk. "I'm sorry. Look, can you take a break soon?"

"No."

Mamá walked over. Ramón hung his head. How could this night get any worse?

"Mom, I'd like you to meet Julieta Campos."

Julieta wiped her hands on her apron. "It's so nice to meet you, Señora Montez."

Mamá scowled at Julieta. "Well, I can't say the same."

"Mom, please."

"Ramón. Stop embarrassing yourself and me. She's the help, for Christ's sake."

"Dammit, Mom!"

Julieta's lower lip trembled. "She's right. Seriously. I need to get back to work."

Julieta scampered off. Ramón went after her, but she slammed the service door in his face.

Ramón went back to the fountain to find his mom.

"Mom. You have no manners or class."

"Me? Ramón, you're making a fool of yourself. We are at a high-end wedding with people who know me, know your father."

"Who cares about your reputation? You pretty much ruined that when you started cheating on Dad."

Mamá grabbed him by the hand. "You know nothing about our marriage. Your father worked all the time. He left me alone in that big house. I had no friends."

"You had us, Mom. But you ignored your children."

Her face softened toward him. "And I adored you, but you were children with your own needs. Nothing is lonelier than being in a loveless marriage. Your father never really loved me. He was always hung up on this girl he met in Mexico."

Her words hit Ramón like a brick.

"Why did you marry him?"

She placed her face in her hand and gave a tragic sigh. "He was so young and dashing and ambitious and had so much passion. I was instantly drawn to him. I wanted to be around him, but we were so different. He liked to work; I wanted to travel. I will never regret marrying him, because it gave me you and your brothers, but you need to be happy and have something in common to make a marriage work."

"You're right, Mom," Ramón said. "And you deserved better than to be forgotten."

His mom hugged him.

Nausea swirled in Ramón's gut. "And so did Dad. You shouldn't have cheated, and he shouldn't have abandoned you."

He stepped back and walked away, ignoring Mamá's shocked gasp. He just wanted to find Julieta.

CHAPTER THIRTY-FOUR

Julieta hadn't returned Ramón's calls since running into him at
the wedding, which was a week ago.

She had cleared out Las Pescas without even telling him. All the
artwork and personal details were gone. Ramón's father had begun
planning new construction immediately. The place would be fully
renovated, and a team of chefs was about to be brought in to create a
new menu. It would be nothing like Las Pescas, but it was more like
Papá's original restaurant. A plain, simple menu. Fish tacos and beer.

And today Ramón was going to do what he should've done all
along—stand up to his father.

Ramón drove to the restaurant, but there was no place to park. Protesters swarmed the streets with big signs and even bigger voices. Ban-
ners that read WE SHALL NOT BE MOVED. WE WANT JUSTICE. NO
CHAINS. NO TACO KING.

Ramón recognized one of the protesters right away—Tiburón.

Ramón parked a block away. He walked down the sidewalk with
his head held high as the residents shouted at him.

Julieta must've been waiting for him. She ran toward him from Las Pescas, a sad look on her face.

She looked beautiful, as always. But it didn't matter.

"Ramón. I'm sorry."

He ignored her and kept his gaze forward. He didn't blame her for quitting, but he couldn't forgive her for ghosting him. Not when he had told her he loved her. Even worse, he meant it.

"I wanted to call. I just didn't know what to say."

Ramón kept walking. "Got it."

"Can't we accept that me working for you will never work? Just like you and I will never work?"

Anger flared through Ramón like a tornado. How could she say that now? "I never lied to you," he hissed. "You accepted the job knowing what would happen. And I don't blame you for quitting. But you shouldn't have walked out on me. I've always tried to do right by you."

"I know, I know. But it is your company that is shutting my restaurant down. And all the other businesses. I can't separate you from your name."

"'What's in a name? That which we call a rose by any other name would smell as sweet,'" he said, snidely.

"It's not that simple."

"Actually, it is, Julieta. Let me go."

"Ramón, I'm so sorry."

All he'd ever wanted was for someone to have his back, no matter what. For him to be worth risking something for, and it was clear to him that Julieta had chosen her family and her community over him.

The heat of the crowd suffocated him. He was the enemy. The chants got louder. *Go back home. We don't want you.*

Ramón walked to the front of the restaurant and took a deep breath. "I know that you don't want us here, and I understand all the reasons why. And you are right, but the building was for sale. Someone had to buy it, and we were the ones."

The crowd booed.

"I am a proud Mexican man. I appreciate and love our culture, but we have to evolve. I'm working toward a solution to do right by your community. Our community. And I pray that you give us grace, and the space, to fix this mess."

The chants started right back up. Ramón walked inside to face his father.

"Ramón, what are you doing here? We have this under control."

Ramón looked at the barren walls and shuddered. All of Julieta's love and character for this place was erased.

"I came to do what I didn't have the guts to do before."

"You are quitting?" His father's fist clenched, and his face reddened. "'Bye, go. Who needs you?"

Ramón never truly hated Papá until that moment. "Well, you do. But I'm not quitting. I spoke with Señor Gomez and told him your plans for the block. As you know, our lawyers were still drawing up the final papers. We had never executed the final agreement."

"What are you saying?"

"I'm saying you no longer own this block. I do." Ramón's mouth widened into a devilish grin. "And I'm telling you to get out."

Papá stood there, his jaw dropped, and his eyes went wide as saucers.

"I can't believe you, Ramón. I started this business."

"Yes, on the back of Julieta's mom's recipe. And guess what? Now I'm going to save our company. Oh, by the way, Father, the board of directors convened this morning. They were very interested to learn how you put the company at risk by taking over a restaurant whose founder you also stole our main recipe from a lifetime ago. For what, Papá, some misguided love vendetta? Grow up. They have begun an investigation that will result in your removal. Or you could save us all the trouble and humiliation and resign."

Papa's hands shook. "How could you? After all I've done for you. The life I've given you."

"I appreciate that. But you're on a power trip and need to be stopped. I won't allow you to destroy Barrio Logan. The man you once were, the Brown Beret who fought for this community, who chained yourself to these pillars, would be disgusted by you right now. You know I'm right. And I'm my own man now. You were the one who taught me how to lead without regret. And I'm finally doing it now. Get out of my restaurant."

Papá sneered at Ramón and left out the back door.

And for the first time in a very long time, Ramón was proud of himself.

Chapter Thirty-Five

Julieta climbed into the van with Mamá after she left the protests. Mamá reached out to her. "Mija."

Julieta threw up her hand like a stop sign. "Don't, Mamá. I don't want to hear about it."

"I was just going to say that I understand." Julieta's mom squeezed her hand. And Julieta let the tears fall. "Ah, mi amor, I know. I know."

"I loved him, Amá."

"I loved his father, too. I loved him more than I loved the sand on the beach. But we were not right for each other. What I had with your papá—that was true love. We shared the same values, the same vision, the same goals. And that is what is important in life."

"But why, Mamá? Why can't this work?"

"Relationships are hard work even under the best of circumstances. I know you remember your papá and me always having a great marriage, but that just was not the case. We fought all the time. We fought about money when you were younger, and childcare, how to raise you. It's incredibly difficult, but you have to be on the same page. Ramón does not share your core values."

"But Mamá, that's not true at all."

"Will you ever feel comfortable in his world? You told me how you felt the day that you saw him at the wedding."

Julieta nodded but wasn't sure if she agreed with Mamá anymore. "Aren't the best relationships when you learn from each other? When you grow together?"

"It is better to be with someone who is like you."

Julieta wasn't so sure. So what that Ramón had been raised with a silver spoon in his mouth? He had already taught her so much. How to enjoy her days off. How to have more of a work-life balance.

How to find a hobby that she enjoyed.

How to love.

And she had taught him stuff, too—it wasn't one-sided. Julieta had seen the way that Ramón had come alive when he played the guitar. That was who he was—not this asshole in a business suit. That was his job, not his real identity.

But it didn't matter. He was gone. She'd broken up with him, and Ramón wasn't the type to take her back.

And maybe Mamá was right. What kind of life would they have had together? Her family would never accept him, and she wouldn't be accepted by his—especially by that mother of his. She no doubt wanted Ramón to date a girl who had Ivy League degrees and came from a rich family. Julieta had tattoos, and Ramón had Teslas. They were like oil and water.

Julieta went back into Mamá's house. The place seemed colder now than before.

There were cracks in the paint and holes in the wall. But this was her home. She had grown up here. She loved it. But even keeping this roof over her head would be a challenge now that she'd quit her job.

Back when Julieta had met Ramón, she'd thought the worst thing that could ever happen to her was to lose the business. But it wasn't. It was finding love and losing it. It was getting a taste of happiness only to have it be snatched out from under her.

That was the worst.

Julieta paused by the photo of Papá. What would he tell her today? He had been such a hard worker, even until the end. He would never, ever let a setback stop him. He would get up the next day and do the same thing.

After all, mañana was another day.

CHAPTER THIRTY-SIX

Ramón woke up a month later with a hangover and a hard-on. He missed sweet Julieta, her voice, her scent, her mouth.

He had been so angry to see her holding that sign that he hadn't been able to forgive her. But time had made him second-guess his decision.

Las Pescas was vacant for now, the rent increases had been called off, and the protests had stalled. But Ramón still hadn't told the business owners what was happening.

He had to make some decisions. Real decisions about the properties in Barrio Logan.

Ramón grabbed his guitar and strummed, but a cacophony of noise came out.

Just like before he met Julieta, his song had gone silent.

But then, something hit him.

Yes, that would work.

He picked up the phone and dialed the one woman who might make this okay. She answered on the first ring and reluctantly agreed to meet him.

Ramón drove to Barrio Logan, but this time he took his Jeep.

He waited for her in the park.

She approached. "Hi, Ramón."

"Hi, Linda. Thanks for agreeing to meet."

She exhaled. "Ramón, what is so urgent you couldn't tell me over the phone? We have nothing left to say to you. You have taken everything from us. What do you want now?"

"Please sit."

She sat on a stone picnic table. The murals seemed a little less bright today, and no kids were playing in the park. But Ramón hoped his plan could bring some light back to Barrio Logan.

"Linda, I talked to my father. Well, a while ago. I begged him to compensate you for the recipe, but he wouldn't. I ordered him not to close Las Pescas or raise the rent, but again, he said no."

"I know this, Ramón. Why did you need to meet me to tell me this?"

He grinned. "Because I told Señor Gomez what my father planned to do. He rescinded his offer to the Montez Group and sold the block directly to me."

"To you?" Her eyes widened, but she gritted her teeth. "And what do *you* plan to do with our block?"

Ramón reached into his pocket and handed her an envelope. "I'm going to give it to you."

Linda slowly opened the flap. She took the letter out and read it. Tears welled in her eyes.

Her eyes narrowed. "Are you serious, mijo? Why are you doing this? What's the catch?"

"There is no catch. It's the right thing to do. Barrio Logan should be owned by the residents."

She clutched the paper to her chest. "It is mine? Las Pescas is mine?"

Ramón nodded. "Not just Las Pescas, but the entire block. It is fair compensation for the recipe my father stole from you. Of course, you will have to sign the papers and agree to not sue the company for the past unauthorized use of your recipe, but if you want the block, it's yours."

Linda embraced Ramón, and he hugged her back.

"I was so wrong about you, mijo. Julieta was right. You are nothing like your father. You are a good man."

Ramón didn't even want to talk about Julieta. He hadn't given the block to Linda to get back together with her daughter. Julieta didn't owe him anything.

"Gracias. Our lawyers will be in touch."

And with that, Ramón left Barrio Logan. Without Julieta and without the block, Ramón had no reason to return.

CHAPTER THIRTY-SEVEN

Julieta read the email and couldn't believe her eyes.

She called Ramón, but he didn't answer.

Mamá had vanished, too. She'd said she had an errand to run and hadn't returned. Julieta had called her, and she hadn't answered.

What was happening?

She read the email again, then ran from her house to the café.

Was he serious? Was this some joke?

Señora Flores was at the espresso machine, making a Mexican mocha.

Señora Flores asked, "Did you get the email?"

"Yes."

"Is it for real?"

"I don't know. Let me call him." *Again.*

She dialed his number, but he still didn't answer. She couldn't blame him—she had been so awful to him.

The street buzzed with theories. No one believed the email, though all the owners on the block received the same one. They were certain he would flip-flop tomorrow.

They gathered in front of what used to be Las Pescas. Julieta tried to open the door, hoping that Ramón would be inside waiting for her, but it was locked.

Seconds later, Linda emerged from around the corner with a set of keys. She opened Las Pescas. Hadn't Arturo changed the locks?

Whoa, what was happening?

Linda held a piece of paper and flashed it to the business owners. "What is that, Amá?"

She spoke loudly to everyone in the street. "Everyone! It's my deed to this land. I'm the owner of the block! Barrio Logan will never change!"

The tenants from the street erupted in applause and hugged one another.

Julieta grabbed the paper. "What? How did that happen?"

"Ramón fixed everything. He told Señor Gomez about what his father was going to do to Barrio Logan and convinced Señor to sell to Ramón instead."

Julieta's face contorted. "Then why do you have it?"

"Because he gave it to me. For his father stealing my recipe. It's ours, mija."

Ay, Dios mío. She had been so wrong to doubt him. How could she have been so foolish? She had to go find him.

She hugged Mamá. "I have to go."

Julieta got in her car and drove to Ramón's house. She spied him sitting on his balcony, drinking a beer and staring at the waves.

She parked her car in front of his house and grabbed a rock, which she threw on his deck.

"'O Romeo, Romeo, wherefore art thou Romeo?'"

He stood up, walked over to the edge of the railing, and smiled.

He disappeared in his house, only to emerge a few minutes later on his lawn.

It had been too long. Tall, dark, and handsome. This Aztec god stepped toward her, and her heart fluttered.

She reached up and touched his chin. "Is it true?"

He looked into her eyes. "Yup."

Julieta embraced Ramón. "How did you pull this off?"

Ramón smirked. "Well, after I convinced Señor Gomez to amend the deal, he sold it directly to me. I got my father kicked off the board of directors. Then I met with a team of lawyers. They figured out a percentage of what my dad would've owed your mom. So, I gave her stock options, which equaled the amount of the purchase price in Barrio Logan."

Julieta couldn't believe her ears. Ramón was brilliant, but she knew that. "So now—"

"So now, she's the owner of the block."

Julieta wrapped her arms around Ramón's neck. "What about you?"

"I'm good. I'm now the boss and don't have to listen to my dad. Though I'd love to invest in a sexy chef's restaurant, if she would let me."

Julieta couldn't help but tear up.

"But why? Why did you do this? After I was so awful to you."

"Because I love you, Julieta. And you have changed my life. I was stuck in a rut and had lost my way. And even if you never came back to me, I knew it was the right thing to do. And I'm sorry, too. I should've stood up to my father sooner. I needed to lose everything to find my way."

Julieta caressed his chest. "But you knew I'd come back."

He smirked. "Well, if you didn't, I would've come after you. We are meant to be."

She kissed Ramón. "I love you."

"I love you, too."

EPILOGUE

"M ija! We are going to be late!"

"Ah, Mamá. I can't believe I agreed to go to this. You swore to me this year that we wouldn't have to work Day of the Dead again."

"I know, but Ramón is working late anyway. We can celebrate tomorrow."

Julieta could never win. And she was annoyed that Ramón had to work on the one-year anniversary of their meeting.

But that was about the only complaint she had. Ramón was an amazing boyfriend. They now lived together in Coronado in a single-family home with her dog, Taco.

They talked about the future all the time, about how they wanted to have kids and travel and raise them to be bilingual.

Julieta had achieved more of a work-life balance. She took days off and she'd started yoga. She even enjoyed golfing once a week with Ramón and his mother, who was reluctantly beginning to accept her.

And even Mamá was happy. She'd officially retired and only

stopped into the restaurant once a week. She kept making remarks about how she couldn't wait to watch her unborn grandbabies.

And Las Pescas was thriving.

It had received a Michelin star. It was on several Best of San Diego lists. Ramón had taught her so much about the financial aspect of her restaurant. And she had brought fresh and sustainable authentic Mexican seafood back to the fast-food market. And she and Ramón were already planning the new vegan location in Encinitas.

The grand reopening of Las Pescas had been held at the beginning of July. There was even a block party. Ballet Folklórico dancers performed, and mariachis played music, and there were paleta carts and frutas vendors, and kids playing in the streets, and everyone was joyous. Crowds filled the streets. Señora Flores's cafe was also renovated and expanded. Mamá even started a new community garden.

Ramón had not yet reconciled with his father, but they had begun therapy.

All the businesses on her block were safe from gentrification now that Mamá was the landlord.

"Julieta, put on your dress."

"I don't see why I have to get in costume."

"Just do it!"

"Mamá. I thought you retired."

"Oh, it's just one demonstration. This time, we will take a break to honor your father with the altar."

That was a good reason to get dressed. Julieta couldn't believe it would be her second Day of the Dead since Papá had passed away. A year ago, she had been a wreck. This year, she was much more stable. She'd created a beautiful altar for him at the restaurant, and this time, she did not feel as guilty about working on Day of the Dead.

"Where's your makeup?" Mamá asked.

"Amá, you're insufferable."

"It's a traditional event. Anyway, reporters could be here—they may take pictures. You always want to look your best."

She looked at Mamá, who was breathtakingly beautiful. "Fine."

Julieta applied the makeup. She drew in her lips, but Mamá didn't have any patience for her.

"No, let me." Mamá snatched the pencil from her grip and began the makeup herself.

Just as she had a year ago, Julieta's mother applied rhinestones to her face and created a spider motif on her forehead. She drew black lines in her lips as if her lips were sewn shut.

They arrived in Old Town, where the celebration was in full swing.

Julieta grabbed her chiles and walked toward the square.

A year ago, she had been so sad, and now she couldn't even imagine being happier.

Julieta quickly began prepping all the ingredients. In addition to the tacos, there would be enchiladas and chicken—mild and hot—spicy salsa, tres leches cake, and guacamole and nachos.

Mamá talked about the evolution of fish tacos in America, and how she had inspired the Taco King. Then they taught the children how to make sugar skulls.

After the event was over, Julieta made sure not to miss the procession to the graveyard. She lit her candle with Mamá and walked in the line behind all of the other people to the cemetery.

Though Ramón was not by her side this year, there was still something so magical about being with a group of people who were all honoring their loved ones. Many people thought the Day of the Dead was like Halloween, or had something to do with devil worshipping, and neither of those was true. To be surrounded by a group of people who all understood the holiday was priceless.

"This one's for you, Papá." She filled a shot glass with tequila from a flask, just as Ramón had done a year before. She toasted to Papá, and then filled another and left it for him.

What a night. On her way back to the car, she stopped in the garden near the fountain where she'd seen Ramón. How handsome he was, how he'd looked at her, how he'd made her feel.

Mariachi music boomed louder in the distance.

She looked up, and there was Ramón, backed by a huge mariachi ensemble.

Shock washed over her. "Ramón!"

He smiled and kept singing—her favorite: "Abrázame."

A crowd soon surrounded them on all sides. Enrique and Jaime stood together in the crush.

Ramón had become an even better musician on the guitarrón. Hearing him backed by a full ensemble made Julieta swoon. She loved the sounds of the violin, the trumpets, and the vihuela coming together to create the perfect song.

The song ended, and she ran over to Ramón.

She wrapped her arms around him and kissed him on the cheek, smearing his makeup.

"You came!"

"Of course. I wouldn't miss it for the world. It's our anniversary." His voice deepened. "'*O, wilt thou leave me so unsatisfied?*'"

Julieta gave him a kiss, but he pulled away.

"That's not what I want, Julieta."

She bit her lip. The crowd was watching them. "What do you want?" she whispered.

"'*The exchange of thy love's faithful vow for mine.*'"

She laughed. "You're so silly. Stop quoting Shakespeare."

"I'm not trying to be silly."

Then he dropped to his knee and pulled out a small velvet box.

Ay, Dios mío!

"Julieta, you are the most beautiful señorita I have ever seen. My world didn't begin until I met you. I was so unhappy, and I didn't even know it. My life consisted of work, more work, and greed, until you showed me the way. You are everything to me. I cannot imagine my world without you in it. Would you do me the greatest honor of becoming my wife? Will you marry me?"

Julieta couldn't even respond. She stood there as tears welled in her eyes. She couldn't believe this was happening.

"Yes!"

He swept her up and kissed her. Then he slipped the ring on her finger. It was a pink diamond. In a rose gold setting.

"I love you, Julieta."

"Te amo, Ramón."

Love was truly alive on the Day of the Dead.

AUTHOR'S NOTE

Thank you so much for reading this book. Authors are often asked which of their books is their favorite, and that is usually a very hard question (I have written thirty books), but not for me. *Ramón and Julieta* is the book of my dreams. I literally fantasized about writing this book for two years before I tapped out a single line. I teased my incredible agent with the concept but wouldn't send it to her for months after I had finished the pages. Honestly, I was scared to write this book. I had made a career writing tropey romances. This book seemed bigger, more important, and scarier than anything I had ever written. Could I pull it off?

But I ultimately felt called to this book. I had to write it. I wanted to show Latinx joy. I wanted to celebrate our culture and shed light on some of our traditions. And as much as I wanted it to be a fun and frothy rom-com on the surface, I also wanted to address class issues in our community and discuss what it meant to be accepted and feel Mexican-American enough, something I've struggled with all my life.

At the beginning of the book, Ramón has lost his way. Though he is outwardly successful, internally he is struggling. Who is he? Is he doing right by his community or is he led by greed? And how can he rectify his business aspirations with his conscience?

Julieta also needs to learn how to balance the success of her business and the loyalty to her community and her family.

Issues of gentefication and cultural identity are very prevalent. Members of historically ethnic communities are being pushed out with rising housing and real estate costs. How do communities move forward and grow while still preserving the heart of their barrios? In the 1970s, Chicano activists fought to preserve Barrio Logan. It is up to the younger generation to make sure that these areas that are now considered hot and good investments aren't stripped of our culture.

Writing this book has been like therapy for me. Like Ramón, I became more in touch with who I was in college. All my idealistic dreams and passions. My determination to make a difference. I'm honored to celebrate my culture with you.

ACKNOWLEDGMENTS

Wow. There are so many incredible people to thank for this amazing opportunity I have had writing *Ramón and Julieta*, my dream book.

First, I would like to thank my brilliant and kind agent, Jill Marsal. You are so insightful and wonderful, and I am so grateful that you believed in my writing and have always been so supportive.

To my awesome editor, Sarah Blumenstock. From our very first conversation, I felt an immediate connection with you and I'm so honored and humbled to work with you. You have completely changed the way I write, slowed me down, and let me savor my words. I adore you and hope to work on many books together.

To my film agent, Carolina Beltran. Thank you for taking a chance on *Ramón and Julieta*! I love your energy and am so blessed by the incredible opportunity to work with you.

To my producers Gina Rodriguez, Kristen Campo, and Molly Breeskin. Ay, Dios mío! I'm over the moon about the opportunity to work with such amazing, strong women for this series. I can't wait to see what we will create together.

To Dailyn Rodriguez. Am I dreaming? You are such an inspiration. Latinx joy, here we come!

To my write-or-die team: Kelli Collins—I would never write a book without your input. Lauren McKellar—you make my words shine! Gwen Hayes—plotting goddess. Jo Machin—your enthusiasm makes my day. I believe in you. Tamara Lush—thanks for listening to me whine. It's finally our time to shine. To Nicole Blanchard and Mia Searles—thanks for being there for me from day one. My DD peeps—you are all my favorites. To all my students in my classes—thank you for inspiring me. My PA, Savannah Avila— thanks for all your hard work. To Jessica King—thanks for always being my partner in Paw Patrol. We've saved so many dogs together and I would've given up years ago without you.

My publicity and marketing team: Jessica Mangicaro, Daniela Riedlova, Lauren Burnstein, Stephanie Felty, Keely Platte, Madison Ostrander, Crystal Patriarche—I'm so honored to work with you all on this release.

To my amazing illustrator, Carina Guevara—thanks for bringing *Ramón and Julieta* to life. To my talented cover designer, Farjana Yasmin—I'm so obsessed with your beautiful design.

To my copy editor, Marianne Aguiar, proofreaders, Lisa Davis and Alaina Christensen, and production editor, Jennifer Lynes— thanks for your eagle eyes and for not editing out my Spanglish.

To my family. None of this would ever be possible without you. To my late father, Joseph Chulick Jr. You are the reason for everything I do. I miss you more every day. To my mother, Diana. You are so beautiful and supportive. I would've given up writing years ago without your encouragement. I love you. My brother and sister-in-law, Joe and Susie Chulick, thanks for always believing in me and supporting me. To my in-laws, Ron and Pam Albertson, thank you for your kind words and encouragement about my publishing career.

To my two beautiful sons, Connor and Caleb Albertson. Everything I do is for you. You are the best part of my day and of my life. I'm so proud of the wonderful young men you are. I love you.

To my supportive and loving husband, Roger. What a rollercoaster ride. Thanks for always bringing my coffee and food during my binge-writing sessions. I wouldn't have this career, family, or life without you. I love you.

And to all my fans—I write for you!!! Thank you for loving my characters.

Ramón and Julieta

Love & Tacos

Alana Quintana Albertson

DISCUSSION QUESTIONS

1. *Ramón and Julieta* is set against the culturally rich landscape of Barrio Logan. How does the setting contribute to the themes of the novel? How do the towns of La Jolla and Coronado contrast with Barrio Logan?

2. Ramón struggles to find his place in his culture. How does he reconnect with his heritage and come to peace with balancing his work and his conscience?

3. Julieta is accepted by her community. How does her loyalty interfere with her love life and her career trajectory? As a woman of color, is she expected to sacrifice her happiness and success in order to remain true to her culture? Is this fair?

4. How does Ramón's relationship with his father compare to Julieta's relationship with her mother? How do they contrast?

5. How does *Ramón and Julieta* explore issues of wealth and privilege? Does Ramón's wealth affect his view of issues affecting his community?

6. How would you describe the portrayal of gentrification in *Ramón and Julieta*? Do you think neighborhoods can maintain their cultural identity when they become developed? Why or why not?

7. Julieta's aunts bond during Lotería night over food. What cultural traditions do you share with your family?

8. Why do you think cuisine culture is so prevalent in the book? What does food reveal about the characters?

9. Music is threaded throughout Ramón and Julieta's romance. How is music used to strengthen the narrative?

10. Ramón's father founded Taco King due to his love of authentic fish tacos. Over the years, his recipe devolved and was nothing like its original inspiration. How do issues of cost and profit margin change the visions of other entrepreneurs? How can they maintain their visions yet still be profitable?

11. Ramón and Arturo both felt deeply connected to their cultures and their passions when they were younger. Can you think of examples in your own life when you lost your passion for causes that were once important to you?

12. Surfing is Ramón's outlet to center himself. Do you have an activity that helps you find clarity?

13. In the 1970s, Arturo was part of the Brown Beret movement, which focused on farmworkers' rights, educational challenges, and

other issues facing Mexican-Americans. What do you think happened for him to have lost his conviction to serve his community? Do you think Ramón and Julieta will lose their passion for their community? Why or why not?

14. Chicano Park is a real historical landmark in San Diego, California, which commemorates the struggles and joys of the Chicano community through murals, sculptures, and gardens. It is a place for the Latino community to come together and celebrate. Why do you think the author chose to include it in the book? What role does setting, and specifically Chicano Park, play in the novel?

Photo by Meg McMillan

ALANA QUINTANA ALBERTSON has written thirty romance novels, rescued five hundred death-row shelter dogs, and danced one thousand rumbas. She lives in sunny San Diego with her husband, two sons, and too many pets. Most days, she can be found writing her next heart book in a beachfront café while sipping an oat milk Mexican mocha or gardening with her children in their backyard orchard and snacking on a juicy blood orange.

CONNECT ONLINE

AuthorAlanaAlbertson.com
AuthorAlanaAlbertson
AuthorAlanaAlbertson
AlanaAlbertson